Death Returns

Mortis Series: Book Seven

J.C. DIEM

Chapter One

Geordie was the first to hear the disturbance. He turned towards the faint sound and the rest of us followed suit. The noise had originated somewhere beneath the surface of the blasted world that we were so desperate to leave.

Dust sifted down through the minute cracks in the silver ceiling when the ground trembled a couple of seconds later. The tremor was barely noticeable and only lasted for a few moments. "Was that an earthquake?" the teen asked.

In this instance 'viltarquake' would be more accurate, since we were on an alien planet.

Gregor brushed the dirt out of his already filthy dark blond hair before querying our Kveet allies. "Is Viltar prone to underground disturbances?" Dressed in the ragged garb of a decommissioned robot rather than one of his usual tweed suits, he was far from his usual suave and sophisticated self. We were all in dire need of bathing and a change of clothes. Unfortunately, we didn't have time for either.

M'narl, the leader of our Kveet allies, waited for his pet droid to translate. Once he understood the question, he shook his head. The tiny alien had only known us for a short time, yet he'd already taken on some of our mannerisms. At an average of two feet tall, our allies had brown skin and heads like dried up apples. I hadn't yet decided if they were cute, or ugly. Maybe they were a mixture of both.

"On the surface, Viltar is a ruin, but its core has always been stable," he said. His voice was amusingly high pitched. It was far less amusing when it came from their kin after they'd been transformed into the larger, far more muscular and ravenous clones.

Translating Kveet into English so the rest of my friends could understand, the robot watched me with glowing scarlet eyes. The Kveet had captured him and had reprogrammed him to obey them instead of his original Viltaran masters. Despite their complete dominance over the droid, they'd removed his arms and legs. The limbless automaton was much lighter and easier to drag around for the miniature aliens without the extra weight.

Grey skinned, red eyed and pointy-eared, he'd been made in his maker's image. The droid was a type that acted as the Viltaran's personal slaves. They'd all been programmed to lie to everyone except their masters. Although this particular robot couldn't lie to us, I was pretty sure it still had the capacity to be evasive. We'd learned fairly quickly upon finding ourselves on Viltar that none of the droids could be trusted.

Pointing at the metal man, I crossed the silver floor until I was looming over him. "You know something." The automaton flicked his glance away, a sure sign he knew what had just happened. Just a short time ago, I'd discovered that our ancient ancestors and current arch enemies were most likely headed towards Earth. The quake had something to do with the escaped aliens, I just didn't know what it was yet.

M'narl also suspected the artificially intelligent droid was hiding important information from us. "What have the Viltarans done?"

Unable to resist answering his Kveet master, the droid responded. "As the vampire deduced, the Viltarans have set a course for Earth. Before leaving, they ensured they would not be followed by destroying all other space crafts in their fleet."

"You mean we're trapped on this rock forever?" Geordie asked. At times of high stress, he tended to look even younger than his fifteen mortal years. In reality, he'd been undead for two centuries. Until a few nights ago, he'd still had a faint ring of blue in his irises. After drinking Viltaran blood, his eyes had turned completely black. He, and my other five close friends, had gained some of the attributes that had previously set me apart from the rest of my kin. Like me, they could now sleep as if they were human. They'd become stronger and faster and, also like me, their eyes glowed red whenever they felt strong emotion.

Only a short while ago, we'd also discovered that they shared my gift, or perhaps curse would be a better description, of immortality. Geordie's head had been torn off by one of our adversaries during our last battle. Normally, being beheaded meant instant death for our kind. Instead of disintegrating into mush, the teen had remained in two pieces until I'd repositioned his head next to his body. To our immense relief, it had become reattached without any visible sign that he'd been grievously wounded.

We hadn't had time to ponder the implications of this new development yet. I was cautiously optimistic about it, but I didn't want to commit myself to happiness just in case it somehow turned out to be a bad thing after all.

Gregor flicked his longish hair back in a gesture that was habitual and slightly theatrical. Handsome and cultured, he was easily the smartest man, or vampire, I'd ever met. He was also a master strategist and could think several steps ahead of our opponents. Unfortunately, even he hadn't seen this one coming. We'd all believed the lie that Robert, the first robot we'd ever met, had told us. He'd led us to believe that the Viltarans had been unable to map the route back to our home planet.

Now well aware of their ability to tell untruths, Gregor pinned the metal man with his black stare. "Did they destroy *every* spacecraft that could convey us back to our home world?"

Shifting his red gaze away again, the robot clearly didn't want to answer the direct question, but couldn't resist due to his programming. "They did not," he ground out. "There is one ship still remaining. It is a Seeker that sustained some damage during its last flight. It is currently being repaired."

"What is a 'Seeker'?" Ishida asked. He might be incredibly ancient, but the former emperor was interested in all things modern and electronic. His interests now included alien technology.

"The Seekers are sent out in search of new planets that might be capable of sustaining the Viltarans," the droid explained. "There is only one left now. The others were decommissioned when fuel became too scarce to sustain more than one Seeker."

Ishida's usually well controlled expression showed a hint of excitement at that news. "Where is this ship?" Like Geordie, he'd been young when he'd been turned. Twelve in mortal years, he had ruled as the emperor of a small nation of Japanese vampires for over ten thousand years. He and Kokoro, the former prophetess who had turned him, were all that was left of their people now.

Kokoro was the oldest vampire still alive. Around forty-thousand years old, she'd been stricken blind when her life had been stolen from her by her maker. When her sight had been taken, she'd been gifted with visions and the ability to read minds.

Long ago, she had foreseen the eventual doom of our species. A vision had shown her that Ishida would guide their people to salvation. I doubted her vision had told her just how few of their nation would survive what would turn out to be a vampire apocalypse.

Neither of them seemed to blame me for causing the end of their nation's existence. Not that I'd killed them all myself. By being turned into a vampire, I had inadvertently set at least two prophecies into motion. It had been foreseen by both Kokoro and a Romanian prophet that I would destroy the bulk of our kind. The only good news I'd read in either prophecy was that a remnant of our people would remain. No one had foreseen that the remnant would be a mere seven vampires.

Not all had been doom and gloom since the humans had turned against us so spectacularly. Surprisingly, a romance had sprung up between Gregor and Kokoro. The

Japanese and European nations had been at war for thousands of years. It had been instant death for a European to set foot on Ishida's island.

The boundaries between their people had begun to dissipate when we'd banded together to take down the Second and his nine brothers. All enmity had been put aside and the warring vampires might have been able to bury the hatchet permanently, if any had survived. We seven were joined in a common cause and had formed a small family. Petty prejudices weren't going to come between us now.

Ishida supported their romance and wasn't about to ruin Kokoro's chance for happiness. He had also gone through a significant change by abdicating his throne. He'd decided it was pointless being the emperor of an all but extinct people. He was trying his best just to be one of us now.

"Answer the question!" M'narl ordered the robot. Geordie stifled a giggle at the Kveet's attempt to be stern.

"The ship lies to the north and east," the droid hedged.

Our enemies might have fled, yet instinct alerted me that another threat was imminent. Sending out my senses, I picked up on something that I hadn't sensed before. New life forms were showing themselves on my internal radar. They appeared as dull silver dots in my mind's eye compared to the light blue of the Kveet and the yellow of their imp clones. The Viltarans had been bright red, when they'd been within my range. My kin showed up as bright white dots.

Seeing one of the life forms only a yard away from me, I opened my eyes and they were looking straight at the droid. Closing them again, I saw the dull silver figures of a robot army numbering in the hundreds only a short distance away.

"What can you sense?" Igor asked me. Russian and fifteen thousand years old, he appeared to be around fifty in human years. His thick black hair was an unruly mess. His face was far too craggy to ever be considered handsome and his manner was usually gruff, bordering on rude.

I'd secretly been intimidated by him when we'd first met. Igor was Geordie's mentor and one of Luc's oldest friends. I'd come to care about him as much as the rest of our tightknit group. Igor was part of my family now. I knew he would have my back in a fight, just as I would have his.

Luc, my one true love and the final member of our team, wasn't speaking to me at the moment. He was doing his best to pretend that I didn't exist. Six feet tall, lean and well-muscled, he had short black hair and a beautiful face. Up until very recently, had been the only man who had ever loved me.

Thanks to my deep-seated insecurities, I'd momentarily harboured the theory that fate had forced us seven together. Based on that theory, I'd believed that their affection for me had to be false.

Luc had asked me if that meant my love for them was also false. In the biggest mistake of my life and subsequent undeath, I'd replied that I didn't know. Before I'd become the living dead, I'd been extremely average in looks. I was still average in height, but I was now almost too slender. My hair hadn't changed. It was still brown with blonde highlights and fell to halfway down my back. A couple of nights after I'd been turned, I'd gained an unholy beauty that had gradually increased over time.

All of my former imperfections were gone and my face and body were flawless. That might be true, but some part of me would always be plain old Natalie Pierce. A clothing store manager who'd worked long hours and rarely, make that never, socialized, I'd been all but invisible to the opposite sex, hence my insecurities.

Getting back to my relationship problems, I'd quickly realized my theory was bogus and that I really did love them all, especially Luc. Unfortunately, the damage had already been done and it couldn't be reversed. I had no idea how to fix our shattered bond, but my personal problems would have to wait for now.

"He's been stalling us," I advised my friends. "I can sense a bunch of murderbots closing in on us." Murderbots was the name I'd given the almost plain looking silver droids that served as the Viltarans' armed forces.

Geordie gaped at that pronouncement. "How is that possible? I thought you could only sense the living and undead. Since when can you sense machines?"

"Since now, I guess."

"I am afraid the question and answer session will have to wait," Gregor said and ushered us towards the closest door. "We do not want to become trapped in this room."

No one disagreed with him. Enough death had already been dispensed within these four walls. It was time to leave before more blood flowed.

Chapter Two

We skirted around a gigantic metal table that had been turned on its side. It had acted as protection for my captors when my friends and the Kveet warriors had stormed to my rescue.

I might be the dreaded Mortis, but even I could be dumb enough to fall for a trap sometimes. It appeared that I'd divulged too much information about my strengths and weaknesses to Robert. He'd snitched on me to his masters and they'd devised a way to hold me captive in a container.

I'd still be trapped inside the jar as an eyeball, chunks of flesh and whirling particles if I hadn't been rescued. I shied away from the memory of how I'd managed to free myself from captivity. It was a mystery that I had no explanation for.

Reaching the end of the table, I spied my new samurai swords and snatched them up off the floor. The Kveet had made them for me at Ishida's request. They were a replacement for the pair I'd left behind on Earth. They might be made of alien metal, but they worked just as well as the originals.

I took a last look at the war room before striding out through the twin doors. The furniture was far larger than was comfortable for humans, or vampires, to use. Somewhere between ten and eleven feet tall, the Viltarans were all heavily muscled, including their females. They reflected their superiority over their servants by making their droids only nine feet tall.

Our arch enemies were a confusing contradiction. They might be technologically advanced, but they were also brutish and disturbingly bloodthirsty. We'd learned from the Kveet that their evil overlords lived to kill. War was their favourite pastime.

Igor bent, grabbed the sturdy ropes that were attached to the translator bot's trolley and dragged it along behind him on soundless wheels. He could move it a lot faster than the diminutive Kveet could. M'narl gathered his people together out in the hallway and quickly explained that a large number of enemies were on their way. Fear lent them speed as they stampeded away from the war room.

Ishida made his way to the front of the crowd, being careful not to trample anyone and guided them towards the closest elevator. The teen carried a wafer thin, portable monitor that was roughly twelve inches wide and six inches high.

He'd quickly learned how to use the alien technology after a brief tutorial given by one of our allies. One of the handy uses for it was its ability to provide maps. He'd also figured out how to operate the elevators that were cleverly hidden in the walls.

Based on the information he'd just been given by the droid, he would attempt to get us as close as possible to the spaceship that would hopefully be able to take us home. I didn't want to contemplate the possibility that the ship was still out of commission.

Fate will make sure it's working. It wants us back home. The thought gave me some comfort, yet it also disturbed me. It wasn't much fun being at the beck and call of an entity that I still had trouble believing in.

Stopping at a blank wall, Ishida operated the monitor. A door slid open to reveal an elevator.

"Wait!" M'narl called before the former child king could send some of the tiny warriors into the carriage. Panting for air after his mad dash through the halls, the Kveet elder tried to catch his breath.

"There is little my people can do for you now," he said. "I will send a small team with you, as well as the droid to program the craft. The rest of us should return to the safety of our cave."

After a glance at Gregor for confirmation that he was ok with the change of plan, Ishida made an adjustment to the elevator's destination. "This carriage will take you close to your caves," he explained as the miniscule aliens boarded the carriage. They crammed in together, standing shoulder to shoulder until it was full.

M'narl paused before entering. He tilted his head back to stare up at me. "I am not sure what providence brought you to this world, but my people and I are very grateful. Without you, we would have forever lived in perpetual fear of the Viltarans and their robot armies. Now we will be able to live free from their oppression. We can finally leave the caves where we have been dwelling for so long."

The planet was riddled with underground buildings that had been made by the Kveet slaves under duress. Now that their oppressors were gone, they could make the structures into their new homes. They'd have to make extensive changes to the size of the furniture, but they'd proven to be adept at working with the dull silver metal that pretty much everything was made from.

Geordie made a sound that was close to a snivel. Crying was impossible since we weren't able to produce snot or tears anymore, but we could still dry sob. The teen could be a sentimental fool sometimes. Apparently, so could I because my reply lodged in my throat.

Gregor, ever the diplomat, came to the rescue. Going down on one knee, he offered his hand to M'narl. "It was our pleasure to assist you in the liberation of your people. You and your warriors were a great help. You should be proud of what you have accomplished." M'narl gingerly allowed Gregor to shake his hand.

"Say goodbye to the octosquids for us," I said to the pint-sized Kveet leader as he stepped inside the elevator. His warriors jostled each other to give him some room.

"I will," he said gravely and was gone before the droid could translate his words.

Ten black, hideous beyond description alien sea creatures shared the caves with M'narl and his people. They'd also been snatched from their planet and were all that remained of their species. I felt kind of bad that they would be stuck on Viltar forever. They needed water to survive and this blasted rock had very little liquid left.

Worry about saving your own people, my alter ego advised. *You weren't fated to save aliens.* I hardly even thought of humans as my people now that I was no longer one of them. My sympathy for earthlings had waned considerably. They'd quite literally shot me in the back and had then gone on to kill and torture the rest of vampirekind.

With M'narl and most of his warriors gone, there were just us seven vampires, four Kveet and one semi-traitorous robot left.

Ishida used his monitor to change the elevator's destination and we piled inside. I sensed the group of killbots quickly closing in on our position. They were only a few hallways away and they would soon be nipping at our heels. Much larger than us, they would only be able to fit ten at a time inside the elevators. Hopefully, that would slow them down long enough for us to be able to escape from this hellish planet.

Zooming along at an unknown speed, I steadied myself with one hand on the wall just in case we came to a lurching halt. My other hand held the swords that were almost a match for the pair Ishida had gifted me with on his small island. The island, and all of its inhabitants, had been bombed by the same man who had sent us into space.

Colonel Sanderson, the rat bastard, I thought. My upper lip curled in a combination of anger and betrayal.

Sanderson hadn't just turned on me, he'd betrayed my entire species. He'd killed as many of us as he could find, but had kept a few alive to be tortured in the name of science. The only vampires that had escaped from his purge had been the Comtesse and some of her sycophants and servants.

My old nemesis had made a deal to rat out her fellow vampires in order to save her own life. The deal might have saved her people from being culled, but it hadn't saved any of them from my wrath. Even if the prophecies hadn't foreseen that I would take their lives, I would have ended their existence anyway. I'd made a vow to myself to murder anyone who stabbed me or my friends in the back. It was a policy I would be happy to enact on my enemies.

If we managed to return to our home planet, Colonel Sanderson was going to be in for one hell of a surprise. It would be my utmost pleasure to educate him on what happened to people who made the grave mistake of stabbing me in the back.

Chapter Three

Our ride came to a smooth stop and we stepped out into yet another silver hallway. The Viltarans had zero imagination or appreciation for art. Consequently, their underground facilities were almost entirely identical in size and appearance. We'd traversed through dozens of these dwellings and hadn't seen even a shred of decoration. The ceiling, walls and floors were all made of the same dull silver metal as my samurai swords.

Before the Viltarans had destroyed their cities, the buildings had been uniform in colour and general appearance. They'd cared more about conquering other worlds than in art, literature or bettering themselves as a species. Not surprisingly, their favourite form of entertainment had been blood sports. More specifically, death by combat.

I couldn't help but compare them to earthlings. Humans had once had the same kind of sports arenas where the combatants would have to fight for their lives. It didn't bode well for my former species that they were so similar to the Viltarans in so many ways.

How long will it be before another world war breaks out and the humans start firing nuclear bombs at each other? That might not ever be an eventuality now. Not with a ship full of alien invaders on their way to take over the planet. Once the Viltarans arrived, nuclear war would be the least of the earthlings' problems.

We came to a halt just long enough for Ishida to orient himself and to attempt to pinpoint exactly where the ship was. "How far are we from the craft?" he asked the metal man.

The droid was reluctant to respond. The Kveet who carried a monitor that was identical to Ishida's gave him a direct order. "Answer the question." The young alien had helped us out more than once during our hunt for the rulers of Viltar. He was more of a technician than a warrior. His tech skills would assist us once we reached our goal.

"Go north for four facilities then east for two," the droid said in a tone that carried the robotic equivalent of sullenness.

With Ishida in the lead, we jogged at a pace that our much shorter allies could keep up with. I'd hoped to evade the pursuing automatons, but I sensed the first group arrive only minutes behind us. Instead of waiting for more of their comrades to join them, they hastened in our wake. They were moving at a fast run and would be on us long before we'd be able to make it to the ship.

"I'm going to hang back for a minute to kill a few droids," I told the others. "I'll catch up to you soon."

Normally, Luc would have protested at being separated from me. This time, he barely glanced in my direction and kept on jogging.

"We will see you shortly," Gregor responded and urged the group to continue.

Depressed by the continued cold shoulder I was receiving from my beloved, I turned around and backtracked for a few hallways. I didn't have to wait long for the robots to appear. When the first pair rounded the corner, my swords went into action before my adversaries could react.

All ten were armed with the weapons that fired darts full of nanobots at their victims. I'd already been hit with around fifty of the projectiles. I knew how much it hurt to have the microscopic robots squirming around in my system.

Due to the weirdness of being Mortis, my body had assimilated the infusion of micro-robots and had turned them to my advantage. It still wasn't clear exactly how I'd been altered, but I'd no doubt discover the changes soon enough.

Metal arms, legs and heads flew as I carved my way through the small unit of droids. When the last robot fell, I turned and sprinted back towards my friends and allies. Another wave of walking machines would be on their way shortly. They would be slightly more cautious now that they knew I might be lurking around the corner ready to pounce. They hadn't been programmed to feel much emotion, but caution seemed to be one of them.

My friends and allies had reached our destination by the time I caught up to them. A larger than usual door swished open as Ishida approached it. A solitary spaceship resided inside the gigantic room.

Our new ride was tiny compared to the craft that had rescued our spaceship and had conveyed us to Viltar. About the size of a small jet, it would be large enough to carry us all home. Dead black, it crouched on the floor almost menacingly and reminded me of a humongous bug.

I flashed back to the giant roaches we'd encountered in the fallen city that we'd briefly used as a hiding spot. Around the size of a small dog, the critters had been the usual brown colour of a normal roach, but had a cluster of large, creepy, purple eyes on the tops of their heads. I could imagine the screams of humans if they ever saw them. I'd come very close to screaming like a little girl when I'd first seen them.

"Have the repairs been completed?" Igor asked the droid.

He paused before answering, presumably using his remote uplink to check the ship's status. "They have," he replied at last.

"Has the craft been refuelled?"

Pausing for another moment, the android gave the affirmative.

"Is there enough fuel to carry us back to Earth?" Ishida asked.

The robot automatically translated his words for our allies once more. "Yes. Barely," it responded with reluctance that was implied, if not actually conveyed in its tone.

"Then program it to do so," the Kveet technician ordered.

"Use the same coordinates that the Viltarans used," Gregor told the robot. That was a smart idea and I was once again grateful to have him on our side. God only knew what route the droid would have programed otherwise. He might have taken us on a scenic trip that would have added a few extra days to our journey.

My senses alerted me that a large number of mechanical enemies were almost on us. "We've got company," I told the others.

"How many?" Igor asked.

"Several dozen are sneaking up on us and a few hundred more are on their way." I could feel them inexorably closing in on our location from three different directions. Thankfully, there only seemed to be one entrance to the room. We would be hard pressed to defend even one door with just our small team against so many adversaries.

"Try to hold them off while the droid programs our route," Gregor commanded then followed the four Kveet inside the craft as they hauled the droid up the ramp.

It didn't bother me to take orders from Gregor. I was supposed to be in charge, but my ego hadn't overridden my common sense. Unlike most vampire leaders, I didn't expect servile obedience from my people. Sycophants and butt kissers would be of no use to me. I needed people who were intelligent, talented and strong of mind on my side.

What possible use could Geordie be to you then? I gave a mental gasp of outrage at my inner voice's sly remark. *Leave Geordie alone! I'd choose him over you any day!* With a huff, my alter ego stalked off into the deeper recesses of my mind.

I ignored my concern that normal people didn't have conversations like this with themselves. For me, it was fairly standard. Sadly, I'd been like this long before I'd become a creature of the night. I couldn't blame being Mortis on that particular mental abnormality.

As ordered, the six of us raced back to the door. We took up positions where we could shoot the oncoming unit of droids without leaving ourselves open to attack. We each carried death rays, weapons we'd appropriated from the corpses of automatons we'd dispatched to robot hell.

The weapons had two settings. One could destroy flesh and the other could destroy metal. Ours were set to take down the droids. All we had to do was wait for them to step into our line of sight then open fire.

Moments later, four killbots appeared at the far end of the hallway. We waited for them to be within range before leaning out and firing. Bright violet bursts of lights lanced down the hall, obliterating all four bots and leaving shallow gouges in the walls and floor.

Thankfully, it also destroyed their nanobot guns. I sincerely hoped none of my friends would be hit with the darts. They might be immortal now, but they weren't immune to pain. The agony of having the new infusion of micro-robots crawling through their veins was something I didn't want any of them to suffer.

Despite the heavy losses we doled out over the next few minutes, the droids just kept on coming. They'd been ordered by their recently departed masters to kill us. They wouldn't stop until either we, or they, were dead. Putting whatever rudimentary caution they possessed aside, they tried to overwhelm us with sheer numbers.

Glancing back at the ship during a short lull in battle, I saw one of the Kveet warriors waving madly. I gave him a quick nod then turned my attention back to the fray. It was strange to see my friend's eyes glowing scarlet as the battle lust tried to take them over. They were all much older than me and even Geordie could master his urge to rend and tear with his bare hands. I'd had enough practice now at being a berserker to be able to contain the rage that fighting always roused within me.

The instant there was a lull in the shooting, I grabbed Ishida and Geordie and hauled them towards the ship. Luc, Igor and Kokoro needed no urging. They were right behind us as we thundered up the ramp. Almost too quiet to hear, the engine had powered up. The hull vibrated beneath our feet.

Standing in the belly of the Seeker ship, we were surrounded by metal. It was a uniform black rather than the dull silver I'd grown used to. Twenty seats ringed the room. All were sized for the much larger Viltarans. There were five on each side and we all chose a seat and clambered up. The ramp closed and the craft lifted into the air. Too tiny to be able to climb up into a chair, the four Kveet huddled in the centre of the floor beside the droid.

Picturing the tons of rock and dirt that was between us and the poisoned air high above, I waited for the ship to crash. Surely it would explode once it hit the ceiling. We'd be torn asunder and our body parts would rain back to the ground.

Instead of crashing, I heard the groan of vast doors sliding open an instant before we zoomed upwards.

Once free from the subterranean facility, we travelled sideways for a short distance then landed. Dust from the nightly storms swirled inside as the ramp slid open. The four Kveet hustled down it quickly, dragging their droid servant behind them on his trolley. His red eyes shifted to keep me in sight until he disappeared. He was silently damning me for the annihilation of his former masters. His will might have been hijacked by the Kveet, but whatever passed for his metallic heart would always belong to the Viltarans.

Causing death and annihilation wasn't exactly new to me. I'd killed two megalomaniacal vampires who had tried to take over our home world. The First had created an army of imps who'd been intent on enslaving and eating humankind.

The Second, along with nine of his long banished brothers, had created an army of rabid and ravenous fledgling vampires. Their plan had also been to enslave and eat the humans.

One thing all ancient and insane vampires seemed to have in common was their desire to enslave the human race. If I ever started having thoughts of absolute rule, I'd know I was nearing the edge of madness.

Now the Viltarans were on their way to our world, presumably with the same plan in mind. I wasn't sure if the aliens would actually have a hankering for human flesh or not, but their imps surely would.

Stopping the Earth from being taken over by vampires, imps and now aliens is getting really old, I complained mentally. *Can't fate dredge up a new kind of threat for a change?* If it ever did, I wasn't sure I'd want to confront it. *Be careful what you wish for,* my subconscious told me darkly. *You just might get it.*

Geordie leaned forward, teetering on the edge of his seat as he waved at the Kveet as the ramp began to close. I caught a glimpse of their small hands lifting to wave in return, then the ramp sealed shut. Seconds later, my stomach dropped all the way to my feet when the ship caromed into space.

Unlike the craft that had sent us into space, this one kept a semblance of gravity. I felt much lighter than usual, but didn't quite float when I jumped to the floor. I wasn't the only one who was curious and the others followed me to the door. It whooshed aside as I approached and revealed a cockpit that was far more advanced than anything I'd ever seen before.

Examining the console, I quickly gave up trying to decipher what any of the strange looking dials, levers and buttons did. Gregor had remained in the cockpit during our abrupt take off. He sat on one of the two large chairs. He looked almost child sized with his feet swinging in the air.

His expression was solemn as he turned and looked down at us. "I hope the Viltarans do not have too great a head start on us."

"Who knows how much havoc they will wreak before we catch up to them?" Igor wondered.

"Do we know where they are heading?" Geordie asked.

I had an answer to that question. "I'm pretty sure they're going to target New York."

Ishida swivelled his head to study me. "Did your dreams show you this?"

I nodded unhappily. "I've had two dreams about Earth since we landed on Viltar. Both were of Manhattan."

"What happens in your dreams, *chérie*?" Geordie asked. Sensing my unease, he slipped his hand into mine. He had a well-developed ability to tell when others were upset. I wondered if his empathy was natural or if it had come to him after being turned into the undead.

"In the first dream, everyone was dead and the sky had turned yellow and poisonous," I explained. "In the second dream, everyone was dead and the city was full of droids and human imp clones."

Gregor's fist went beneath his chin in his usual thinking pose. "Neither dream sounds very promising. The humans put up no resistance to the Viltarans at all?"

"Not in the first dream, but in the second one a few army choppers turned up. The Viltarans shot them down with some kind of electromagnetic pulse ray before they could land." I remembered them falling out of the sky and everyone on board dying in their collision with the ground.

"We have no way of knowing which of the two fates Manhattan will suffer," he mused.

I couldn't hide my expression of loathing at his choice of wording. Fate, if it really did exist, had once more sunk its claws into us. It had killed off most of our species then had kicked the rest of us off our home world. All but seven of the twenty-nine who'd been exiled from Earth were now dead. It now appeared that we were expected to return home and save the very beings who had attempted to eradicate us in the first place.

"I can see what you are thinking, Natalie," Gregor said. "We have already agreed that we cannot allow the Viltarans to destroy humanity."

"Even if they do deserve it," Igor said darkly. I was mollified that at least one person shared my point of view.

Experience had taught me that struggling against my duty was useless. "I know," I replied and my shoulders slumped in defeat. "We have to kill the Viltarans. It's our 'destiny'." My sarcasm was thick as I made the required quotation marks with my fingers.

Kokoro's next words effectively put an end to our discussion. "All of us must do what we feel is right. I have no love for humans, but I cannot stand by and watch them being enslaved by our ancient ancestors."

I was somehow certain that I wasn't the only one who felt the irony of our situation. Millions of years ago, the Viltarans had created their nanobot technology. They had gained the ability to create armies of clones. They had used them to invade and conquer every planet that contained intelligent beings within the reach of their ships.

Eventually, they had run out of worlds to destroy and had turned on each other. Their planet had become all but uninhabitable beneath the toxic clouds of yellow gas. In desperation, they continued to send out ships to search for new planets to destroy.

One of these Seekers had crash landed on Earth. The droid on board had waited through the millennia until humans had developed enough intelligence to be turned into imps. It had injected the First with the nanobots that would eventually turn him into a Viltaran clone. The fact that he hadn't been instantly converted into a grey skinned imp strongly hinted that the micro-robots had been faulty.

According to Gregor, fate had screwed up when it had allowed the ship to land on our planet. It had taken steps to ensure the error would be rectified. I was the solution that it had come up with. With my coming, events had been set in motion that had resulted in my friends and me being the only survivors. Now here we were, heading back to Earth to finally end the cycle.

"Is it just me, or is fate suffering from some kind of major malfunction?" I asked the others.

With his fist still beneath his chin, Gregor was slow to answer. "I am no longer sure of anything when it comes to our destiny."

His words were heavy and far from reassuring. The most intelligent person in our team had no idea where our destinies now lay. There was no telling what would happen to our small cadre of vampires. Whatever chance had in store for us, I doubted we'd be in for an easy ride.

Chapter Four

"How long will it take us to reach home?" Geordie asked after the contemplative silence stretched out for longer than he could bear.

"There is something you need to know," Gregor replied, instead of answering the question directly. "I discovered quite by accident that M'narl's droid had been withholding information from us. I asked him to repeat the diagnostic report that Robert the robot first ran on our spaceship. He did so, but very reluctantly."

No one showed surprise at learning that. While the droid's return uplink to its former masters had been severed, it could still access information from the other robots on the planet.

"It seems that we had been drifting through space for a number of years before the Viltarans found us," he said.

"How many years?" Kokoro asked. Her trepidation was shared by us all.

"Nearly ten."

My mouth dropped open in shock. "Ten years? But I was only asleep for a short time before I woke up to find myself a vampsicle."

Wry amusement glinted in Gregor's dark eyes. "Your slumber must have been far deeper than it seemed."

I'd left no family or friends behind to mourn me when I'd been bundled into the spaceship and sent into outer space. But I was still shocked at how long we'd been gone. *At least you weren't asleep for a thousand years,* my inner voice ventured. Who knew what sort of changes might have occurred back home during that length of time?

"It won't take us another ten years to return will it?" I asked. Our fuel had run out after a few hours, so I wasn't sure how fast we'd been moving through space. Hopefully, the Viltaran Seeker ship would have enough fuel to carry us home far more quickly than it had taken us to arrive in this distant galaxy.

Gregor shook his head. "These ships can move very quickly, according to the droid. It should only take us a little more than four months to reach home. Apparently, this will consume almost all of our fuel. On the bright side, the Viltarans' fuel will also be greatly diminished. This will be a one way trip for them. They will never be able to return home again."

I wasn't sure how that was a plus for us. The aliens would be left with no choice but to succeed in taking over our world, or die trying. Their desperation would make them even more dangerous. Not just to us, but also to the humans they were intent on conquering.

"Weren't they carrying any extra fuel?" Ishida asked.

"According to the droid, their fuel is extremely rare and difficult to manufacture," Gregor explained. "Their reserves were almost gone. The rest was stored in the factory we destroyed. Apart from the fuel that was already in their ship, and ours, there is no other fuel left."

"If Earth is just within their reach, why have they not discovered it and invaded long before now?" Ishida asked. Understanding dawned and he answered his own question. "They sent their Seekers out searching for worlds to conquer. They did not hear back from the one that crashed on our planet."

"I have a question," Kokoro said. From the way she was looking directly at me, I suspected it wasn't going to be about the Viltarans. "How did you break free from your glass prison?"

That was a question I had been hoping to avoid simply because I didn't have an answer to it.

"I want to know how you can now sense the robots," Geordie added.

Looking down at me from his seat high on the chair, Gregor's expression was shrewd. "What happened to you when you went hunting for the Viltarans by yourself?"

I mentally squirmed beneath their stares. Luc was the only one who wasn't watching me. He stared out through the window into the darkness of space. We were moving so fast that the stars were just a momentary blur as we streaked past them. My beloved's expression was serene, but his jaw was tightly clenched. I wished I could probe his mind and see if there was any chance that we could ever be a couple again.

Knowing that they would pester me until I answered their questions, I surrendered to the inevitable. "After I killed a bunch of them, I sensed all of the Viltarans gathered in one room. I fought my way past a giant octosquid imp and found them waiting for me. There were no droids in sight and it looked safe enough, so I figured it couldn't hurt to hear what they had to say."

"It was a trap," Igor guessed.

"Yep. They waited until I was halfway across the room before springing it."

I was alive and well, yet Geordie's chin trembled anyway at the thought that I might have come to harm. "What did they do to you, *chérie*?" he asked in a small voice.

"They'd rigged up dozens of nanobot guns in the walls. They didn't appear until after Uldar told me I was a worthy warrior, but that I'd made the mistake of underestimating their technology. I outran the first wave of darts, but the door closed just as I reached it. I was hit by about fifty or so flying syringes."

Gregor winced, most likely remembering what had happened to Aventius after he'd been hit by a single dart. The former Councillor hadn't been transformed from a vampire into an imp smoothly. His body had fought against the infusion of new nanobots. His flesh had bulged and swelled while it tried to decide what form would take precedence. He'd suffered horribly before his follower, Cristov, had put an end to his misery.

"How did your system react to the nanobots?" Gregor asked.

I gave a half shrug. "Apart from feeling like my veins were being eaten away by acid, there were no physical changes." None that I'd noticed anyway.

"How did they get you into the container?" Ishida asked.

"Uldar shot me with a death ray, then sucked my particles up with some kind of vacuum cleaner." Uldar was the self-appointed leader of the remaining Viltarans and my new main target to kill. "I managed to form a hand and an eyeball, but the space was too small to re-form my whole body. Then they transferred me into the larger jar. My hand wouldn't fit through the opening into the container. I had to break it down into chunks. My eye stayed whole so I could see what was going on, but they had air blowing around constantly so it was almost impossible to put myself back together." I'd have found a way out eventually, but my friends had come to the rescue before I'd managed to think of a way to escape.

"I saw your eye whirling around inside the jar," Geordie said. "Then the Viltaran tore my head off and I didn't see what happened next." Kokoro put her hand on his arm in silent commiseration when he shuddered at the memory of being beheaded.

Even Luc turned to look at me as they waited for an explanation for how I had escaped. "I'm not sure how I broke out of the container," I confessed. "When I saw what the Viltaran did to Geordie, I kind of went berserk. One second I was trapped and the next instant I was free and whole."

"And naked," Ishida interjected. The teens shared a snigger, then quailed at Igor's warning frown.

Kokoro shivered at the memory of what I had done next. "You moved so fast to tear out the alien's heart that I was unable to follow you with my eyes."

Gregor's chin rested on his fist, deep in thought. "The nanobots have altered you in ways that I would not have thought possible."

"I'm Mortis," I reminded him unnecessarily. "I'm pretty sure nothing is impossible when it comes to me." I wasn't bragging, it was a factual statement based on the weird and wacky things that I was able to do.

Igor shrugged off Gregor's misgivings with his usual gruff practicality. "Your new ability to sense the droids should come in handy when we reach Earth and start hunting them down."

"Do you think we will have to cooperate with the armed forces once more?" Ishida queried.

Again, my upper lip curled at the thought of seeing Colonel Sanderson. He and three of his men had tossed me out into the sun. They'd then shot me in the back with their prototype weapons that had been designed exclusively to kill our kind. What they'd done to me had been pretty bad, but what they had done to my friends and allies had been far worse. "The instant I see Sanderson, he's a dead man," I vowed.

I wanted to eradicate the entire US government but, after nearly a decade, new people would most likely be in charge by now. I was brewing a quiet animosity towards all humans, but even I couldn't justify killing the innocent for something that their predecessors had done. *Can I?* I asked my inner voice. *Probably not,* it responded. *Not unless you want your friends to think you've gone nuts.* It had a point, so I shelved the idea of murdering hundreds, or even thousands of meat sacks in revenge.

"Is that your answer for everything now?" Luc asked, interrupting my short internal debate. "Kill everyone who displeases you?"

Numbed to silence by his sudden accusation, I couldn't think of anything to say. Close to tears, I turned and walked out of the cockpit.

"If Nat kills everyone who annoys her, then why are you still alive?" Geordie said nastily to my one true love.

"Behave yourselves, children," Igor warned as the door slid open before me. I almost smiled at Luc being called a child, but my lips refused to move. The door closed behind me and I was as alone as I could possibly be on a small craft that had only two rooms.

Murmurs came from within the cockpit, but they were too low for me to make out. Luc's jab had hurt, just as he'd intended. *Where did that accusation come from,* I wondered. I had never, to my knowledge, killed anyone who hadn't deserved it.

Oh, really? Are you sure about that, my inner voice asked. To be completely honest with myself, there had been one death that might not have been completely justified. A young vampire by the name of Joshua had been killed at my whim. He'd been brash, hot headed and a general pain in the butt. He'd been warned not to cause trouble, but had been unable to keep his mouth shut and his opinions to himself.

The truce between the Japanese and European vampire nations had been precarious. Joshua had known this and he hadn't cared. He'd opened his mouth once too often. Aventius had sired the young vamp and he had also been the one to execute Joshua. If he hadn't done the job, I would have.

Belated guilt hit me that I had so casually dismissed the life of one of our own. Joshua, along with most of our kin, had been doomed anyway. But that didn't excuse what I had done.

I hadn't turned power mad when I had voted myself to be the temporary leader of our small army. It had just seemed to be a necessary action at the time. In hindsight, I wasn't sure what I would have done differently.

If Luc thinks I make such horrible decisions, then maybe he *should be in charge.* As soon as the idea hit me, a weight dropped off my shoulders. From now on, someone else could make the decisions that would affect the few of us that were left. Since I was being so honest at the moment, I had to admit that I was vastly underqualified for the job anyway.

Backtracking to the cockpit door, I poked my head inside when it whooshed open. "I'm stepping down as your leader."

The momentary silence inside the small room was short, but profound.

"But you are Mortis," Kokoro pointed out. "It is your destiny to…"

She trailed off as I cocked an eyebrow at her. "It was my destiny to get most of our kind killed. That mission has been accomplished and we are 'the remnant that remains'. My job is done, unless there is another prophecy that I'm not aware of?" I waited for someone to drop a bombshell that there was indeed another prophecy that I didn't know about, but they remained silent. "Then I quit. Pick someone else to be in charge from now on."

Feeling free for the first time since I'd realized I was chained like a beast of burden by fate, I left them to discuss their options. Choosing a chair, I jumped up and made myself comfortable. Closing my eyes, I forced myself into a sleep that I didn't really require.

Chapter Five

Opening my eyes what seemed like only a second or two later, I was slightly disoriented when the room seemed to be moving. A narrow bunk bed was above me. It matched the one I was lying on. Springs from the cot above sagged down almost to my face, which probably meant the bed was occupied. A loud, wet fart from above confirmed my suspicions.

Rolling sideways, I escaped from the noisome, yet invisible butt fog before it could completely envelope me. My feet hit the floor and I cautiously stood. I pin-wheeled my arms to keep my balance when the floor pitched sharply.

Spying a small round window, I lurched over to it and grabbed hold of the rim. Pressing my face up against the glass, I saw only darkness outside. Water splashed against the pane and I jerked back. I finally realized that I was on a boat when it wallowed and almost tipped over beneath a large wave. The reek of fish should have alerted me to where I was, but the fart had momentarily drowned out all other smells.

Several more men slept on the bunk beds that lined one wall. All were unshaven, grizzled and dark skinned. I wasn't sure what their nationality was. I wouldn't be able to tell unless one of them woke up and spoke to me. None woke as the ship tilted back once more as it climbed another wave. They were accustomed to the seesaw sensation.

Far from used to walking around on a floor that pitched and rolled, I kept one hand on the wall as I made my way over to the hatch. The door was open. It had been pinned in place to stop it from banging backwards and forwards and waking up the crew.

Stepping through the opening, I looked up and down the narrow corridor. Stairs at one end most likely led to the upper deck, so I negotiated my way over to them. I held onto the railing with both hands when we crested the wave and went into a short fall.

Curses sounded from someone who was tossed out of his cot to the floor. Other sailors grumbled at being woken from their slumber. I felt a momentary pang when I realized they were Italian. Luc had been born in Italy over seven hundred years ago, but I'd rarely heard him use his native tongue.

When the ocean temporarily smoothed out again, I quickly climbed the stairs. The hatch squealed in protest when I shouldered it open. The door was ripped out of my hands by a howling wind and rain instantly drenched me. A wave slapped at my feet and I closed the door before the boat could become flooded. I knew I was dreaming, but it was so realistic that I might have actually been there in person.

For a moment, I marvelled at the sight of a sky that wasn't a sickly yellow. Low clouds hovered above the boat as the angry clouds lashed us with rain and wind. The boat turned into another wave that threatened to tip us over. I stumbled back against the hatch as the nose of the boat rose. The wave grew and almost seemed to hover over us before it came crashing down. A torrent of water swept over me, knocking me to my knees.

A dark form appeared and at first I thought it was another, much larger wave. Then darkness enveloped the boat and a stench unlike anything I'd ever smelled before assailed me. The wind and rain disappeared, leaving an eerie silence behind. Tilting my head backwards, I could no longer see the sky at all. *I think we just sailed into a cave.*

We drifted through darkness for a short while, then the bow of the boat began to tilt downward as we reached a precipice. Still on my knees, I slid across the deck. Sailors screamed in terror from the bridge behind and above me as the boat tilted forward at a sharper and sharper angle.

Landing against the railing, I held on tightly and stared down a vast, dark waterfall that didn't seem to have an end. I closed my eyes as the boat fell into the void.

A hand on my shoulder woke me from my dream before the boat could hit the ground, assuming there eventually was one. "Are you all right, Natalie?" Geordie asked me quietly.

Looking around, I saw that everyone except Luc was strapped into their seats. My beloved was still in the cockpit. "I'm fine," I reassured the teen. "I was just having a weirder than usual dream."

"Was it another premonition?" His dark eyes were large with apprehension.

"I doubt it. I was on a boat and we sailed into a cave, then fell over a really long waterfall."

Relieved that, for once, my dream had been just a dream, Geordie checked that no one was listening to us, then dropped his voice down to below a whisper. Even sitting right beside him I could barely hear him. "When are you going to fix things between you and Luc?"

My expression hardened slightly, but that was to prevent myself from bursting into dry sobs rather than in anger at my love life being put to the question. "I'm open to suggestions," I said.

I had a feeling that the teen's experience with romance was even more pathetic than mine. Realizing he had no suggestions to offer me, his face fell. "Why can't you just apologize so he can forgive you and you can go back to being happy again?"

"I tried that already and my apology wasn't good enough. Being who and what I am, nothing is ever going to be that easy," I said glumly. "I don't think I'm destined to be happy." It was a new and dismal thought.

Geordie frowned in puzzlement. "What do you mean?"

"I was created for one thing; to dole out death." Mortis was actually Latin for death and it was a fitting name for me. The irony of being named death by a now dead language wasn't lost on me. "It doesn't say anywhere in the prophecies that I'm supposed to have a happily ever after ending." In fact, both prophecies had predicted nothing but horror for me and our kind.

"We have moved beyond the prophecies now," Geordie said. "No one knows what is supposed to happen anymore. There is no reason why you and Luc can't have a happily ever after together."

Forcing a sigh from my airless lungs, I slumped back against the uncomfortable metal seat. The harness was far too large and pooled in my lap, but it would keep me from being tossed to the floor in case of an unexpected collision with space debris. "This isn't a story, Geordie. This is real life and real life rarely turns out how you want it to."

Studying my face, his bottom lip pooched out in a pout. "So, you're just going to give up on the man you love?"

"Why not?" I asked with a bitter glance towards the cockpit door. "He's already given up on me."

Geordie's chin trembled and he subsided into tearless sobs. Covering his face with his hands, he muffled the noise as best as he could so he wouldn't wake the others. Kokoro opened one eye, saw us trying to have a private moment and closed it again. I was inordinately grateful that she could no longer pick up on the self-pitying thoughts that were whirling around inside my head.

As I patted my young friend on the shoulder, I wondered who was going to comfort me in my time of need. Luc had been there for me from the first moment we'd met. We'd fallen for each other and had become almost inseparable. He'd been the one good thing that had happened to me since my untimely death. Then I'd made one small mistake and he had thrown away our hopes of a future together.

Theoretically, you can all live forever now, my subconscious whispered insidiously. *Why would someone as hot as Luc want to spend eternity with* you? I wasn't sure why my inner voice sometimes turned against me. I'd listened to it the last time it had offered its advice and it had destroyed my relationship with Luc. The damage had been done, so there was no need for it to continue to poison me against my former beloved. It claimed it was just trying to keep me from being hurt, but I wasn't so sure that was true. Some part of me obviously wanted to wallow in misery. Maybe, deep down, I believed I deserved to be alone forever.

The next four months passed in a tense blur. Thanks to imbibing Viltaran blood, none of us were starving yet. Geordie complained of feeling hungry every now and then, but his cheeks didn't turn hollow from lack of food during our lengthy journey. We would still need to feed, of course, but not nearly as often as before.

Like me, the rest of the group could sleep true sleep now instead of falling into a death-like coma when the sun came up. I was pretty sure we still shared the Viltaran allergy to the sun. While we would still be horribly injured if we came into contact with its burning rays, it no longer had the power to make us die for the day.

Luc and Gregor spent most of their time seated in the cockpit. I remained in the hold, upholding my former love's wish to avoid me. I spent most of my time pretending to doze, mainly to avoid the pitying glances my friends sent my way.

Eventually, we had our first sign that we were drawing close to our destination. "A shutter has just descended across the cockpit window," Geordie said as he took his usual seat beside me.

"We must be drawing close to Earth," Ishida surmised from his seat to my right. The Viltarans would flash fry if the sun touched their flesh. The shutter had to be a protective measure.

We were almost home and I should have been ecstatic about that, but instead my stomach felt leaden. It might be selfish, but I was more concerned with my lack of a love life than I was with the impending invasion of our home world.

"Have you picked your new leader yet?" I asked the teens. Not all of my naps had been forced. It was possible they'd had a meeting to discuss this issue while I'd been slumbering.

Leaning forward, they exchanged careful glances across me, unsure of how to answer. "If you and Lucentio would air your grievances like adults instead of sulking like children," Ishida said, "you could possibly solve your issues and the point would be moot."

"So, you haven't chosen a new leader then."

Geordie gave me a sour glance. "*You* are our leader. You promised you would keep us safe."

"Yeah, just look how well I kept everyone safe," I responded bitterly. "Everyone except us is dead. Besides, you're all immortal now. You don't need me to keep you safe anymore."

Gregor, Igor and Kokoro were in the cockpit with Luc, so we three were alone. Ishida checked to make sure none of the adults were in sight then gestured at the samurai swords on my lap. "I would like to test that theory. I want to see if I am able to reattach my limbs as both you and Geordie can."

Appalled at the idea of dismembering my young friend, I automatically shifted the swords out of his reach. "I'm not going to chop one of your hands off!" I replied in a whisper-shout.

"I'll do it!" Geordie said eagerly and tried to snatch one of the weapons from me. He distracted me long enough for Ishida to snag one of the swords he'd asked the Kveet to make for me. A second later, his left hand thumped to the ground. All three of us stared at it as black blood sluggishly oozed from both of his stumps.

At the sound of the door sliding open, we turned to see Igor watching us suspiciously. I was certain I looked just as guilty as the teens. "What are you three up to?" He turned a stern glare on us that made me feel like a naughty five year old. Igor had practice at that since he'd been a father once, a long, long time ago. Then he'd been turned into a monster and had killed his entire family. His maker must have been a colossal douchebag to force him to feed from his own wife and children.

He'd gotten his revenge in the end and had forced his master's horse to stampede over a cliff. Vampires weren't able to survive murdering our makers, but he'd proven that there was no rule against engineering their deaths.

"We're not up to anything," Ishida said, hiding his wounded arm behind his back.

The Russian's gaze latched onto the severed hand then flicked to the sword in the teen's attached hand. Shaking his head, he crossed the metal floor and snatched up the appendage. "I take it this is yours," he said as he handed it back to the former child king.

Ishida tossed the sword back to me since he'd been busted in a lie and took the offering. "It is mine," he confessed. "Thank you, Igor," he said with stiff dignity.

The sight of his fellow adolescent holding his own hand struck Geordie as funny and he giggled. My lips trembled, then we were both howling with laughter. The dour expression on Igor's face made me laugh even harder.

Ishida's shoulders moved in silent mirth as he held his detached hand to his stump. He waited for a few seconds, but nothing happened. My laughter dried up at his panicked look. "Give it some more time," I urged him. "It'll work." Putting a hand behind my back, I surreptitiously crossed my fingers.

With a look of fierce concentration, Ishida held the raw edges of his wrist together again. It had taken a while before Geordie's body had accepted his head. The same thing happened to Ishida. After a few more moments, the ends melded. A thin red line was the only sign his hand had, for a very short time, been apart from him. The line would soon fade and then no one would be able to tell that he'd performed the experiment at all.

That thought conjured up memories of what they'd all been through in the secret government facility in Colorado. I'd rescued twenty-eight of my kin from cells where they had been tortured in the most horrific manner the humans could devise. I shuddered to think what they would do to us if they got their hands on us again.

Hearing the door open again, I turned to see Kokoro and Gregor standing in the doorway. Instead of wearing looks of disapproval, they studied Ishida as he tested his hand by opening and closing it. "I believe it would be prudent if we all experienced reattaching severed limbs," Gregor stated.

I offered the sword to Kokoro first. For someone who had been blind for forty millennia and had only recently regained her sight, she handled the weapon as if she'd had extensive training with one. For all I knew, maybe she had been trained to fight. Her lack of vision had never seemed to slow her down much. She'd once told me that, when her eyes were open she was blind, but when they were closed she could see very well. It hadn't made much sense to me at the time. Frankly, it still didn't make much sense to me now.

Twirling the sword in an arc, she neatly sliced off her right hand then handed the weapon to Gregor. His hand thumped to the ground next to hers a second later. Igor took the sword, then Gregor bent to retrieve his and Kokoro's hands. Geordie covered his mouth to politely hide his gag reflex as they held their still bleeding hands to their stumps. Apparently, it wasn't quite so funny to him anymore. Again, it took half a minute or so before their bodies accepted their severed appendages.

Igor was next to perform the experiment, but he chose to hack off one of his feet instead of a hand. Geordie giggled at the sight of his mentor trying to keep his balance on one foot and hold up his pants leg while hacking at his limb. Ignoring his apprentice, Igor picked up his severed foot and placed it against his sluggishly spurting shin.

When it was safely reattached, he tested its performance by swinging a kick at Geordie. Shrieking with laughter, the teen cringed against me and drew his legs up to avoid the blow. His mood swings were sometimes enough to make me dizzy.

Taking the weapon when Igor had wiped it clean and offered it to me, I wasn't surprised when no one offered to give Luc the opportunity to test his healing skills. I figured he was far too busy brooding to bother interacting with the rest of us.

Chapter Six

It was impossible to tell how fast we were moving in the artificial gravity of the ship. I couldn't tell we were moving at all unless I looked out through the cockpit window. Only the automatic closing of the shutter a few days ago hinted that we were nearing our destination.

The droid had grudgingly followed Gregor's instructions when he'd programed our craft's journey. It would land at what would hopefully be a safe distance from where the Viltaran ship had touched down. Presumably, the only way we'd be able to tell we'd arrived would be when the ramp slid open to let us out.

I was wondering how close we were to Earth when the ship suddenly lurched sideways and went into a shuddering nosedive.

"I suggest we should all strap ourselves in," Gregor said with false calm as he reached for the oversized harness on his seat. "It appears that we are about to crash."

From the way the ship was dropping, I didn't think we would be in the air for much longer. The quiet sound of the engine had been snuffed out. It had to be from the same electromagnetic pulse ray that I'd seen the Viltarans use against the army choppers in my dream.

Already strapped in, I braced myself for impact and didn't have long to wait. With a tortured groan, the ship hit a solid surface. It skipped for what felt like a few hundred yards, then quickly began to sink. I reflexively pulled my feet up when the ramp opened and water spewed inside.

Unbuckling his harness, Igor jumped down into half a foot of water that was rapidly rising. "Quickly, we should escape from the ship before it settles to the bottom and we become trapped."

We were all willing to follow his advice and slid to the floor. The door to the cockpit opened and Luc joined us. A deep gash on his forehead from where he must have hit it on the console was already healing. It faded completely before he reached us.

Igor was the first to dive into the water and make his way through the opening. Geordie went next, followed by Ishida, Kokoro then Gregor. Luc brushed past me, leaving an ache in my chest where my dead heart lay.

The water was now up to my waist and would quickly be over my head. I wasn't worried about drowning, since I no longer needed to breathe. However, I was in danger of being trapped in the hulk of the downed ship when it settled on the bottom of whatever body of water we were in.

I'd be able to break myself down to minute particles and escape easily enough, but I'd have to leave my clothes behind. Like the others, I was dressed in the castoff clothing of robots. The clothes were black, unimaginative and had been adjusted to fit us by clever Kveet tailors. Gregor had very reluctantly donned his outfit. He still managed to seem more sophisticated than the rest of us while wearing it.

Holding both of my swords in one hand, I dived into the water and followed the thrashing figures of my friends. The sun was down, so it would be safe enough for us to surface. Igor wisely swam underwater for some distance from the ship before heading upwards. He stopped just beneath the surface. No spotlights searched the area, so he deemed it to be safe to rise.

When my face met fresh air, I accidentally swallowed some salt water and coughed it back up again. Thrashing around in a half circle, I saw the familiar Manhattan skyline looming over us. It felt almost strange to be home again, even if we were in a foreign country. If we'd been on solid ground, I would have been tempted to drop to my knees and kiss the soil.

Expecting to see the skyscrapers in ruins, I instead saw lights blazing from intact buildings. Tilting my head back, I was relieved to see a normal black sky and bright stars instead of a sickly yellow hue and madly boiling clouds. The air smelled of salt water and pollution, but I detected no hint of rotten eggs. Whatever the Viltarans had planned for the city, they hadn't launched it yet.

"What forced our ship down?" Luc asked. He treaded water gracefully and with a minimum of movement. In comparison, my hands and feet clawed at the river in an attempt to stay afloat. I held my swords tightly, wishing I had sheaths for them both so my hands could be free.

Gregor searched the sky for an answer. "It must have been the Viltarans."

Geordie tried to peer between the buildings, but there were too many of them to catch a glimpse of the aliens. "Where are they? Have they attacked the city yet? I don't hear any humans screaming."

Igor turned his wet, shaggy head to me. "Can you pinpoint where they are?"

Closing my eyes, I forgot what had happened the first time I'd used my newly enhanced skills back on Viltar. Opening my mind wide, I was instantly inundated with human lives in an almost incomprehensible number. Attempting to catalogue every life that it picked up, my consciousness automatically shut down in self-defence before I could become overwhelmed. Our brains might be like highly sophisticated computers, but mine had its limits and I'd just reached it.

When I woke, it was to the unlovely sound of screams. I lay on the filthy ground in a dark, narrow alley. Geordie was crouched beside me. One of my swords was clutched in his hand. The other lay on the ground beside me. He'd presumably stayed behind to guard me, which I found both amusing and endearing. He could easily protect my unconscious body from humans, but I wasn't so sure he'd be able to stop a bunch of Viltarans from dismembering me in a murderous frenzy.

The teen started in surprise when I sat up. "How long was I out?" I asked. I doubted it had been long. My hair and clothes were still dripping and so were his.

"Not long," he confirmed, brushing his hair out of his eyes absently with his free hand. "Ten minutes, maybe." Sparing me a strained smile, he turned his attention back to the mouth of the alley. A dumpster blocked most of his view and he leaned sideways to peer around it. Humans moved past in a steady stream. Most were sobbing, wailing or screaming in terror. The familiar high pitched cries of Kveet imp clones carried even above the humans' cacophony. Their endless quest for food had ceased and now they could feast to their heart's content.

"Where are the others?" I asked as I grabbed my sword and climbed to my feet.

"They are assessing the situation and will be back soon." Standing, Geordie offered me the other sword, knowing I would be able to defend us both from harm. He pulled his Viltaran death ray out of the waistband of his pants and checked the setting. "Are you feeling well?" he asked in an abrupt change of topic.

Nodding, I swung the swords in an arc, limbering up my wrists. Not that they needed it. "I'm fine. I just forgot how much stronger my ability to sense things is now."

"What happened?"

"I didn't filter my senses and opened them up too wide." Remembering the barrage of coloured mental dots that had filled my head, I froze the image and sorted through it. Humans had shown up as bright yellow dots that covered the globe. Thousands of imp clones and murderbots had been placed all throughout Manhattan. They were our main concern.

I would ponder about the other coloured dots I'd sensed when I had the time. They were a surprise that I found very disturbing.

Keeping a tight rein on my senses this time, I cautiously sent them out in search of our friends. I found them only a block away and heading towards us. "The others are on their way back," I told my companion.

Geordie grabbed my arm and pulled me into the shadows as a small unit of droids jogged into view. There were twenty in total and all were armed with nanobot guns. Aiming at the fleeing earthlings, they opened fire.

Halting in mid-step, several humans screamed in pain as their bodies were instantly transformed. In seconds, they were almost the exact image of the seven foot tall, grey skinned hell spawn I remembered so well and had loathed so much. Only their eyes were different. They were scarlet instead of orange. I figured the orange eyes had been due to the faulty micro-robots the First had been infected with.

Naked, since their clothing had been torn apart during the cloning process, the imps eyed each other in approval. All were heavily muscled, even the ones who'd been scrawny before their transformation.

"Food?" a female queried in the guttural Viltaran language. The only way I could tell she was female was from her rudimentary breasts and lack of male genitalia.

Pointing at the humans, who were frozen in horror at the sight they'd just witnessed, a male answered her. "Food!"

As the newly made clones loped after their fleeing meals, violet bursts of light streaked towards the androids. Five were disintegrated before they realized they were under attack. Geordie shot another one from the safety of the alley as our friends closed in.

Holding my swords tightly, I raced forward to engage the nine foot tall robots. Any that weren't disintegrated by the death rays fell beneath my weapons.

Slicing the legs off the final machine, I kicked it over onto its back then stabbed it through both eyes. It was a fatal wound for the bot. Both hands reached for the sky, clenching and unclenching as it gave a buzzing squeal that slowly petered out. Silence descended in the immediate area, but screams of terror and roars of triumph came from a few blocks away.

"How are you feeling, Natalie?" Gregor asked me when I'd yanked my swords free from the corpse of the droid.

"I'm fine. I was overwhelmed by the sheer number of humans on the planet for a moment, but I have it under control now."

"I do not suppose you know how many droids and imps we face?" Ishida asked.

"There are seven thousand, nine hundred and eighty droids," I answered, to their surprise and mine. "As well as twenty-two thousand, one hundred and eleven Kveet clones and five hundred and fifty-nine human imps." Pausing, I amended the number. "Make that six hundred and seventy human imps."

We all knew the numbers would increase with each human that was shot by a nanobot dart. With so many robots on the march, the numbers of fresh clones would shortly grow out of control if we didn't find a way to stop them.

"There are so many!" Geordie exclaimed in dismay. "How are we going to fight them all?"

Gregor and Luc looked at each other, then at me. I knew I wasn't going to like whatever they had cooked up between them. I suspected I knew what their solution would be. "Don't even think about it!" I warned them in a dark tone.

"What choice do we have, Natalie?" Gregor asked me, striving to be reasonable. "We seven do not have the capacity to stop this invasion alone. Like it or not, the American troops have the necessary firepower to destroy the clones and the droids."

"You have stepped down as our leader," Luc said far more bluntly. "You no longer have control over our decisions."

Narrowing my eyes that had begun to glow scarlet in growing anger, I could see that they had already made their decision. "You're kidding yourselves if you think you can trust Colonel Sanderson. The first chance he gets, he'll shoot you in the back," I prophesized.

"We are immortal now," my former one true love said carelessly. "What can they possibly do to us that we cannot eventually repair?"

"Reattaching a hand or a foot is very different from piecing your entire body back together, Lord Lucentio." It might have been my imagination, but he appeared to flinch slightly at my cool tone. "I hope none of you finds out just how difficult it can be."

Drawn by their comrades' deaths, a double contingent of androids arrived. We scurried into hiding moments before they marched into view. Armed with their death rays, they searched for enemies and found only empty streets. The Viltarans must have recognized our ship to be one of their own before they'd shot it down. They knew we were here and that we would be a pain in their butts. Exterminating us probably wouldn't be a priority, but they knew what we were capable of and they would be wary.

Crouched behind a car with Geordie at my side, I raised an eyebrow at Gregor. He and Kokoro were hunkered down two cars away from us. The vehicles would make effective cover only as long as they existed. A shot from a death ray on the correct setting would leave us exposed. Weighing up our options, Gregor gave me the nod. Silently cautioning Geordie to stay down, I dashed out from behind the car.

Violet light reflected from the storefront windows, but I moved too fast for the rays to hit me. With blinding speed, I chopped, sliced, hacked and stabbed my way through the forty metal men. Battle lust sang through my veins that were clogged with the black ooze that passed for my blood. Killing droids was less satisfying than rending and tearing living enemies. My teeth clenched against the urge to hunt down some imps and rip their flesh apart with my bare hands.

Gregor's chin rested on his fist when I was done and trotted over to join the group. We remained silent to give him the time he needed to think up a strategy. "We should target the droids first," he concluded. "We must stop them from converting more humans into clones."

"Wouldn't it be a better idea to go after the Viltarans first?" Ishida queried. "If we kill them, the droids and imps won't have anyone to order them around. They will hopefully become easier to hunt down."

"Where are the Viltarans, Natalie?" Gregor asked. Once debonair, he was now bedraggled.

I pointed up at the sky. We couldn't see their ship, which meant it had to have some kind of camouflage ability. They couldn't hide from my senses and I knew they were hovering high above the city. "They're hiding out on their spaceship."

Nodding, as if I'd just confirmed his hunch, Gregor explained his reasoning to Ishida. "The Viltarans might be unreachable, but their droids aren't. If we take down the robots, we can then concentrate on eradicating any clones they've created, as well as the Kveet imps."

Ishida's expression was wry. "In that case, we will definitely require assistance. There are far too many enemies for us to face alone."

Shaking his head as if he couldn't believe what he was about to say, Igor spoke. "The quickest way for us to contact Colonel Sanderson would be to use a police radio." He pointed at a pileup of cars at an intersection half a block away. Red and blue lights flashed from the black and white police vehicle. They were an almost festive touch on an otherwise bleak street.

Chapter Seven

A sense of unreality swept through me as Gregor headed towards the police car. Several vehicles had been involved in the accident, creating a jumbled mass of twisted metal. I wasn't sure if the collision had occurred before, or after the city had come under attack. Steam still rose from an engine that had been crumpled in the crash.

No bodies were evident and there was no sign of the police officers. They'd either fled, or had been changed into ravenous monsters. Their car was parked haphazardly across the street and was pointing the wrong way. I expected to see blood soaking the seats, but they were stain free.

Taking a seat behind the wheel, Gregor reached for the radio. Noise erupted through the speakers when he switched it on. Panicked cops babbled about the horrors they were witnessing.

Gregor waited for a break in the noise before he spoke. "My name is Gregor McIvor. I was one of the twenty-nine beings that were exiled from Earth a decade ago."

A short, astonished silence followed his statement. Then a harried officer replied. "Look, pal, I don't know what kind of prank you're trying to pull, but you might have noticed we have something of a crisis going on here."

"This crisis is the result of you humans sending my people into space," Gregor said coolly. "My friends and I have information that will be of great help to your government if they wish to defeat these droids and clones. I suggest you contact Colonel Sanderson and advise him that Natalie Pierce and her kin have returned. We will be waiting for him in the vicinity of this police car."

"Are you talking about Natalie the *vampire*?" the stunned officer squeaked. I was momentarily embarrassed that my fame was still fresh in their minds. "Jeez, I thought we'd gotten rid of you lot for good." After another pause, he made a decision. "I'll make sure General Sanderson is contacted asap. Now get off the radio and let us do our jobs."

Replacing the radio in its cradle, Gregor's eyebrows rose. "It appears Colonel Sanderson has been promoted several times during our absence."

Geordie scowled at the news. "They probably pinned a bunch of medals on him as soon as our ship left the atmosphere."

"He is going to be very surprised to learn that we have returned," Ishida said with satisfaction.

Kokoro's eyes met mine and they were full of fear. The soldiers had done their best to rid their world of us forever. They wouldn't be happy to learn that their mission had failed.

"I bet you a billion dollars that Sanderson blames us for the invasion," I said to no one in particular. I didn't have one dollar to bet, let alone a billion.

"That is a wager I would not be foolish enough to take," Igor muttered.

"How long do you think it will take Sanderson to get here?" Geordie queried. He was unhappy with the tension that had sprung up in our group. He held his death ray tightly and threw frequent glances over his shoulder in search of danger.

I could have reassured the teen that we were the only living, or unliving beings in the area. The closest robots were blocks away. I chose not to share that information. It wouldn't hurt for him to be on high alert.

Luc's black eyes also searched the streets and buildings and pretty much anywhere that I wasn't. "I imagine the soldiers will already be on their way by now," he said.

Remembering my dream of the army helicopters being shot down by an electromagnetic pulse, I crossed my fingers that Sanderson's ride would crash and burn. We might require aid, but I wouldn't lose any sleep if my most hated enemy crashed in a blaze of fire.

A couple of hours later, we heard several large vehicles approaching. Unfortunately, they were trucks rather than helicopters. Apparently, they weren't seen as a threat by the aliens. They entered Manhattan without being blasted to pieces by the hovering ship.

Parking several blocks away, hundreds of soldiers approached on foot. They quietly swarmed the area in a pathetic attempt to sneak up and surround us.

Sharpshooters climbed up to the rooftops. They appeared as yellow beacons in my mind when I sent out my senses. No red dots from their scopes had appeared on our bodies yet. I had no doubt that they would show up shortly.

Waiting until his men were in position, Sanderson strode into view. He had mastered his shock at hearing we were back, but he couldn't hide his displeasure. His blue eyes were hard and unmerciful when they swept across us.

We hadn't changed in appearance since he'd bundled us into the spaceship and sent us to our doom, but he had aged. The lines in his forehead were deeper than ever and grey was speckled through his short blond hair. He would be somewhere in his mid-fifties by now, but he was still trim and fit.

After briefly studying my friends, his attention settled on me. "After ten years of relative peace, we're suddenly facing what appears to be an alien invasion. Why am I not surprised to see you here in the thick of it?" His tone was accusing, as I'd known it would be.

My upper lip had instantly curled back again at the first sight of the soldier. New medals decorated his chest, just as Geordie had predicted. He wore a snazzy officer's suit rather than the normal fatigues he'd once donned.

"Don't speak to me, worm," I told him coldly. "If it was up to me, I'd tear your throat out and leave you to bleed to death on the street like the dog you are." Actually, I had a higher regard for canines than this particular human and I'd never been much of a dog fan.

At my threat, dozens of red dots appeared. They didn't just target me, the dots speckled my friends as well. Sanderson held up his hand to prevent anyone from firing. They were all armed with the weapons that had been designed specifically to blow our kind apart. "Who should I speak to then?" he asked with a strong undertone of sarcasm.

Gregor stepped forward. "You may address me, if you wish."

"I remember you, Gregor." The soldier's nod was almost civil. "Your surname is McIvor, I presume?"

"You presume correctly." Geordie smothered a snigger at Gregor's polite reply and received an elbow in the ribs from Igor. The Russian was aware that any abrupt movement could startle the soldiers into shooting, but his apprentice was less conscious of that fact.

"Your presumption that we are responsible for the Viltaran invasion is incorrect," Gregor told the general.

Clearly disbelieving the claim, Sanderson's smile was a wry twist of his lips. "It is just a coincidence that you have arrived at the same time as the alien spacecraft then?" Some of his men shifted uneasily at the faint sound of screams. While we were standing around arguing, their people were either dying, or were being converted into monsters.

Far less diplomatic and patient than Gregor, Igor took matters into his own hands. "You have only yourselves to blame for this predicament. If you had not sent us into space, the Viltarans would not have learned about Earth. They learned of your planet's location from the ship you expelled us in."

Forgetting my warning not to speak to me, Sanderson turned to me. "Is this true?"

"Yep. You walking blood bags are finally going to pay the price for betraying us. You are directly responsible for the crap that is about to rain down on this city." My satisfaction was profound and I didn't try to hide it.

"If you feel that way, then why are you even here?" he shot back.

"I've abdicated my position as their leader," I told him. "They're in charge now." I swept my hand across my friends, then turned my back on the soldier to signify that I was done speaking to him.

"What can you tell us about these," he paused to remember the name Igor had used, "Viltarans?" he asked my friends.

Gregor took charge and gave the American a quick summary. "They are our distant ancestors. It was their ship that crash landed on Earth so long ago. Luckily, their ship was too badly damaged to contact Viltar and advise them they'd found this planet. A droid survived the crash and eventually transformed an unfortunate human into the first vampire."

According to vampire lore, the droid had been the being they'd referred to as their 'father'. I'd once thought of the sire of our race as a demi-god, since it had lived for a million years or so before perishing.

We'd all been wrong about that and the prophecies hadn't corrected our mistake. Not for the first time, I wondered exactly who or what sent us our visions. *Maybe fate is behind them,* I pondered. It wouldn't really surprise me to learn that Gregor was wrong about one thing. Maybe none of this had been a mistake at all. Maybe it had all been very deliberate.

That thought chilled me to the core. What kind of being could orchestrate events that spanned millions of years? *God?* I dismissed that thought. This wasn't the work of

God, but something far more Machiavellian. If I'd believed in Satan, I might have lumped the blame on him.

"Their technology has evolved over the millennia," Gregor continued. "The nanobots they now use leave their hosts almost bereft of any intelligence. The clones they now create have only the desire to eat and to kill."

That explained why the Kveet imps had been so lacking in conversational skills. The human imps we'd witnessed being transformed into their new bodies had been just as stupid. None were capable of thinking for themselves, which would make them malleable slaves. An added bonus was that they wouldn't have the brains to be able to plot against their masters.

"The Viltarans captured our drifting spaceship and took us to their planet," Gregor explained. "We waged war against them and only we seven remain of the twenty-nine vampires who you banished from Earth." I mentally clapped at his not so gentle dig at Sanderson's betrayal. "We managed to whittle their numbers down to twenty-one. Before we could eradicate them completely, they fled from Viltar and headed here."

I didn't trust the general at my back and half turned so I could keep him in my peripheral vision. He appeared to feel the same way and kept darting glances at me. "What kind of forces did they bring with them?" the soldier asked.

Gregor recounted the statistics I'd relayed earlier, minus the droids we'd disabled. The remains of the bots I'd sliced apart were still lying in a jumble on the street. Some of the soldiers eyed the no longer functioning metal men curiously.

"I suggest you target the droids first," Gregor counselled the general. "Their weapons can destroy both metal and flesh, but your weapons should be sufficient to terminate the robots. The Viltarans have an electromagnetic pulse ray that can disable your vehicles. It would be unwise to allow any of them to arrive via the air."

"Where are these aliens?" Sanderson swept his eyes around the area, as if expecting his adversaries to pop out from hiding and wave hello.

"We believe they are directing the attack from their spaceship. It is hovering above the city." Some of the soldiers automatically looked up, but most kept their guns trained on us.

Assessing his options, General Sanderson made up his mind. At his curt gesture, the red dots that had been speckling our bodies disappeared. "It looks like fate has thrown us together once more." *If he only knew how accurate he is,* I thought dismally. Fate had been manoeuvring all of us in a game that only it knew the rules to. "I propose that we instigate a truce while we deal with this threat," Sanderson said.

"The instant you think we're no longer useful, you'll either gun us down, or try to turn us into science experiments again," I predicted loudly enough for his closest men to hear me. "Just like you did the last time."

Lowering his eyes in a semblance of shame, Sanderson didn't bother to deny my accusation. Some of his troopers were young enough that they would have been teenagers when we'd been booted off the planet.

This was the first time our side of the story had been heard, but it wouldn't make any difference. We were a superior species and were therefore a threat to their kind. When the dust settled from our war with the Viltarans, we would face treachery from the humans again. I didn't need to be a prophet to know our truce would end in disaster.

Chapter Eight

Unseen with my eyes, but picked up by my senses, movement from high above drew my attention. I followed the direction the invisible spaceship took and realized they were drifting towards the river to our east. Framed between two buildings, the Brooklyn Bridge was an icon that even a foreigner like me recognized.

Hundreds of cars were crammed together on the structure as panicked people tried to escape from Manhattan. Many had abandoned their vehicles when the way had become clogged and were fleeing on foot. Some made it to the far side, but the vast majority were about to become casualties in our campaign against the aliens.

The ship lowered, then momentarily became visible just above the skyscrapers. My friends and I could see it clearly enough, but it was just a dark blob against the sky to the humans. Several blasts of violet light issued from beneath the ship and streaked towards the bridge. This time, it wasn't an electromagnetic pulse, but something far more damaging. A gaping hole appeared in the middle of the structure as cars, steel, bricks and people were blasted apart. With a tortured scream, the bridge collapsed into the river, taking hundreds of lives with it.

"Dear God," Sanderson breathed in horror. "They're making sure no one can escape from the city." Pulling his radio from his belt, he called for backup. The ship was already heading for the next bridge. It would shortly cut off any hope of escape for the people who resided in, or had the great misfortune of visiting, the city.

Several loud explosions went off a few blocks away. The noise came from the same direction that Sanderson and his men had appeared from. I detected several contingents of droids heading towards us as thick black smoke billowed into the sky.

"I hope you brought a lot of spare ammunition along, General Sanderson," Ishida said to the soldier as he whirled around at the noise. "You and your men are stuck here with us now and I am guessing that your vehicles have just been destroyed by the robots."

"Natalie, what do you sense?" Gregor asked.

"Eighty killbots are heading straight for us from two directions." I pointed towards where the explosions had just gone off to the southeast and directly to the north.

Thinking fast, Sanderson deployed his men. "Teams one and two, head for the rooftops. Teams three and four, spread out and take cover." His men followed his orders and scattered. He'd brought eight hundred soldiers along, which gave us far better odds than just us seven. They were all equipped with vampire killing guns. They probably also carried the small bombs that could destroy several of our kind at once. The Kveet had used a similar type of explosive device and they had proven to be effective against the droids.

Gregor motioned for us to hide and we hunkered behind the cars that had been abandoned up and down the street. Sanderson kicked open a door to an apartment building and stepped into the foyer. Half a dozen of his men followed, quickly ducking out of sight. Speaking into his radio, he gave his men further orders. My hearing was exceptional and his order easily carried to me. "Wait until they are all visible before you open fire. Our ammunition isn't infinite, so choose your shots wisely."

The metal men converged on our position. They moved almost stealthily for such large contraptions. A few low mutters were issued and were quickly stifled when the first bots came into sight. Far plainer than the translator droid we'd left behind on Viltar, their features were rudimentary, but they shared the same pointed ears, red eyes and mere slit for a mouth.

We waited for all eighty automatons to enter the street before the first shot was fired. The surprised droid looked down at the small hole that had just been punched in his chest. Before it could attempt to extract the projectile, the bullet exploded and tore it apart.

Another murderbot screeched a warning and fired at the unseen sniper. The violet blast petered out before it reached the third floor of the seven story building. Now aware of the limits to their enemy's weapons, the soldiers stepped out of hiding and focussed on eradicating the automatons.

Letting the soldiers handle the fight, I crouched beside Geordie and peered out from behind a battered piece of junk that was at least a decade older than me. The droids were methodically cut down one by one beneath the barrage of fire. Efficient and ruthless, they reduced the robots to twisted chunks of dull silver metal.

Sanderson only lost two of his men during the fracas. I'd expected more of them to die during their first major tussle with the alien robots. The general hadn't grown complacent during our absence. Maybe he'd expected us to return one day and that we'd bring trouble with us when we did.

Instructing half of his force to keep watch from above, the general cautiously left his position to take a closer look at the carnage. One of his men fished a small video camera out of his backpack and filmed the fallen androids.

I doubted it would be the only footage that would be taken of the invaders. I was fairly certain that almost everyone on the planet carried a cell phone, or some other type of device that could record videos. If any of the civilians survived this invasion, they'd make a fortune selling their images.

Taking out a radio that didn't look like it had evolved much during our absence, Sanderson contacted his people to give them an update. "This is General Sanderson. I would like to speak directly to the President."

"This is Vanessa Rivers," a female voice responded almost immediately. "What can you tell me about the situation in Manhattan, General?" Her voice was slightly gravelly, indicating she was, or had once been, a heavy smoker.

I was momentarily shocked that the Americans actually had a female president. She sounded capable and determined. I wouldn't be surprised if she turned out to be just as treacherous and cowardly as the former president who'd ordered us to be expelled from our world.

Sanderson advised his leader of the type of threat and numbers we were facing. "We require backup, Madam President, but it might not be safe to send anyone in by air."

"The police have reported that all avenues in and out of the city have just been destroyed, General Sanderson. How else are we going to send more men in? By boat?" Her tone was sarcastic, but hinted that she wasn't entirely joking.

"The Navy has submersibles that we might be able to use, ma'am."

After a brief hesitation, probably to confer with her advisors, she responded. "They'll be readied for transportation as soon as possible, General. Sit tight and remain available."

"You have a *female* president," Geordie said with almost insulting surprise when the radio went silent.

"President Rivers is the most competent person I've met so far who has held the Presidential position," Sanderson told the teen. "I have faith in her capabilities."

Ishida shared Geordie's astonishment that a female was in charge of the American government and its people, but wisely kept his mouth shut. Even Kokoro's eyes were wider than normal at the news.

Sensing trouble coming, I warned the large gathering. "Two hundred robots and five hundred Kveet clones are heading this way."

"What the hell is a 'Kveet clone'?" one of Sanderson's men wondered. A full dozen soldiers were keeping their eyes on us without openly pointing their weapons in our direction. They probably thought they were being subtle about being ready to blow our heads off at the slightest provocation. My powers of observation had sharpened considerably since leaving my mortality behind. It helped that I wouldn't trust any of these men and women as far as I could throw them.

"Pray that they do not get close enough for you to find that out for yourself," Igor told the human.

"Do we fight, or do we run?" Sanderson asked Gregor. One thing I'd admired about him, before he'd betrayed us all so horribly, had been his willingness to listen to our counsel. We knew far more about our mutual enemies than he did and he had no trouble bowing to our experience.

Gregor's answer was short and succinct. "We run." With the soldiers carrying minimal ammunition, they would quickly run out. Each man wore a small backpack that presumably held extra bullets and explosives. It wouldn't be nearly enough firepower to destroy all of our enemies. *It was pretty stupid of them not to bring a stockpile of ammo along.* If they had, it had been blown up along with the trucks.

Sanderson ordered everyone who was keeping watch in the surrounding buildings to descend to the ground while the rest of his people fell in behind him. They might have a female president, but they still didn't allow many female soldiers on the front lines. Only a handful were scattered amongst the troops.

Gregor urged me into the lead. I was our best chance of escaping without running into robots or clones. I guided my friends and despised allies through the mostly empty streets towards the west. Not everyone in the city would be aware that they were under attack, but word would surely spread quickly enough. Pandemonium would break out when they realized they were trapped.

Like sheep in a pen, they would be rounded up to be either eaten, or converted into imps. I couldn't dredge up much pity for them. For reasons that were beyond me, my friends still cared about the humans. For their sake, I would cooperate with the soldiers, but I wouldn't be stupid enough to trust Sanderson ever again. He didn't know it yet, but he was a dead man walking.

Sensing droids around the next corner, I motioned for the others to be quiet. "A unit of twenty robots is just ahead," I whispered to Gregor. I might have to work with the soldiers, but that didn't mean I had to interact with them directly.

Gregor conveyed the news to Sanderson. "Since your ammunition is limited, allow us to destroy these droids for you," he offered.

Sanderson didn't waste any time arguing. "Fine. We'll wait here."

Drawing into a small circle, we listened to Gregor's plan. "Natalie, I'd like you to circle around them. Try to get their attention while the rest of us fire on them from behind."

"Will do," I responded immediately. I didn't mind being the bait when it meant I'd have a break from being in Sanderson's presence. Shooting a brief glare of intense hatred at the general, I sprinted down a side street and came out on the far side of our quarry.

I peered around the corner to see the droids searching the buildings for victims. One held a small device that could most likely locate potential prey. My senses reported that most of the buildings were empty. A solitary human remained towards the far end of the street. The person was either paralysed, or was in a death-like sleep and had missed all the excitement.

Sauntering out into the middle of the street, I waited for the droids to spot me. A robot turned its head to scan the area and went still when it saw me. "There! A human," it said in the guttural Viltaran language.

"Guess again," I murmured when they swung their nanobot weapons towards me. I might look like a human, but I was an entirely different and far more dangerous being.

"That is not a human," the killbot with the monitor advised. "It's one of the vampires. Change weapons." It reached for the death ray that had been fixed to a nifty tool belt at its waist. Dozens of refills for the nanobot gun were lined up in a neat row on its belt. The darts were full of a glowing fluorescent yellow liquid. The fluid was a combination of Viltaran blood and the nanobots that transformed sentient, intelligent creatures into moronic, grey skinned clones.

Spreading out, the droids fired their death rays at me, but I was already on the move. They didn't stand a chance of tracking me. I easily dodged their shots and streaked towards them. I sheared the arms off two of the droids as violet light bathed them from behind.

My friends closed in, picking off targets as I sliced my way through their front ranks. Set to destroy metal, the beams from our weapons were harmless to me at the moment. Since they were extremely harmful to my swords, I shielded them from the blasts with my body.

Our exchange with the enemy hadn't gone unnoticed by the soldiers. "My God, did you see how fast she moved?" an incredulous trooper whispered from the corner where he'd watched the short skirmish. He had no idea I could hear him.

"I saw," the general replied grimly. "She wasn't that fast ten years ago."

A small smile touched my mouth. Sanderson had no idea just how much I'd changed since he'd seen me last. All of my naivety had been scoured away. I would end his life without a qualm at the first wrong step he took. In fact, I was kind of looking forward to it.

Fate owed me after all that it had put me through. Surely it wouldn't be so unkind as to deny me the joy of pinning Sanderson down with a foot on his back and tearing out his spine.

Chapter Nine

A voice came through Sanderson's radio before we could head out to hunt down some more targets. "Sanderson? This is General Hart." He sounded stern and around Sanderson's age.

"I'm here, Hart," Sanderson replied.

"Reinforcements will be arriving at the Wall Street Heliport in five minutes."

"Roger that. We'll head towards the heliport immediately."

I heard the choppers approaching and they rapidly drew closer. Dozens of the flying machines swarmed towards us like angry wasps on the warpath. A quick count told me that they carried a thousand troopers on board. Despite Gregor's warning, they'd sent their people in by air. I shook my head in warning, but Sanderson ignored my silent disapproval.

Geordie sidled up to me and huddled in close. "Why do you not want more reinforcements to arrive, *chérie?*"

"More men means there will be more of them to turn on us later, but that's not the problem."

Overhearing us, Ishida moved closer. "Then what is the problem?"

I simply pointed towards the incoming machines that had just come into our view. Four of them were framed between the buildings closest to the river. A second later, bursts of violet light streaked towards them from out of nowhere. My dream came true and the first dozen choppers, now without power, dropped out of sight into the water. The rest veered away and beat a hasty retreat. Two more went down before the Viltarans stopped firing. I could almost feel them up above us, chortling in glee at shooting down the force of soldiers. Fighting earthlings would be child's play to the far more advanced aliens.

Staring at the spot where his men had just lost their lives, Sanderson lifted the radio to his mouth again. "I don't think it would be wise to send any more soldiers in by air, Hart. They were just shot down by an electromagnetic pulse." He flicked a glance at me and I kept my expression neutral rather than mocking. While it might be fun to goad him, it probably wouldn't be very wise. You could only push someone so far before they would snap. I didn't want to test his tolerance at this early stage of our already fragile alliance. "Have the submersibles been readied yet?"

"I'm sorry to say that they aren't available. Apparently, the entire fleet has been taken out on an exercise." The general had the grace to sound embarrassed by the admission even though they belonged to the Navy rather than the Army. "It'll take two days to get them back and have them readied."

Far from a master strategist, even I knew it was doubtful we'd last two days against a superior force that had advanced weaponry on their side. Sanderson lifted his eyes heavenward before responding. "We'll hold tight and work with the vampires to take down as many of these robots and clones as we can."

"So, the blood suckers are really back?" General Hart might be a highly decorated man of war, but he sounded as scared as a kid who'd found himself in the middle of a nightmare. It was a fitting description for what we were facing.

"Yes, they're really back. And they brought a whole lot of trouble with them." Sanderson muttered the last bit beneath his breath, but we undead heard him anyway.

I slanted a look at Gregor and he nodded in acknowledgement of my warning. The flesh sacks were willing to team up with us again, but their leader held us responsible for the invasion, just as I'd known he would. If anyone had taken me up on my bet, I'd be a billion dollars better off right now.

I should have bet a hundred billion dollars. A billion probably isn't worth all that much now. It was still a shock to realize that ten years had passed while we'd been floating around in outer space. So far, nothing much seemed to have changed. Manhattan didn't seem to be all that different from the dozens of movies I'd watched that had featured the city. The skyscrapers still scraped the sky, stores still had enticing displays in their windows and cars still ran on the ground instead of hovering in mid-air.

Sanderson motioned for everyone to gather around and gave a short speech. "Since our reinforcements are cut off, we have little choice but to attempt to whittle down the enemy's numbers as best we can."

Sensing a small mob of enemies wandering in our general direction, I put a finger against my lips in the universal sign for everyone to be quiet. "We can start whittling them down right now," I said in a low voice and gestured for everyone to follow me.

The nearly eight hundred humans were anything but silent as they crept through the empty streets of one of the greatest cities on the planet. I smoothed out my grin when Gregor narrowed his eyes at me suspiciously. Understanding at my amusement dawned when he heard the piping, high pitched queries for food.

I'd decided it was high past time for our allies to meet the Kveet clones. Gregor slanted a frown at me for my childishness. I managed to curb the impulse to stick my tongue out at him, but it was a struggle. Seeing the humans panic at their first sight of the alien clones was the only enjoyment I would be likely to have over the next few days, or possibly weeks to come.

"What is that noise?" one of the men behind us asked when we were one street away from our next target.

"It sounds like birds," another man whispered. "Lots and lots of birds."

"They aren't birds," Geordie said without turning around. "They're Kveet clones and they're very, very hungry." His solemn words were more effective than if he'd run screaming in terror. With audible swallows, the soldiers braced themselves for a battle.

Choosing thirty of his men and women to follow him, Sanderson snuck up to the building on the corner. Mannequins from a clothing store watched us with creepily blank eyes. The latest fashion seemed to be sheer shirts and micro shorts. They were so tiny that my butt cheeks would have been visible if I were to don them. Geordie and Ishida eyed the outfits in appreciation, but refrained from making any juvenile comments.

Sanderson peeked around the corner at the clones that I could sense huddled together. Two and a half feet tall, grey skinned and red eyed, they almost looked like dolls. Until you saw their razor sharp teeth. "Food?" a clone cried pitifully.

I knew someone would do or say something stupid and I made sure I was right beside the soldiers when one did. "Aw," said a man who was peering over Sanderson's shoulder. "They're so *cute*."

The clones' hearing was almost as good as mine and their heads instantly whipped around. "Food?" several hell spawn queried as they slowly began to shuffle down the street towards us.

Spying the cluster of humans, a clawed hand rose to point. "Food!"

The soldier's face drained of colour and he took a step back before he gathered his courage. "Do you still think they're cute?" I asked from right behind him. Ears flushing red in embarrassment, he tried to pretend he wasn't terrified of the small herd of creatures that was now stampeding towards us.

"Can normal bullets kill these things?" Sanderson asked me calmly. His serenity was a façade. He might be able to control his expression, but I caught a whiff of the sweat that popped out on his skin. Fear was never a lovely odour.

I shrugged. "Probably." Then I cursed myself for forgetting that I'd decided I wasn't going to speak directly to him.

Waving the rest of his men forward, the general made an adjustment to the oversized weapon they all carried. He fired a short burst of normal bullets rather than explosive rounds at the rapidly approaching imps. Blown off their feet, they weren't like monsters in a horror movie that kept popping up no matter how many times they were shot.

Bright yellow blood leaked from their small, broken bodies. They reminded me of the imp baby that I'd watched claw its way out of its dead mother's womb what seemed like a thousand years ago. It had also been pitiful after I'd sliced it in half. Of course, it had tried to eat me as soon as it had seen me. I hadn't felt much remorse for killing it.

When all two hundred or so clones were either lifeless, or twitching in their death throes, the soldiers shared shaky glances. For most of them, this was their first encounter with alien life forms. A few veterans had been present in the First's cavern of doom when Sanderson and I had forged an alliance the first time. Even they were grey faced at seeing the Kveet imps up close and personal. While the earlier clones had been humanoid, these were clearly from another planet. It was still a shock to me that other intelligent beings existed. We'd thought we were alone in the universe. We'd been wrong.

"If you think they're bad, wait till you see a human that has been turned into a clone," one of the veterans said to his younger comrades. He looked vaguely familiar and had probably been with us during the battle with the First or possibly his protégé, the Second.

Word quickly spread through the group that they could expect to face monsters much larger than the ones they'd just encountered. The humans who had been turned into alien clones would be an average of seven feet tall. They would be far more formidable than the Kveet imps.

Drawn by the sound of battle, five units of silver automatons hastened to investigate. I took refuge with my friends. We watched from the safety of an alley as the human and robot armies clashed.

The death rays cut through metal and flesh easily enough, but had no effect on brick or concrete. Sanderson lost a few more men before they managed to subdue our enemies. The soldiers automatically reloaded and checked their ammunition after the last droid went down.

Sensing movement high above the city, I searched the sky, but the ship remained invisible. I followed its unseen path northward and had a premonition of disaster. Seconds later, a searing bar of orange light shot from the ship.

The vessel momentarily became visible as the ray hit its target. Loud enough for even the humans to hear it, an explosion ripped through the buildings. Too many skyscrapers hid the catastrophe from our sight, but a massive cloud of dirt billowed up, then spread out to enshroud the entire city. I felt the sudden absence of thousands of human lives.

"What the hell was that?" Sanderson barked. His eyes watered from the orange glare that still lit up the horizon to the north. Most of his troopers shaded their eyes with their hands and squinted at the brilliance.

"I am fairly certain that was the weapon the Viltarans almost destroyed their entire planet with," Gregor replied.

His prediction was proven to be correct as the sky turned a sickly shade of yellow.

Geordie wrinkled his nose as the sour smell of rotten eggs wafted to us on a breeze. The humans gagged uncontrollably, losing their last meal in most cases. Far across town, thousands, then tens of thousands, then hundreds of thousands of human lives winked out. The survivors began fleeing southward to escape from the deadly fumes. They unwittingly ran directly towards the murderbots and hell spawn that were waiting for them.

"Christ! It smells like a giant stink bomb," one of the soldiers gasped, then heaved again.

"That stink bomb just killed over four hundred thousand people," I told him.

"How can you possibly know that?" General Sanderson rasped. Taking a sip of water from his canteen, he swirled it around in his mouth then spat it out. His face was almost as pale as mine and sweat gathered on his forehead. His breath hitched again, but he controlled himself this time.

"I've changed, Sanderson," I told him ominously. "I've gained abilities that would make your hair turn white if you saw them." I glanced at the grey in his hair. "Make that whit*er*."

"I am afraid you will just have to trust that Natalie's information is correct," Gregor intervened before I erred and said too much. The soldier and I stared at each other for a long moment. Neither of us was willing or even capable of trusting each other at this point and neither of us was about to break eye contact first. It was a given that I would win. I could go for a very long time without blinking. Decades if I had to.

"General, we're going to run out of ammo long before we can subdue the droids and those…imp things," a soldier with a few medals on his chest warned his boss.

Nodding, Sanderson used the interruption as an excuse to break our staring contest. Turning his back on me, he addressed Gregor. "Is there any chance your people could retrieve the ammunition that went down with the choppers into the East River?"

Gregor was ostensibly in charge, but he wasn't our absolute ruler. He looked at each of us for our opinion. Everyone gave him a nod and I gave him a shrug to say that it was his choice. It hadn't been my decision to call for Sanderson's help so they could deal with the details. "We are willing to try. After you, General," Gregor invited the soldier with a small bow.

I remained on full alert as we jogged eastward to where the choppers had gone down into the murky water. Sanderson had kept in shape while we'd been floating around in space as frozen vampsicles. He was barely breathing hard when we came to a stop near the dark water just north of the Brooklyn Bridge.

The area was deserted now that the bridge no longer offered the way to freedom. Dozens of bodies lay strewn in the wreckage and bobbed in the water below. My stomach tried to lurch at the thought that the victims would become imp snacks once the clones came across them. *At least they're already dead.* The humans that were being held captive throughout the city would still be alive when their captors began to eat them. The earlier version of human imps had preferred to cook their meat before eating it. Somehow, I doubted these clones would even be able to figure out how to start a fire.

Sending some of his people out to scout the water, Sanderson waited patiently for several minutes until his radio came to life. "General, this is Sergeant Wesley."

"Go ahead, Sergeant."

"I've located where the choppers went down, sir."

"Where are you situated?"

"I'm roughly halfway to the Manhattan Bridge, General."

"Stay put, we'll be there shortly."

We moved at a fast jog and it didn't take us long to reach the waiting soldier. A number of men wearing army uniforms floated in the river. Their corpses helped us to pinpoint where the helicopters had disappeared.

"Will you advise the soldiers if you sense danger approaching?" Gregor asked me as Sanderson deployed his men to strategic positions around the area. The Manhattan Bridge had also been destroyed, as had any other avenue that had once offered a way to safety.

Glancing at the smelly, polluted water, I nodded. "I'll keep watch. It beats going back in there." Kokoro's delicately beautiful face briefly registered disgust as a dead rat floated past. Waterlogged and bloated, it showed clear signs that it had been feasted upon by its fellow critters. With ropy intestines bulging out of its torn stomach, it wasn't a pretty sight.

Not happy about leaving me behind, Geordie opened his mouth to protest. Igor picked him up and threw him into the river before he could utter more than a startled squeak. The Russian tossed the teen an empty backpack a soldier handed him, then took one for himself. My other five friends followed him beneath the surface and disappeared from even my keen sight.

"Don't they need to come up for air?" someone asked quietly after several minutes had passed.

"They're undead, stupid," a female soldier replied with a hint of derision. "They don't need to breathe."

"Oh, yeah. I forgot about that." With a sheepish smile, the male soldier subsided into a watchful silence.

Dozens of lifeless bodies were retrieved by a small group of their comrades as they waited for the ammunition to be rescued from its watery grave. They placed their deceased in a neat, respectful row. The rest of the soldiers would still be entombed within the choppers that rested on the bottom of the river. It would take hours for my companions to retrieve all of the ammunition from the metal coffins and I didn't envy them their task.

No one could have lived through a fall from the height the choppers had been, so they didn't bother to search for survivors. That didn't stop me from sweeping the river in search of anyone still clinging to life. Once their lives ended, I could no longer sense the humans. I wasn't surprised when I came up empty.

My clothes were now dry and no longer clung to my skin, but they were filthy and tattered. The closest enemies were a dozen blocks away and none were moving in our direction. I decided it would be safe enough to get cleaned up and to find a change of clothes.

Picking one of the soldiers at random, I pointed at him. "You. Come with me."

Blanching at the command, he sent a mute glance of appeal towards his superior officer.

"What do you want with Corporal Higgins?" Sanderson asked suspiciously.

Forcing out a completely unnecessary sigh, I explained my intentions. "I'm going to take a shower and find something else to wear. If I sense anything coming this way, your man can radio a warning to you."

Searching for a flaw in my logic, the general finally nodded his permission, not that I was seeking it. "Make sure he comes back in one piece," he warned me.

"Make sure he comes back in one piece," I mimicked in a high pitched undertone as I walked away. The soldier following on my heels suppressed a snigger. We both knew the general wouldn't do anything to me. I could pull my new lackey apart with my bare hands and leave him in a dozen pieces if I really wanted to.

We all knew that Sanderson needed my talents, and the help of my friends, if he wanted his people to survive this invasion. Even with our help, there was no guarantee that we'd be able to stop the alien invaders from becoming Earth's new evil overlords.

Chapter Ten

Heading to the closest apartment building, I ignored the elevator and trudged up the stairs to the first floor. The smell of mothballs coming from the first apartment strongly hinted that an elderly person lived there. I continued on.

Checking doors that had mostly been left open when their occupants had fled in a panic, I finally found an apartment on the second floor that had housed two young women. Sorting through a chest of drawers, I pulled out a pair of jeans and checked the size. The US sizes were very different from the Australian sizing system, but they looked like they would fit me.

"Wait out in the hall," I told Higgins. The last thing I needed was a stranger hovering nearby while I showered. "I'll yell if I sense anything coming." He gave me a salute and retreated from the apartment.

Locking the bathroom door automatically, I stripped off my filthy clothing and turned the hot water on full blast. I used a quarter of a bottle of shampoo and conditioner before I was convinced my hair was finally clean. My skin was bright red from the boiling water when I was finished scrubbing it. I was no longer affected by extreme temperatures. It might as well have been lukewarm to me.

Wrapping a fluffy towel around my body, I blow dried my hair, glad the power was still on in the city. Combing it into a semblance of neatness, I stared at my reflection. Despite my lingering insecurities, even I had to admit that I was now beautiful. My pale skin was flawless and my features were perfectly formed. *I might look gorgeous on the outside, but I guess I'm still plain on the inside,* I thought sadly. Maybe if my personality had been more vibrant and loveable, Luc might not have given up on me so quickly.

Fighting down the childish impulse to smash my fist into the mirror, I sorted through the chest of drawers again for more clothing. I found clean panties that were my size, but the bra was two cup sizes too small. The other occupant of the apartment was larger than her friend and her bra was a better fit.

Returning to the first bedroom, the jeans I struggled into were a tight fit. They'd have been in danger of cutting off my circulation if I'd had any. The plain white t-shirt and red hooded sweater fit me well enough. The sneakers I found beneath the bed were a size too large. I tied the laces tightly so they were in no danger of falling off.

When I joined the soldier in the hall, he stared at me as if he was seeing me for the first time. "You really are gorgeous, aren't you?" he asked me in wonder.

Now that my disguise of several layers of dirt was gone, my magical vampire hotness was on display. "Yes," I replied honestly. "Let's go."

Scrambling to catch up to me, Higgins walked at my side, sneaking frequent glances at my face. "Can I ask you something?" Average in height, weight and looks with brown hair and eyes, he was the sort of guy who could blend into a crowd and not easily be remembered. His expression was earnest and curious. It made a nice change from the hostility displayed by some of his fellow troopers.

"If you must." His instinctive fear of me must be abating if he felt comfortable enough to play twenty questions.

"What happened the day you and General Sanderson fought the crazy vampire that called himself the Second?"

Being in his mid-twenties, the trooper would have been a teen at the time. "*I* fought the Second," I corrected him. "Sanderson and his three stooges waited for me outside while I entered the abandoned castle in Bulgaria."

I remembered it well. To me, the episode in question might only have happened a few months ago rather than a decade. The crumbling ruin had been half taken over with clinging vines. The Second had used it as a lair to stash the beginnings of an army of newly made vamps. My task had been to stop him from creating more servants. I'd snuck into his hideout at dawn. Some might call it a cowardly act. I considered it to be practical. Doing so had meant I'd only needed to battle the master of the ruins rather than dozens of his devoted minions.

Skipping most of the details, I stuck to the main points. "I had a one on one battle with the Second and turned him into a slimy puddle of ooze. I then headed downstairs to polish off his lackeys. When I finished stabbing the vampire fledglings to death, I called out to Sanderson that it was safe for him and his men to enter the castle." I remembered the then colonel's betrayal very clearly and doubted I'd ever forget it.

"His men rushed inside, grabbed me and tossed me out into the sun. Then they shot me with their guns," I gestured to the weapon in his hands that was now standard issue, "and blew me apart. They stomped my bones to pieces and let the sun turn me to ash. Lastly, they sealed me inside a metal box and threw me into the sea. After that, they either killed, or captured my friends and allies and performed horrible experiments on them."

Doubt was reflected in the soldier's eyes. "That's not what they said happened." I guessed the 'they' he was talking about had been the government at that time.

"What story did they tell you?"

"That you went power mad and tried to hypnotize the General and his men. They were forced to imprison you and your people to prevent you from attempting to take over the world."

For a moment, I was too astounded to speak, then I started to laugh. Wiping dry eyes that would have been streaming with tears if they'd been able to, I finally regained control of myself. "If I'd wanted to hypnotize Sanderson, he wouldn't have been able to stop me. As for taking over the world, I don't even want to rule my kind let alone your kind."

"Why not?" he asked curiously as we headed down the stairs.

"I don't have the slightest interest in ruling anyone," I responded. "If my friends were to create an army of our kind, we'd be constantly at war with you humans. Only the really old vampires want absolute rule. And some of the crazy ones," I added as an afterthought.

When I really thought about it, the ancient vampires tended to be crazy anyway. Kokoro, Igor and Ishida were some of the oldest vamps I knew. So far, they seemed to be sane enough. Igor was just too practical to turn insane and Kokoro and Ishida were too self-disciplined to succumb to madness. Not that I was an expert on mental illness. If any of us was likely to go mad, it would probably be me.

"Why would your friends have to create an army? Can't you do it yourself?"

"I'm different from the others in that way. My blood is toxic to humans." Actually, it seemed to be lethal to all life forms. I'd yet to be bitten by anything that had actually survived the attack.

"Oh." He pondered that news silently, then changed the topic back to our current enemies. "Do you think these Viltarans," he stumbled over the unfamiliar word, "are crazy, or are they just evil?"

My brief moment of hilarity had already faded. "I'm pretty sure they're both," I told him. My senses detected enemies approaching. I held up my hand to stop him from asking any more questions. "You'd better tell your boss that some Kveet imps are heading this way."

"How many are there?" he asked as he reached for his radio.

"About five hundred."

"General Sanderson," he said into his radio, "this is Corporal Higgins."

"Go ahead, Higgins," his boss responded.

"Natalie has advised me that five hundred or so of those little grey monsters are heading in our direction."

"Roger that, Corporal. Head back on the double."

"Yes, sir."

I kept pace with the soldier as he sprinted down the stairs and through the streets back to his team. Sanderson's expression was grave as he walked towards me. "I know you hate my guts and I don't blame you for feeling that way." *Gee, how nice of him to give me permission to despise him,* I thought snidely, but he continued speaking before I could voice it. "I'm asking you to put aside the animosity you feel towards me. Like it or not, we're going to have to work together until this mission is done."

I briefly wondered which of us hated the idea of being allies more and suspected it would be too close to call. "Then you're going to shoot me in the back again, I suppose?" I said cynically. Higgins peeked at me from the corner of his eye then tried to pretend he hadn't heard my remark.

"Which direction are these clones coming from?" the general asked, ignoring my question and the heavy sarcasm that had come with it.

"From there and there." My hands pointed west and north. Relaying the information to his men, Sanderson then ordered radio silence. "I have a question for you, Sanderson," I said quietly.

"Make it quick." He flicked a glance at me then went back to scanning the area for threats.

"What did you do with my original swords?"

His eyes dropped to the plain, yet functional samurai swords in my hands. "I took them to a scrap metal yard and watched as they were melted down." I heard no satisfaction in his tone, yet sensed it anyway.

"That was stupid. They were thousands of years old. You could've made a fortune if you'd sold them to a

94

collector." I felt a stab of pain that my prized weapons had been lost beyond any hope of recovery, but I kept my expression neutral. He'd done his best to wipe away any trace of my existence, but he'd failed. I was back and soon he was going to pay. The destruction of my weapons was just one more crime he would answer for.

A small pile of ammunition rested on the street after being retrieved from the river by my friends. Dripping with water, they were otherwise still in good condition. I was pretty sure being immersed in water wouldn't render the bullets useless. The soldiers wouldn't have bothered to send us in after them if the ammo didn't work.

Kokoro's head broke the surface, drawing the attention of a soldier. She swam over to hand her loaded backpack to him. While she held it up easily with one hand, he gave a grunt of effort and grabbed it with both.

She spared an envious glance at my dry state and clean clothing before accepting an empty backpack and diving to hunt for ammunition once more. While some of the ammo had broken free from their containers, some intact boxes had also been retrieved. Just as I'd suspected, small bombs sat alongside the magazines that contained bullets and explosive rounds.

I heard the twittering cries of the approaching clones long before they came within range of human detection. A few of the soldiers cursed beneath their breath when they caught sight of the army of ravenous imps. They were questing for food and none would stop until they had either eaten their fill, or were dead.

Snipers began picking off the small critters, but they barely made a dent in the numbers. More soldiers had been stationed on the first floor of the nearby buildings.

They could shoot their targets without the risk of being eaten by them. At their leader's signal, they leaned out of windows and opened fire.

The hell spawn milled in confusion as dozens of their companions were blasted off their feet. Then one spotted a soldier who peeked too far around the car he was hiding behind. With a high pitched cry of glee, the clone sped across the road. Remaining calm, the soldier put a bullet into the creature's brain, but hundreds more were fast on its heels.

Surrounded by heavily armed soldiers, the tiny terrors were gunned down unmercifully. They lacked the intelligence to understand the concept of surrender. Even when their numbers had been whittled down to a bare handful, the clones continued to attack. Climbing over the bodies of its kin, one of the final remaining imps scurried towards Sanderson. Scarlet eyes were trained on the general's face as it dodged bullets more by accident than on purpose.

Standing beside the man who'd betrayed me, I made no effort to stop the gremlin as it raced across the graveyard of its fallen brethren. It came within ten feet of Sanderson before Higgins finally managed to blow the creature in half.

Leaving its body from the waist down behind, the starving Kveet imp stubbornly clung to life. It doggedly used its claws to drag itself a few inches closer before finally collapsing. Taking a stride forward, Sanderson calmly pulled his pistol from the holster at his hip. Pinning the dying alien down with a boot on its back, he pumped two rounds into its head. Its skull exploded, staining his boot with brains and bone. The image was very similar to the one I'd had of ripping the human's spine out of his back. I doubted he'd appreciate the comparison and batted my lashes innocently at his suspicious glare.

Nearly twenty men had fallen beneath the wave of starving mini demons before they'd finally been cut down. Bare skeletons with chewed bones were all that remained of the deceased soldiers. Still trembling in a combination of fright, horror and adrenalin, a few men picked their way through the carnage. They stripped the weapons and ammo from the corpses of their comrades.

"That's what you sent us to face," I said to Sanderson's back. He looked over his shoulder at me as he reloaded his weapon by touch. "We found ourselves on a planet that was almost completely devoid of life. The only creatures that were left were the Kveet, ten aquatic aliens, various types of clones and the Viltarans.

"The Viltarans are so warlike and bloodthirsty that they almost killed each other off when they ran out of other worlds to conquer. They turned their planet into a wasteland. They have to live beneath the ground because their air is no longer breathable. Now they're here and, if we don't stop them, they'll do the same thing to our planet." After a brief silence while he contemplated this bleak future, I continued. "If it were up to me, I'd let the Viltarans turn you all into their food and slaves for what you did to my kind."

"I'm sorry," he forced out through stiff lips. The gun in his hand twitched as he turned around. I knew he wanted to point it at my face and pull the trigger until the clip was empty. "I'm sorry I was ordered to betray you and for what my government did to your people." I noted how he neatly avoided taking responsibility for the deaths and torture of my kin. "Surely, you don't want your own planet to become an uninhabitable ruin like Viltar?"

"No. I don't want Earth itself to be harmed. I just want the people that inhabit it to suffer."

He waved his empty hand at the chewed up skeletons of his men. He swept it northward, presumably indicating the civilians that were currently being rounded up. "Don't you think there has been enough suffering by now?"

My smile was small and tight. "Not by a longshot."

"What happened to you?" he asked quietly. "You used to care about humans. Don't you have even a shred of compassion left? Don't you have a heart anymore?"

"*You* happened to me, Sanderson. I used to feel compassion and cared about your kind, but that was before you turned on me. Now my heart is as cold and dead as the rest of me."

"Why did you come back then? Your friends seem eager enough to help us, but I don't understand why you're here if you hate us so much."

He was truly bewildered and it would be my great pleasure to explain my motives. "Isn't it obvious?" At his blank stare, I spelled it out for him. "I'm here for revenge."

"You want to kill me," he said flatly.

"That's the general idea, no pun intended." Hovering nearby, still trying to pretend he wasn't listening in, Higgins stirred slightly. He didn't point his weapon at me for threatening his boss. Now that he'd heard my side of the story, maybe he had some doubts that I'd turned into a power mad vamp and had tried to take over the world.

Sanderson didn't smile at my quip. His hard blue eyes bored into mine. "If I promise to hand myself over to you when this is all done, will you give me your word that you will do your best to assist us?"

"Your promises mean nothing to me, Sanderson," I scoffed. "Besides, handing yourself over to me won't be any fun. I'd rather hunt you down, like you did to my kind." His face paled and he shifted his grip on his gun slightly. "Don't even think about it," I warned him quietly. "If you, or any of your people fire at me or my friends, I will shove my hand down your throat and rip your intestines out through your mouth." I wasn't sure where that idea had come from, but I liked it immensely. It was an even better threat than tearing his spine out would have been.

Quailing from my dark promise, he turned and walked away. Higgins sent me a wide eyed stare before turning away to keep a lookout for approaching enemies.

Are you having fun baiting Sanderson? My inner voice sounded dry as it asked me the question. *I'm having more fun than I've had in years,* I responded airily. Physical pain was only one way to torture someone. Mental anguish was turning out to be far more satisfying.

Chapter Eleven

A faint blush of light touched the horizon when my friends finished hauling the last of the ammunition to the surface. The soldiers had quite a cache by now. It still wouldn't be enough to destroy all of our enemies, but it would help to cut down the numbers of murderbots.

The fewer droids that were running around firing nanobot guns meant we'd have fewer clones we would eventually have to destroy. I didn't kid myself that this would be in any way easy. We had a long, hard fight ahead and it didn't look like backup was going to arrive any time soon.

Squinting against what was searing brightness to us and barely noticeable sunlight to the humans, Gregor had a quick word to Sanderson. "The clones will be seeking shelter from the sun by now and my friends and I must do the same."

"They'll be heading for the subway, I assume?" Sanderson asked.

Gregor arched an eyebrow at me in silent query. I'd been keeping track of our adversaries as they headed into the dark tunnels the humans had thoughtfully made for them and nodded. "So it would seem," Gregor replied.

Sanderson had been on enough monster hunts against nocturnal creatures to know their habits. He was well aware of our limitations as well and knew we would also need to find shelter. "I'll have some of my men escort you to the nearest subway entrance," he said. "The rest of us will join you shortly."

Corporal Higgins was one of the men chosen to be our escorts. He nodded at me politely as he jogged past.

"He seems awfully friendly," Geordie said suspiciously as he walked at my side. Dripping wet, he peered through his dirty blond hair.

"Higgins escorted me when I took a shower." The teen's eyes bugged at that and Luc's head twitched in my direction. For a moment, I debated about pretending that I'd fed my flesh hunger on the human to make Luc jealous. Then I realized how ridiculous that idea was. A vampire as worldly and attractive as my one true love would never be jealous of an ordinary human. "He waited out in the hall just in case I sensed any enemies approaching," I explained.

Geordie gave a weak laugh. "For a moment there, I thought you'd fed your..." he trailed off when Igor frowned threateningly at him.

"Natalie is choosy about who she shares her flesh hunger with," Ishida said with a sly glance towards my ex-beloved. "She had the choice of several humans on our island and she refused them all."

"Sex with humans is overrated," Geordie said with a careless wave. "They are far too fragile and break easily." I hid my smile, wondering how many humans he'd had sex with since he'd been turned. Something told me it would have been few. The sardonic look his mentor gave him backed up my theory.

"I disagree," Ishida said with a rare smile. "If treated gently, humans can be very satisfying bed partners."

Goggling at his fellow adolescent, Geordie almost tripped down the stairs. I grabbed him before he could fall and dispel the myth that we had preternatural, catlike reflexes. Most of us did, but even we could be clumsy at times. "You've had sex with a lot of humans then?" Geordie asked.

Ishida nodded almost casually. "I usually shared my bed with three or four girls at a time."

Geordie turned to Kokoro to see if the former emperor was telling the truth. She confirmed his story with a nod. "I really, really wish your island hadn't been bombed," he said mournfully.

"As do I," Ishida replied with a dark look at the soldiers that were flanking us. It had been men like this who had eradicated our kind, even if it hadn't been these particular soldiers.

We descended the stairs into the subway. Apart from rats, I heard and sensed no signs of life in the nearby vicinity. A strong odour of urine came from a dark corner. A pile of filthy blankets and a few flattened cardboard boxes had once been a homeless person's resting place. From the empty booze bottles and syringes lying around, neatness wasn't particularly important to the hobo. When the pile of blankets suddenly moved, Ishida almost blasted it with his death ray. A pair of rats glared up at him before scampering off towards the tracks.

"Can you sense what is happening on the surface?" Igor asked as we gathered into a small group further away from the smell of pee.

Sending out my senses, I confirmed that the imps had all taken shelter. They were either in the sewers, subway tunnels, or inside hastily vacated buildings. Hundreds of thousands of people were currently making their way southward. The rest were huddled inside their homes, hoping to be overlooked in the next robot sweep.

The droids had drawn back somewhere to the north. Any humans they turned into clones would probably burst into flames once the sun hit their flesh. They'd given up hunting and now seemed to be in a state of rest. I described what I'd sensed to the others.

"How many humans have been converted now?" Luc asked without looking directly at me.

"Four thousand or so." Exact numbers didn't matter so much when we were outnumbered so badly. We'd been in a similar situation twice before, but this time we had even less chance of taking down our enemies.

Fighting hordes of the First's imps and then the rabid vampire fledglings made by his disciples had been tough. We'd managed to kill them all with only a minimal loss of human lives. The Viltarans had a weapon that was capable of eradicating all life on the planet. They were going to be much harder to best. They'd already murdered hundreds of thousands of earthlings and they'd just gotten started.

Gregor took a seat on one of the benches and settled into his classic thinking pose. He was already concerned about the numbers we were facing and his worry was about to increase.

"There's something I think you guys should know." Their heads swivelled to me. Even Luc turned in my direction, but averted his gaze as if he couldn't stand to look at me. "The Viltarans aren't alone on their ship. They have more droids up there with them."

"How many more?" Gregor asked with a hint of alarm showing through his calm.

"Thirty thousand."

"*Thirty thousand?*" Geordie's voice was a high pitched tone that sounded startlingly like our Kveet allies back on Viltar.

"They have a few more Kveet imps with them as well," I added. "Eighty thousand in total," I said before anyone could ask.

Igor thumped down on the bench beside Gregor with a weary shake of his head. "If they have so many servants, why do they not just release them all at once?"

"They are most likely testing the humans' defence capabilities," Gregor told him.

"They know about our nuclear weapons," Ishida reminded us. Anything we'd told Robert the robot had been relayed to his master, Uldar. "But they also know how reluctant the armies will be to use them."

Geordie had a different theory. "I think they are toying with us. They like watching the humans squirm."

"We need to disable their ship," Gregor said.

"How?" Luc's tone was despairing. "They will shoot down anything that comes within their reach."

"Do you think they will be able to shoot down missiles that are fired from a distance?" Ishida asked.

Hearing the last part of our conversation, Higgins wandered over. "Missiles need a target to lock onto and the alien ship is invisible to our detection systems." It sounded like they'd already tried to target the space craft and had failed.

"Then there is no hope of blowing it out of the sky?" Geordie asked.

Higgins shook his head mournfully. "Nope." He returned to his team after receiving a sharp glance from a superior officer for fraternizing with the undead.

"They don't know it yet, but everyone in Manhattan is screwed," I said softly enough that the soldiers couldn't overhear me.

"You are giving up on them already?" Luc said almost bitterly.

"Giving up is more your style," I said coldly and stalked off before my temper could turn into sorrow. Dry sobbing in front of the soldiers would be far too humiliating. Disappearing into the darkness of the subway tunnel, my now scarlet eyes lit up the area a few paces ahead of me.

"Where is she going?" Higgins asked.

"To kill some imps," Ishida replied.

It was a good guess and an accurate one. I could sense a small pocket of freshly converted human clones somewhere to the east and hurried towards them. Mindful that being electrocuted wouldn't kill me, but would probably mess up my hair pretty badly, I avoided the rails.

Several subway stations later, snoring rumbled down the tunnel from slumbering imps. Thirty-seven former humans lay on the ground. Far less intelligent than the imps I was used to back in what I thought of as the good old days, none had bothered to find makeshift clothing. Their naked, sweaty, blood stained grey flesh was a mass of muscle. Some had breasts and all had human genitalia. I wondered if these clones could reproduce like the original ones I'd destroyed. Instinct told me they couldn't, so at least that was one less thing to worry about.

Identical of face and form, these particular clones had a pig-like snout and fangs that protruded from their top and bottom jaws. They had the typical long ears that were curled at the ends. None stirred as I moved amongst them.

My swords slid in and out of their hearts and each one died soundlessly and painlessly. The humans they'd consumed would have suffered a far more terrorizing and painful death. A flicker of pity welled up for the civilians who had already died and for those who would suffer the same fate. I stamped down on it before it could grow into the compassion that Sanderson had accused me of no longer possessing.

Working my way through the tunnels, I eradicated dozens of small groups of human and Kveet imps. Eventually, I reached a far larger band and found both types of clones mixed in together. Standing in the shadows of the subway tunnel, I studied the gigantic ex-humans and the tiny Kveet clones. They slept peacefully together, which meant they had been ordered not to attack each other. I'd hoped they would kill their rivals on sight, but that likelihood had just gone out the window.

I'd lost track of time while I'd been hunting and the sun would shortly tuck itself away for the day. I didn't have enough time to stab this entire group of imps to death before they woke up, which meant I would have to improvise.

Remembering how messy it could be when I unleashed the power of my holy marks, I stripped off. I left my clothes and swords a safe distance away from the mess that I was about to create. Naked and seemingly unarmed, I walked to the centre of the slumbering mob and dropped to my knees.

I glanced at my hands before placing one on the head of a Kveet and the other against a former human. Twin indentations in the shape of crosses marked my palms. The original cross that had given me the marks had been large and plain. A much smaller silver cross in the centre had contained exquisitely detailed filigree.

The delicate metal lacework had been perfectly rendered on my palms. They had been one of the first signs that I was the dreaded Mortis. No matter how many times my body was destroyed and repaired itself, the holy marks always came back. They were my greatest weapons. With them, I would never truly be unarmed.

Concentrating, I let the power build up inside me. The imps began to wake as the ground trembled. I let the power grow until it felt like I would burst if I didn't let go. Let go I did and every imp in the area exploded in a barrage of grey flesh.

Splattered from head to toe in ooze, I stood and surveyed the devastation. Bright yellow blood and gobbets of flesh covered the walls, the ground and me. The imps I'd faced before we'd been sent into outer space had had black blood rather than fluorescent yellow. Then again, they had been vampires before finally being transformed into imps.

The nanobots the droid fed to the First must have gone bad over time, my subconscious mused, echoing a thought I'd had earlier. The crash-landed droid had had to wait for a very long time for humans to evolve before they'd become intelligent enough to be converted. It was possible that the micro-robots had malfunctioned due to extreme age.

Right from the start, our physiology had been different from normal clones. Instead of being turned into an imp straight away, the First had simply died then been reborn three nights later as the undead. It had taken thousands of years for him to finally turn into an imp. The vampires he and his disciples had created had retained their human forms, but their shadows had been corrupted by the ooze that clogged their veins. Their shadows had become imps instead of their bodies. Only when they were called to the First had he been able to bring their inner hell spawn out from within them and convert their flesh into his image.

Flicking my hands, more blood speckled the already slick ground. I'd need to take another shower to clean it all off. *Or do I?* Since I was alone and none of my friends or allies were there to witness my possible failure, I tried an experiment.

Instead of breaking my body down into pieces, I envisioned it becoming tiny dust motes just like when Luc had shot me with a death ray. Obeying my mental command, I instantly lost form and became smaller than ashes and as light as the air itself. It took some practice, but I was able to glide across the subway and over to my clothing. It only took a second to re-form and when I did, I was squeaky clean.

"Now that's going to come in handy." I mentally patted myself on the back for my ingenuity. It was a neat trick. I was glad it no longer took me several minutes to break down into chunks before finally becoming tiny motes. I only wished I had the same kind of control over my clothes as well. Alas, they weren't a part of me and were beyond my ability to manipulate.

Dressing quickly, I retrieved my swords and jogged back through the tunnels to the others. I wasn't sure if Sanderson was relieved, or disappointed when I appeared. Luc spared me a glance, then dismissed me completely. Igor rolled his eyes, probably wishing he could smack both of us up the back of the head. If it could have helped our situation, I would have gladly lined up to be walloped.

"How many imps did you kill, *chérie*?" Geordie asked. He was doing his best to ignore the tension in the air. The sidelong glances he kept sneaking at the soldiers told me he trusted them about as much as I did.

"A few hundred. Not enough to make a real difference." His face fell at my glum reply. "At least these still work," I held up my palms to show him the crosses and he automatically flinched away. He knew they couldn't hurt him, unless I willed them to, but their deadliness was well known amongst our kind. They would be difficult for any vampire to grow comfortable with.

"Why aren't you covered in intestines?" Ishida asked.

"I learned a new trick," I replied and winked. We were talking softly enough that the soldiers weren't in danger of overhearing us.

The teen glanced towards our allies and nodded that he understood my reluctance to explain myself. "Are you aware that you are speaking in Japanese?" he asked me.

I laughed at his joke, but none of my friends laughed with me. *He isn't kidding,* I realized. I'd noticed that he had reverted to his native language, but I hadn't realized I'd somehow managed to respond in kind.

"Where are the closest droids?" Geordie asked me casually in French.

"Six blocks away," I replied in the same language.

Igor was next. "Have the clones begun their attacks on the humans yet?"

"Not quite. They are just beginning to leave their shelters now." My Russian was flawless.

Gregor gave Luc a pointed look, which he ignored. It didn't look like I would get to test my ability to speak his native tongue.

"When did you acquire this new ability?" Kokoro asked. She spoke in English for everyone's benefit.

"Probably after I was shot with the nanobot guns." I couldn't think of anything else that had happened to me that could have wrought such a change. It seemed my brain rather than my body had been altered by the infusion of micro robots in my system this time.

"How come you always get the cool powers?" Geordie complained with a pout.

"Because I'm Mortis, queen of death," was my dry response. "Believe me, I'd switch with you in a heartbeat if I could." He was in no danger of that happening. My heart had ceased to beat when my life had ended. The chances of it ever beating again were non-existent.

The teen debated the pros and cons of being a dreaded figure of legend then shook his head. "No thanks. I prefer being a nobody." So did I, but I hadn't had any say in the matter. My fate had been sealed long before I'd even been born.

Sanderson stopped just ahead and waved for us to catch up to him. "If you're ready, we'll head up to the surface," he said when we reached him. He looked tired and I wondered how much sleep he and his troops had managed to grab. I might not be happy about being allied with the Americans but, unfortunately, we needed their firepower. His people had to be fit and ready to fight our mutual enemies. They would be useless if they fell asleep on the job.

My friends and I were showing few signs of tiredness so far. I felt as fresh as if I'd just slept for an entire day. Somehow, I doubted the general would be happy if I pointed that out to him. He already had enough reasons to hate, fear and resent us. I didn't need to rub our overall superiority to his species in his face.

Chapter Twelve

Slowed down by the weight of the ammunition they carried in their packs, as well as the other essentials they'd brought along, the soldiers could only move at a fast trot. When it came to the crunch, they could shed their backpacks if needed and move at a much quicker pace.

We vampires remained in a small group with a wide space between us and the soldiers. Most of the humans distrusted us and were intent on keeping their distance. Despite the treachery he'd doled out to our kind, Sanderson alone felt comfortable mingling with us. He fell into step beside Gregor. "None of your people have fed yet," he pointed out.

"We no longer need to feed as often as we once did."

"Why not?"

Gregor gave the soldier a measuring look. "Let's just say it is a consequence of vacationing on Viltar."

Our entire band of twenty-nine banished souls had fed on a Viltaran shortly after landing on the alien planet. It had been enough to partially reverse their starvation from drifting through space for a decade. Only we seven had fed far more deeply on the blood of our ancient ancestors the next time we'd cornered our enemy. My friends had gained immortality from their second feast. I'd already been unkillable and had only gained enhanced strength and speed.

"What other changes have happened to you?"

"Our eyes turn red when we're angry," Geordie said helpfully. It was a minor change that didn't seem to have any benefit at all. It indicated when we were mad, sad or were in dire need of feeding our flesh hunger.

"We also sleep like humans now," Ishida added. That was a far more useful change. Our bodies no longer shut down into a deathlike sleep which rendered us helpless during the day. Any vampire would kill for that particular talent.

Sanderson waited for more, but no one else offered him any information. "That's it? Nothing else has changed?"

"That's it," Igor said flatly. His expression dared the general to call him a liar. Proving he wasn't stupid, the soldier increased his pace to catch up to his men again.

I'd been worried that Geordie would blurt out that they were all immortal now, but I'd underestimated his level of maturity. We hadn't discussed withholding how much we'd changed from our allies. We'd each individually decided it would be prudent to let them think we were more vulnerable than we actually were. Our truce with the humans was a precarious thing. It could end very abruptly if our fragile trust were to be broken.

While I'd been busy hunting down imps, Gregor had discussed strategy with the general. They'd agreed to continue to focus on the droids and attempt to eradicate them first. Gregor hadn't yet passed on the information about how many more enemies were waiting in the spaceship that hovered far above the city. We couldn't do anything about them anyway and he didn't want the soldiers to give up hope that they might come out of this alive.

I wasn't the only one to notice a small group of soldiers break away from the others and move to the head of the pack. One glanced back almost guiltily as they moved out of our range of hearing. Gregor threw a glance at me, indicating that he was worried they might be plotting something. I shared his concern. "Do you want me to see if I can spy on them?" I whispered.

At his short nod, it was time to test out my newest skill. Concentrating on my right eye, it didn't pop free of the socket as usual, but simply disintegrated instead. Geordie made a startled noise and Igor put a finger to his lips to keep him quiet. Staying together in a tiny clump, the weightless eye particles floated towards the small group in the lead.

My eye re-formed just enough for me to see the men foggily then descended to land on one of the soldier's shoulders. Whole again, it held on with its optic nerves and peered down at the human's hands. He and several others had appropriated death rays that had been dropped by fallen droids. Pushing buttons methodically, none had yet worked out how to use them, but they eventually would.

Recalling my eye, the particles settled back into the empty socket and my orb became whole again. Ishida gave me a quick grin of appreciation at my new ability, but Geordie's was decidedly sickly. For a creature that drank blood to survive, he had an almost pathetically weak stomach at times.

"A few of the soldiers are trying to figure out how to use the death rays," I reported quietly.

"How many do they have?" Gregor asked.

"I only saw six, but they might have more."

"Their ammunition will not last forever," Luc pointed out to his old friend. He spoke so rarely now that each time he opened his mouth it was a bit of a surprise. It occurred to me that I missed his company. I'd come to depend on him always being there and now that he wasn't, I felt bereft. He might be here, close enough for me to touch, but he had become inaccessible and distant.

"I fear the repercussions of humans getting their hands on Viltaran technology," Gregor responded quietly.

"It's far too late to worry about that now," Geordie said despondently. "There are already lots of dead droids lying around in the streets above. Thousands of their weapons will be available for anyone to pick up by the time we finish killing them all."

Bowing to the wisdom of someone who was three thousand years younger than him, Gregor nodded. "You are right, Geordie. There is no use worrying about something that we cannot control."

The teen beamed at the rare praise. When we'd first met, I'd thought of Geordie as childish and irreverent. Now that I knew him better, he was still childish and irreverent, but I knew he was far wiser than he appeared. His heart might be on the wrong side of his body, but it was large enough to encompass us all. The thought of losing him, or any of my friends, was too hideous to contemplate. Now that they were seemingly immortal, my fears for their safety had abated somewhat, but they still hadn't faded completely.

Gregor waited for the soldiers to stop for a brief rest before broaching the subject of the alien weaponry with Sanderson. "Would you like me to show your men how to use the Viltaran death rays that they have appropriated?"

Startled, Sanderson opened his mouth to deny the implied accusation that he'd been hiding the weapons from us, then thought better of it. We obviously knew about the secret they were trying to hide. "I'd appreciate it," he said. "We need every weapon we can find and the alien weapons are fairly effective."

The men I'd secretly spied on came forward at their commander's wave. Gregor pulled his death ray out of his pocket and showed the men the correct buttons to press. One fired his newly acquired weapon at the ground and a long strip of metal tracks disappeared.

"Be careful where you point those things!" Sanderson barked. "I'd like to leave at least some of this city intact when we're done." A few of his soldiers laughed nervously, oblivious to the fact that their general was being serious. I wasn't sure the man even had a sense of humour anymore. Maybe it had died sometime during our battles with our previous enemies.

"To change the setting, push these two buttons and turn this." Gregor demonstrated on his death ray and fired it at the tracks. It passed through the metal harmlessly this time. "You should all practice changing the settings, but I strongly recommend you do not test it on each other," he said dryly.

"You wouldn't believe how painful it is to be disintegrated," I said to the grinning men.

"You mean you've been shot by one of these?" Higgins asked. He always seemed to be just a few steps away from me. Maybe Sanderson thought I'd taken a shine to the corporal and had ordered him to hang around me to act as his spy. From the angle of the general's head, he was listening in on our conversation.

"I was shot with one so I could escape quickly from a Viltaran death pit."

"If you were disintegrated, then how are you still alive?"

"Didn't your boss tell you?" Higgins should have figured it out after I told him I'd been blasted into ashes and thrown into a box. "I can't die." Stunned murmurs sounded and the word spread through their ranks in a hushed whisper.

"But that's…" Higgins trailed off, lost for words.

"Awesome?" Geordie said to finish the soldier's sentence. "I agree. Who wouldn't want to live forever?" He put just enough wistfulness in his question to sound believable. Amusement danced in his eyes when he cut a glance towards me.

"I was going to say 'impossible'," Higgins replied, eyeing me with amazement.

"Nothing is impossible when it comes to Mortis," Kokoro told the soldier. She received wide eyed stares at her pronouncement. I suspected many of the soldiers had a crush on the black haired, pale skinned former seer. None were stupid enough to make a move on her, since it was obvious she and Gregor were an item.

They walked arm in arm, talking quietly most of the time. A lump tried to form in my throat that Luc tended to walk on the far side of the tunnel from me now. *You're going to have to come to grips with being dumped by him sooner or later,* my subconscious pointed out. *Screw you,* I mentally shouted at it and it fled back to the deep recesses of my mind.

It was almost a relief when I sensed two units of droids ahead. The action would prevent me from being able to dwell on my ruined love life, at least for a few minutes.

At my warning of approaching danger, Sanderson sent some of his men into buildings to act as snipers. He cautioned them to climb up to the fourth floor, since the death rays had a short range. Saluting their leader smartly, fifty soldiers crept up the subway stairs. We gave them ten minutes to move into position before heading for the robots.

Back when I'd still been alive, I'd dreamed of visiting Manhattan one day. In my fantasies, it was winter and a light snow was falling. Christmas decorations adorned the stores and the streets were packed with tourists. Instead, it was spring, the stores were locked up tightly and the streets were mostly empty, at least where we were.

Further north, terrified humans huddled together as they waited to meet their doom. Instead of Christmas decorations, the only trimmings in sight were splashes of blood from the dead that had been dragged away for food. I carefully avoided looking at the chewed up limbs that had been left behind.

At Sanderson's signal, the men who were armed with death rays moved to the front ranks and closed in on the unsuspecting killbots. The droids would be armed with nanobot guns as well as death rays. Both weapons were equally dangerous to the humans.

Holding his hand up for his men to see, the general silently counted down from three. When he reached one, he made a fist and his men opened fire. They'd appropriated far more than the six death rays that I'd counted. Forty of their men pulled an alien weapon from their pockets. In a barrage of soundless violet light, most of the droids vanished before they even knew they were under attack.

A few more shots ended the battle that had been as quiet as it had been deadly. Not all of the enemy's weapons had been disintegrated. Any that had been dropped were retrieved and were handed around to those without.

Handling his own death ray, Sanderson examined it with new respect. I shared Gregor's fear that the humans would be able to figure out exactly how the weapons worked. Eventually, they might even be able to reproduce them in large quantities. God help any friendly aliens who might drop by for a visit. They'd be reduced to an ash pile before they could say, 'We come in peace'.

Our attack had been so swift and unexpected that no other droids came to investigate the battle scene. The tactic worked three more times as we stalked the slowly dwindling metal army. On our way towards yet another unit of robots, I sensed a small number of humans and Kveet imps to the east. Remembering the stripped skeletons that had been left behind after Sanderson's men had been devoured, my conscience made a sudden reappearance. I had the sneaking suspicion that guilt would haunt me if I just left the victims to be eaten.

Turning, I searched the crowd and spotted Gregor. I waved to get his attention and he hurried to catch up to me. "I sense some Kveet imps and human captives a couple of blocks away," I told him when he reached my side.

"Where?" He followed my pointing finger to the north-east. They were only a short distance away, but the tall buildings blocked our view. Gregor didn't need to debate about the wisdom of trying to rescue the civilians. He hurried over to Sanderson to relay the news.

Gathering his men, Sanderson explained the situation and picked half a dozen troopers to reconnoitre the area. Higgins was one of the chosen. He raised his eyebrows in a silent invitation for me to join his team. They'd find the captives much faster if I went along as a guide, so I fell into step beside him.

A second later, Geordie pushed his way in between us, shooting an annoyed scowl at the human. Ishida appeared on my other side and gave me a bland look. Rolling my eyes, I kept my mouth shut. Geordie was always jealous when I spent time with anyone other than him. I didn't know what Ishida's excuse for joining us was. He probably just didn't want to miss out on the action. It was also possible that he wanted to give Kokoro and Gregor some time to be alone, or as alone as it was possible to be while surrounded by a small army.

The soldiers slowed down at my signal as we neared the enemy. Soon, we were close enough for even the humans to hear the piping cries of the imps. Higgins' face was pale as we crept up and viewed the small park where the captives were being held. It went dead white when he spied the victims. The soldier came very close to vomiting at the sight of the grisly skeletons that were strewn across the grassy area. He'd already witnessed his fellow troopers' deaths, but he was far more affected this time. Maybe because these had been helpless civilians rather than battle hardened soldiers.

Higgins wasn't the only one to feel nauseated by the carnage. Geordie made quiet gagging noises and I almost joined him. Blood coated the grass. It looked almost black in the lightless gloom. Most of the hell spawn had eaten their fill and were merely guarding the humans rather than feasting on them. Their tiny bellies bulged almost to the point of bursting.

Penned in by a high fence, most of the surviving humans were sobbing quietly. Some had fallen into a state bordering on catatonia. One woman was screaming over and over. She only stopped long enough to take a fresh breath. Her voice had disappeared, possibly irreparably damaged. All she could manage now was a painful croak.

Spying the skeleton of a child, my rage spiked. I had no way of knowing if it had been a boy or a girl. I could tell that they hadn't been much larger than the Kveet imps that had eaten it. Scarlet light burst from my eyes. Geordie and Ishida grabbed my arms to stop me from sprinting into the park and laying waste to the enemy.

Struggling against their grip, I was dragged backwards into an alley as one of the soldiers frantically, but quietly called for backup. Battle lust had me in its grip and nothing was going to stop me from tearing the tiny monsters apart.

The teens stumbled when my sleeves suddenly became empty. Sprinting forward, I re-formed my lower arms. I was secretly amazed that my hands hadn't just remained whole, they had also retained their grip on my swords. I'd disintegrated my flesh and had re-formed it so quickly that my hands hadn't had a chance to fall to the ground.

Crossing the road, I leaped high into the air and landed in the middle of the gluttonous clones. My swords spitted two of the imps and I flicked their lifeless bodies away before the rest of the pack even realized I was there. My hands moved into a blur of motion as I sliced my adversaries apart. Heads and limbs fell and piping cries of rage sounded. Tiny claws and razor sharp fangs reached for me, but few managed to make contact with my flesh.

I wasn't sure how long it took me to turn the clones into minced meat, but I eventually turned in a circle to find none of them left standing. My stolen jeans were tattered in a few places, but any injuries I'd sustained had healed instantly. I saw no dark stains left by my black blood, just bright yellow smears from the deceased imps.

Stunned to see their captors chopped into sushi, the humans huddled together and gaped at me. "What are you?" an elderly male voice asked in a hoarse whisper.

I went with honesty since I doubted they could become more afraid than they already were. "I'm a vampire."

"I remember you," a young woman said and extricated herself from the clutching hands of her fellow survivors. "You're Natalie. I thought you went mad and were sent to a maximum security prison."

"My sanity is intact," was my dry response, but I didn't dispute her assumption that I'd been sent to prison. I couldn't think of a better description for Viltar than a jail.

"Are you here to save us?" a small boy tottered forward to ask. He was bigger than the child that had been eaten, but I doubted he'd be much more than five or six.

Caught beneath his innocent, frightened stare, I nodded. "That's the plan."

With a sob, he lurched forward and wrapped his arms around my legs. My hands and swords were dripping with alien blood. I was reluctant to touch the boy with them, even to get him off me. Searching for help, I saw Higgins looking at me from the entrance to the park with something close to pride in his expression. Geordie wiped away an imaginary tear and held back a sob of his own. Ishida patted the other teen on the shoulder. They obviously weren't going to be of any assistance.

"Can you do something about this?" I said to the young woman and made a helpless gesture at the kid. Clinging to me like a monkey, he was crying hysterically.

She eventually managed to pry the kid loose. By then the rest of our gang had arrived. Sanderson had the unenviable task of trying to figure out what to do with the survivors. Evacuation wasn't possible. No crafts of any kind would be able to enter or leave the city until the mysterious submersibles turned up. He opted to send the women, children and elderly to the dubious safety towards the south.

Once the survivors had been escorted away, fifty-eight men and a few of the tougher, more determined women remained to add to our ranks. They were green and most had never seen any kind of combat before, unless it was through computer games. They were soldiers now, whether they liked it or not.

From their set, if terrified faces, most would rather fight than cower with the children and elderly while they waited to be discovered and turned into tasty treats. If I'd been in their shoes, I wouldn't have wanted to stay behind either.

Chapter Thirteen

Our new civilian troops were given handguns by the soldiers. Anyone who didn't know how to use them was given a quick tutorial. We left the bloodstained park behind and headed towards the closest unit of droids. We were slowly making a dent in their numbers, but it would take weeks for us to eradicate them all at this pace. By then, hundreds of thousands of civilians would have been converted into clones and the city would be lost. The Viltarans would surely move on and target another city rather than wait around to watch the outcome of this attack. We had to think of a way to bring this battle to an end quickly.

Taking quick glances at the nervous additions to our team of allies, Geordie raised a good point. "I am surprised the civilians haven't fought back against the droids and imps yet. Don't most Americans own guns?"

Higgins answered him. "I wouldn't say most of us own guns, but a great many do."

Gregor turned to stare at the teen, then grinned widely. "Geordie, you show rare flashes of true genius from time to time."

"I do?" Bewildered, the teen looked at me, but I just shrugged. No one had ever accused me of being a genius and I had no idea what Gregor was talking about.

Motioning for us to follow him, Gregor hastened through the soldiers and townsfolk towards Sanderson. "General, I've just had an idea."

Halting, Sanderson waved his men to follow suit. "I'm all ears," he invited.

"We need far greater numbers if we are going to destroy this threat," Gregor said. "The Viltarans might be able to stop anyone from coming to our aid, but I believe we have more than enough support in the city already."

Confused, the general frowned, deepening the lines on his forehead. "What are you talking about?"

"We need to get word to the civilians that there are less than eight thousand droids left. Once the robots are gone, the conversions will cease. We will only need to eradicate the clones that have already been made, rather than keep battling new ones constantly."

Latching onto the idea, Sanderson's expression brightened as he realized that all hope wasn't lost. "Your idea makes sense. We should wait until daylight before rallying the survivors. Then we'll only have the droids to face rather than taking on two enemies at once." Reaching for his radio, he outlined the plan to General Hart.

After a lengthy pause while he thought over the proposal, Hart gave a heavy sigh. "I agree, this is our best chance of taking down the enemy. I'll advise President Rivers of your plan. Good luck, Sanderson."

From the little I'd seen of them, the inhabitants of New York were a tough breed. The men and women who'd joined us were willing to lay down their lives for the safety of their people. I hoped the rest of the city felt that way. If they did, we might actually have a chance of saving them.

Edging our way northward, we encountered several lone droid units. The newly acquired death rays took them all down far more quietly than explosive rounds or normal bullets would have. We were able to work our way deeper into the city and leave the way to the south open. The few humans we found were given the choice of joining us, or heading for safety. Most opted to assist us, swelling our ranks even further.

As dawn approached, we were within sight of Times Square. Amazingly, the power was still on and a dazzling array of lights assailed us. Geordie tilted his head back to view the gigantic screens that advertised a range of products to the deserted streets.

To the naked eye, the area was empty, but I sensed tens of thousands of humans cowering inside the buildings around us. We had cleared the immediate area of droids, but many more had converged on Central Park to the north. Even now, I could sense them firing their nanobot darts at defenceless civilians, creating more monsters that we would have to destroy.

As one, the robots suddenly ceased firing and the newly converted imps scurried for cover. They disappeared into buildings, or beneath the ground before the first rays of the sun touched the sky. Momentarily safe from the dawn light due to the cover of the skyscrapers, our small group of vampires also headed for the subway.

Noise blared from behind us as we reached the stairs and we turned to see what the commotion was. High above the street, a gigantic TV screen had changed to a grainy, grey static channel. A few seconds later, a face appeared. The camera pulled back to reveal the vaguely familiar sight of the office of the President of the United States of America.

A woman in her early fifties sat behind the desk, staring at the camera solemnly. Her suit was dark blue, expensive and suitably sombre. Her greying, curly brown hair had been cut short in a no-nonsense bob. Thick glasses perched on her bold nose, magnifying piercing blue eyes. She was short enough that her impressively sized breasts rested on the surface of the desk. Her hands were neatly folded, but clutched each other in a white knuckled grip. Apart from her trembling hands, she gave the overall impression of being calm and in control.

Roused by the noise, faces appeared in windows high above us. Some spotted the soldiers and pointed. Windows opened and questions were shouted down to the troopers. Silence descended again as the president began to speak. "Good morning. For those of you who do not know me, I am President Vanessa Rivers." Her raspy voice thundered through the streets, drowning out the nearby ads and drawing curious humans from within their hiding places. "This might be difficult to believe, but you are under attack from an alien nation."

"Yeah, we kind of figured that out!" a smartass called from the slowly increasing crowd. "The robots and hulking monsters were our first clue!"

"My fellow Americans and visitors who are currently trapped in Manhattan, you have not been abandoned in

127

your time of need," the president continued, blithely unaware of the interruption. "I assure you that I am doing everything in my power to ensure you are rescued from harm. Unfortunately, the city has been cut off and evacuation is not going to be easy. The alien spaceship is circling the city and is preventing any help from reaching you. Some soldiers were able to reach the city before it was cut off. Sadly, they are few in number."

Looking down at her people gravely, she braced herself visibly before continuing. "What I am about to ask you to do may sound harsh, but these are difficult times. I wouldn't ask this of you if it wasn't absolutely necessary."

"Get to the point already," an anonymous woman muttered from within the press of bodies.

Rivers plunged ahead with the plan Gregor had thought of and Sanderson had agreed with. "I ask that you unite with the soldiers against the robots that are terrorizing you. Only you can stop these alien droids from converting your fellow citizens into monsters."

Astonished whispers came from those who had been brave enough to leave their hiding spots.

"Is she saying she wants *us* to fight the robots?" someone asked, then uttered a terrified laugh.

"I know you are frightened and that all hope seems lost," the president continued, "but know this." She paused just long enough to gain the attention of everyone within earshot. "There are less than eight thousand of these robots and there are many, many more of you." She paused again to let the numbers sink in. "General Sanderson is in charge of this operation and he will oversee the resistance. He is in Times Square right now, ready to lead the charge. I urge you all to arm yourselves, then seek out the General. My hopes and prayers are with you all."

The picture faded and the screen went blank. Sanderson strode out into the open as civilians began to converge on the streets. Some were armed, but most were without weapons. Homes would have to be ransacked and, if there were any in the city, gun shops looted.

Already, more and more civilians were arriving, either drawn by the noise, or at their president's plea. Rivers' short speech would have been widely televised. Only those who had gathered in Central Park would be unaware that their salvation would be in their own hands. Once they saw the droids under attack, they would get the idea quickly enough and would join the fight.

Thanks to our allergy to the sun, we vampires would have to sit out this part of the revolt. Sanderson needed every available man and woman to fight, so my friends and I were left to our own devices.

"Are any of you tired yet?" Gregor enquired and received six head shakes. "Then I suggest that we go imp hunting." He said this with a sly wink at me.

I perked up at the prospect of slicing and dicing some more foes. Remaining idle would allow me time to think and thinking would lead to the depression I was trying so hard to avoid. Getting over being dumped by Luc was going to be difficult. Having him so close, yet so distant was adding salt to the raw wound of no longer being the recipient of his love.

There were plenty of targets to choose from stashed away beneath the ground. I led the way to a small pocket of Kveet clones first. Most of the sixty or so creatures were deeply asleep. The rest were hovering on the verge of it. Lying side by side in the subway tunnels, they looked almost peaceful.

Geordie was reluctant to use his weapon on the tiny targets while they were unaware, but Ishida was more practical. Far, far older than his fellow teen, Ishida had survived many wars with the rival European vampire nation. One shot from his death ray disintegrated four clones.

The blasts of light woke some of the others, but we circled them and kept shooting until only their dust motes remained. Kokoro waved the cloud of minute particles away from her face in distaste. It wasn't much fun shooting them when they were half asleep and unable to fight back, but it was necessary, so we continued on through the tunnels.

A few hours later, Gregor stopped and pointed upwards. "How is the hunt for the droids going?"

I sent my senses out to investigate the status of the ongoing battle and relayed what I'd found. "They've wiped out most of the robots. The rest are on the run and the humans are nipping at their heels."

"Where are the robots running to?" Ishida asked.

I followed the progress of the remaining two hundred or so murderbots and my blood tried to run cold. They were heading directly for the small group of humans I'd rescued from the Kveet clones earlier. I tried to tell myself that I shouldn't care what happened to them, but the picture of the little boy wrapping his trusting hands around my legs refused to fade.

Giving in to my newly resurrected conscience, I turned and sprinted down the tunnel. None of my friends asked me what the urgency was. They kept up with me as I raced through the subway tunnels in a blur.

It was midday and the sun was still high in the sky. It would be madness to leave the safety of the subway, but I was going to ascend to the street anyway. I mentally crossed my fingers that the skyscrapers would offer enough shade that none of my friends would burst into flames. The sun had a different effect on me, my flesh tended to boil, then melt right down to the bone. After drinking Viltaran blood, I wasn't sure how my friends would react to direct contact with the sun.

Spying stairs, I raced up them and emerged onto the street a block ahead of the droids. As I'd hoped, deep shadows prevented the sun from scorching me. Even with the shade, the brightness was almost too much to bear and I blinked painfully. Geordie hissed out a curse and covered his eyes with one hand, peeking out through his fingers. Not that long ago, he would have been dead to the world during daylight hours.

Fleeing from certain death, the metal men didn't realize they were running from one danger straight into another until we opened fire. The droids were quick to react and we scurried for cover as they sent retaliatory blasts of violet light towards us. At their backs, the humans closed in, firing either bullets, or death rays. Jubilant screams came from the citizens. After two nights of being eaten and turned into monsters, they could taste victory.

Only two blocks behind us, the people I'd rescued earlier cowered inside the apartment building they'd chosen to hide in. We were being pushed backwards by the droids and they would soon pass us. I wasn't sure if the droids were intelligent enough to use the townsfolk as hostages or not, but I'd rather not find out.

Pocketing my death ray, I raced towards the rapidly diminishing number of bots. Halting their forward rush, I sliced into them. I chopped arms off and stabbed faces while vampires and humans alike closed in to finish them off.

When the last automaton fell, General Sanderson fought his way through the crowd and nodded his thanks to our small group. He took a few moments to catch his breath before speaking. "I didn't think you could be outside during daylight hours."

"We are safe as long as the direct rays of the sun don't touch our flesh," Gregor explained. He didn't add that any normal vampire would be steaming by now and would shortly catch fire before turning to ash. We seven were the only ones who could withstand being outside. Even for us, it caused some pain.

"Is it over?" an overweight man armed with a machine gun asked. From the familiar way he was holding it, I suspected it came from his own personal arsenal. He carried a small backpack that was most likely full of extra ammunition. *He must be one of those weekend warriors I've read about.* They were the type who spent their weekends camped out in the middle of nowhere, taking pot shots at cardboard cut outs of animals. I couldn't fault his hobby, since it had prepared him for an alien invasion. I guessed the doomsday preppers weren't entirely crazy after all.

"All of the droids in the city have been destroyed," I confirmed. Cheers rang out and the nearby crowd broke into a joyous dance. A thin, sallow man grabbed a woman twice his size and whirled her in a circle before staggering and almost dropping her. She steadied him, then leaned down and planted a kiss on his mouth. His grin was dazed as he shyly slipped his arm around her sizable waist. Surprisingly, she cuddled him against her side. True love had been born in the aftermath of battle. I tried to form a cynical snigger, but I was too depressed at the state of my own pitiful love life to manage it.

"How many clones are remaining?" Sanderson asked.

I didn't need to check ,since I'd already scanned the area. "There are still over twenty-thousand Kveet imps hiding out in the buildings and sewers." Groans of disappointment were issued by several soldiers. "Plus more than one hundred thousand human imps." This time the groans were louder and more numerous.

I'd expected dismay from the townsfolk and was astounded when a woman old enough to be my grandmother hefted her shotgun. "What are we waiting for? I say we hunt these suckers down while they're still sleeping." Roars of approval met her words. Their blood was up and they were eager to take back their city.

"Most of them are in the subway," I told Sanderson. "Only a few thousand are hiding in the apartment buildings."

"If I show you a map of Manhattan, do you think you could pinpoint their locations?" he asked. I'd had practice using maps to find my enemies on Viltar. It shouldn't be a problem using the same tactic on my home planet. I nodded, pretending it didn't feel like my eyeballs were boiling from being outside while the sun was still up. A slight tic started up beneath my left eye and I hoped no one noticed it.

"Let's take this meeting back in the subway," Gregor suggested and headed for the stairs to the closest tunnel.

My pain immediately abated once I was beneath the ground again and my tic disappeared with it. The others blinked a few times, but that was the only indication they gave of the discomfort they'd been feeling. Soldiers and civilians crowded into the subway with us. While we waited for someone to appear with a map, Sanderson sent a few soldiers to cut the power to the tracks. It was a smart move and would prevent the unwary from being fried.

A few minutes later, a soldier rushed to Sanderson's side and handed over a map. The general spread it out on the ground and pulled a pen out of his pocket. I hunkered down across from him and pointed out where the imps were hiding. They were spread out all across the city, but stayed well clear of the area that had been blasted with the poisonous gas. The clones weren't immune to the poison and would also die if they came into contact with the spoiled air.

Manhattan had been turned into a prison by the Viltarans and we were about to turn it against their clones. I could easily picture the aliens gnashing their fangs in fury that the puny, less-than-technologically-advanced humans were proving to be far more resilient than they'd ever expected.

Chapter Fourteen

Not all of the survivors were willing to participate in the imp slaughter that was about to take place. Enough volunteered for us to be able to get the job done. Everyone had a weapon of some kind, even if it was just a meat cleaver. Personally, I'd rather slink quietly away and hide if that was the best weapon I could come up with.

Sanderson gathered everyone together and split them into teams. A few soldiers were in charge of the civilians in each group. The chosen team leaders would keep in contact with the general by radio as they spread out and began flushing out the enemy.

It took time to organize the groups. They eventually began to head back up to the surface to search the buildings that had been marked on the map. Other teams took off down the train tunnels in search of enemies. In the past, Sanderson had always made sure he and I were on the same team. This time, we went our separate ways, much to our mutual relief.

"You can join us, if you want," Higgins invited. With a shrug, Gregor followed the young soldier as he hastened after his team leader.

"You like that human, don't you, *chérie?*" Geordie said with a nod towards Higgins as we jogged behind the soldier down a long, dark tunnel. Some of the civilians were still recovering from chasing after the droids. They gasped for air as they struggled to keep up. Flashlights speared through the gloom, lighting the way for those without.

"'Like' is too strong a word," I replied. "He hasn't tried to kill any of us yet, so I'm tolerating him."

"He seems to be very attached to you," Ishida said from my other side. "You should think about turning him into your companion, since Lord Lucentio no longer appears to hold you in his regard." Walking a few paces ahead of us, Luc stiffened slightly.

Ishida had used the word 'companion', but turning someone into one of us would make them into my slave. I'd have complete control over them and they wouldn't be able to defy my direct orders. "I couldn't even if I wanted to. Remember what happened to that fledgling in Africa who accidentally bit me?"

Both teens shuddered at the memory. I'd saved Sanderson's life when one of his men had turned after being drained then fed vampire blood. The undead soldier had chomped down on me after I'd pushed Sanderson out of the way. The black ooze that passed for my blood had eaten its way through the fledgling's stomach, meat and skin. It had melted half of his face off before Sanderson had put a bullet in his brain to end his suffering.

"I'd forgotten about that," Geordie said in a small voice. They gave me pitying looks, as if I'd suffered a debilitating injury that somehow made me less of a vampire. I didn't feel as if I was missing out on anything. The thought of turning a human into my minion horrified me.

My life had been brutally snatched from me and things had gone downhill ever since. I'd never wanted to put someone else through the awfulness of being converted into the undead. Eternal life might sound great but, for me, it had mainly sucked so far. I had a feeling it was going to continue to suck for a long, long time. Possibly forever.

Our group was larger than most. It was made up of a thousand civilians, twelve soldiers and seven vampires. Most of the hell spawn we'd encountered tended to stick to smaller groups, so I doubted we'd have too much trouble eradicating them. We'd be bound to lose some of our teammates along the way. There were always casualties in any war.

Huffing, puffing and wheezing, some of the older humans were in real risk of having a stroke if we kept up this pace for too long. The soldier in charge kept glancing back at me, but he was too intimidated to ask me to join him. I figured he had a question so, with an internal sigh, I made my way to the front of the pack.

"Hey," a wheezing man said and grabbed my arm to stop me. "There's a rumour going around that you're a vampire."

"So?" I tried to disengage my arm, but he held on tight. If I yanked my arm away I might accidentally rip his off in the process. My compassion was still a new and precarious thing. It wasn't going to stretch very far if I became annoyed.

"Prove it." His expression was belligerent and his dark grey suit expensive. His belly hung over his belt and I doubted he'd be able to see his shoes. Clearly, he was the type of guy who usually got what he wanted.

"I don't have time for this," I said and peeled his fingers free. Luckily for him, I didn't snap any off.

"Hey! I'm talking to you!" He lunged after me, but Geordie and Ishida intercepted him.

"Are you certain that you want proof that we are vampires?" Ishida asked the man coolly.

Less sure of himself now that he wasn't confronting a lone female that was half his size, the guy stammered his reply. "Y-yeah."

"How about I bite you on the neck and drain your blood?" Geordie offered. "Will that be enough proof for you?" The two boys were much smaller, not to mention thinner, than the human, but I heard him back away a step anyway as he searched for a reply.

Two slaps rang out and I glanced back to see the teens rubbing the backs of their heads. Igor gave the belligerent American a flat stare. Reaching out, he grabbed the man by the shirt and lifted him two feet off the ground with one hand. "Is this enough proof for you?" he asked around the fangs that had suddenly sprouted from his gums.

"Ok! Ok! I believe you!" Feet kicking in panic, the civilian was on the verge of fainting in terror when Igor dropped him. Losing his balance, he went down on one knee before staggering to his feet and darting away into the crowd.

Catching my eye, Igor gave me a rare grin. His fangs retracted back to normal in the blink of an eye.

"I can't believe they're letting loud-mouthed fools like that carry firearms," Gregor said to me out of the corner of his mouth.

Stifling my snigger, I finally reached the team leader. Short and compact, he had sandy coloured hair and a pug nose. "I'm Sergeant Wesley, ma'am," he said by way of a greeting and gave me a polite, but reserved nod. "Can you tell me how close we are to the targets?"

"They're just at the next station," I replied. "So we'd better try to keep the noise down from now on."

While the civilians weren't being overly noisy, they also weren't making much effort to be stealthy. I doubted many of them had ever been on any kind of hunting trips before, let alone pursuing something that had come from outer space.

Wesley sent his soldiers out to round everyone up and also to warn them to be quiet. Gregor and the sergeant had a brief discussion on our best course of action as the stragglers caught up to the rest of us.

The strategy they decided on was fairly simple. We would creep up as close to the enemy as we could get, then riddle them with bullets. My senses told me that there were less than sixty adversaries ahead. It was decided that an equal number of us would engage the imps. The rest of the team would act as our backup if any of the monsters survived the first barrage and managed to flee.

Our force of twelve soldiers, seven vampires and forty-one humans closed in on the slumbering targets. Sneaking about as effectively as a cow with metal buckets on all four of its feet, the civilians shuffled through the dark tunnel towards the light ahead. A few of the humans carried flashlights. Their beams moved up and down and from side to side like searchlights on the hunt for an escaped prisoner. Someone sneezed and was loudly shushed by half a dozen people. Kokoro shook her head in despair that we had been lumped with civilians that could best be described as inept.

Motioning the small group forward, the soldiers crept up to the imps. No matter how many times I saw the human clones, they always gave me a shiver. Their faces had been transformed into a semblance of the Viltarans', but their grey bodies were still human. They were just far larger and far more heavily muscled than usual. They slept deeply and didn't sense our approach. Bereft of their intelligence, they were too stupid to think of leaving someone awake to stand guard.

When we were close enough that even the worst shooter amongst us would have at least a fifty-fifty chance of hitting a target, Wesley signalled for us to fire. We had nineteen death rays in our group and violet light bathed the slumbering giants.

The clones that hadn't instantly been disintegrated woke up and struggled to their feet. The thunder of bullets was painful and ricocheted off the tiled walls and back down the tunnel as the humans panicked and opened fire. The skirmish was over quickly and with no loss of life on our side.

Two of the soldiers checked to make sure the imps weren't just faking death. They sank kicks into the corpses as cries of triumph rang out from the rest of our team when they ran to catch up to us.

"Are they going to be like this every time?" Geordie complained, wincing at the cacophony.

"Probably," I responded with a grimace. "I have a feeling it's going to be a long day."

It was a long day and the sun had begun to wane by the time we approached a group of clones. This one was far larger than any we'd encountered before. Halting Sergeant Wesley, I advised him that we would be outnumbered by around five to one if we were to engage the enemy.

"I'd better call for backup," the soldier decided and reached for his radio.

"Don't bother," I told him. "I'll take care of it."

Higgins' expression clearly reflected that he thought I was crazy. "You can't take on five thousand of these things alone!"

He turned to my friends for support, but Gregor just shrugged. "Natalie has the capacity to destroy a large number of clones. If she did not think she was capable of eradicating them, she would not have made the offer."

"But...how?" Higgins asked, at a loss of how I could possibly achieve such a claim.

"With these." I tucked my swords beneath my left arm and held my hands up to show him my palms. At the soldier's continued bafflement, I nodded to Gregor. "You explain it to him. The imps will be waking up soon and I'd rather they were dead before that happens."

"I hate it when Nat goes out on her solo missions," Geordie said to Ishida as I headed away from them.

"Did he just call her a gnat?" a tourist said in heavily accented English. "Isn't that a kind of insect?"

Geordie's shrill giggles chased after me as I put on a burst of speed. *Seriously, how many times have I heard that comparison now,* I grumbled internally.

Nearing a convergence of several tunnels, I closed in on the immense group of prone clones. Kveet and human imps were crammed into the tunnels, lying cheek by jowl. Some even lay on top of each other in a hideous parody of affection.

Trembling on the verge of setting, the sun was about to disappear. I didn't have much time to plan my attack. I carefully picked my way through the mob, nudging limbs out of the way so I didn't step on them. As I neared the centre of the group, the sun winked out. Scarlet eyes opened all around me as some of the clones began to rouse.

Being older than their larger brethren, the Kveet imps woke first. In a move fuelled by panic, I captured the closest creatures with my gaze before they could raise the alarm. Quickly shifting my eyes from one tiny monster to the next, I snared more and more of them as I knelt and groped for the heads of two former humans. The pair stirred beneath my touch, but didn't wake.

One of the Kveet that I had yet to hypnotize saw me and pointed with a tiny clawed hand. "Food?" it asked me hopefully.

"Not food," I replied in its own language. Its tiny face fell in disappointment then I had no more time to interact with the imps. Roughly two hundred of the closest clones had gone still and pliant beneath my silent spell.

A thought occurred to me that I almost dismissed. My inner voice backed the impulse, so I decided to act on it. It might be a decision that I'd regret later, but I had a nagging suspicion that my crazy idea just might come in handy. I gave an order to all of the Kveet that had fallen beneath my spell and they scurried into action.

Closing my eyes, I let the power build up until the train tracks vibrated. The imps that were still asleep snapped awake at the sound. The two I had my hands on stood and I was lifted several feet off the ground. I sent a jolt of power through them both that brought them down to their knees. My feet touched the ground and I opened my eyes to see thousands of monsters milling in confusion. Waiting until I felt the power spread out to touch every clone in the area, I finally released it.

The closest imps swelled alarmingly from the pressure of being inundated with my dark mojo and I realized I'd forgotten to undress. I was about to be covered in guts, gore and giblets. Even as the thought occurred to me, I was suddenly standing safely out of range of the carnage.

With a gigantic, wet splat, every hell spawn in the tunnel exploded. The hot smell of innards that were now on the outside was overwhelming. Fluorescent yellow blood, mixed with grey flesh and pink brains, made disturbing murals on the walls.

I searched for survivors and was amazed to realize I'd gotten them all with one blast of power. Mentally patting myself on the back for a job well done, I jogged back down the tunnel and returned to my group.

"Was there an explosion?" Sergeant Wesley asked as I stepped into the light. "I felt the ground shaking."

"That was just my holy marks doing their job."

"It felt like a bomb went off," Higgins said.

"You could say it was a spiritual bomb," Gregor replied. Maybe it was. I was immune to holy water, after all. Although I was marked with holy symbols, I had no explanation for why I couldn't say God, Jesus or Christ out loud. In that way, I was just like every other vampire.

It was nice not to be completely different from my own kind.

"Are they all dead?" Geordie asked me.

"The threat has been neutralized," I confirmed then winced at his shrill giggle. I was starting to sound a bit too much like the soldiers that we were spending far too much time with.

Wesley used his radio to share the news with Sanderson.

"Good work," the general responded. "Head back to Times Square for further orders."

Free to make as much noise as they wanted now, the civilians in our group chatted excitedly about our numerous victories. I'd been wrong about the likelihood that we would suffer casualties. Everyone had survived our below-ground hunting trip. Of course, if I hadn't single-handedly annihilated the group of five thousand opponents, the outcome would have been very different.

The soldiers knew they had me to thank for their good fortune. All twelve gave me nods of respect, which I returned solemnly. Like it or not, we would be working with these men and women for the foreseeable future. While I despised their commanding officer, the rest of them didn't seem to be so bad, so far at least.

Chapter Fifteen

A quick sweep of my senses indicated that the other teams had also been efficient at hunting down their prey. Most of the clones were dead and only a few small pockets remained. Vindictive civilians, led by a few soldiers, blasted the last of them apart while we made our way back through the subway tunnels to emerge near Times Square.

Gesturing to Higgins, I gave him the good news. "Tell your boss that the city is now clone free."

Letting out a whoop of joy, he reached for his radio, then lowered it when he spied Sanderson through the crowd. He ran to update the general in person.

Clapping the corporal on the shoulder, Sanderson gave Higgins a wide smile, then spoke into his own radio. He was too far away and there was too much noise coming from the milling civilians for me to be able to overhear him. I assumed he gave General Hart the good news before putting his radio away.

Several minutes later, President Rivers appeared on the gigantic TV screen. She beamed down on us like a pleased goddess raining praise on her worshipers. "Citizens and visitors of Manhattan, General Sanderson has informed me that all of the androids and clones have now been destroyed."

A resounding cheer went up as relieved civilians and soldiers celebrated their victory. As Rivers launched into a congratulatory speech, I sensed movement high above. Tilting my head back, I followed the progress of the ship that I could sense, but not see as it headed to the southwest.

"I take it the Viltarans are on the move?" Gregor asked. At my nod, he waved to get Sanderson's attention.

"What's wrong?" the general asked after struggling through the press of bodies to reach us. He studied my face, instinctively knowing I held the answer. That might be the case, but that didn't mean I had to relay the news to him.

"The alien spacecraft is leaving the city," Gregor said.

Unsurprised, Sanderson reached for his radio again. "Do you know where they're heading?"

"Natalie can sense only that they're drifting towards the southwest. We do not know their final destination," Gregor responded. "There is something you should know about our mutual enemies."

It was a subtle reminder that we were on the same side, but Gregor was wasting his time. We might be allies now, but the truce wouldn't last once we managed to kill off the Viltarans. We vampires would then become the most dangerous adversaries the humans had. They would feel compelled to try to kill us. They'd be in for one hell of a surprise when none of my friends died from their wounds. Their treachery would amount to nothing more than an annoyance to us. Personally, I wasn't about to let any further backstabbing go unpunished.

Sanderson held his hand up to halt Gregor. "Don't tell me, the ship is full of droids and clones, right?" He'd correctly assumed the attack on Manhattan was only the first of many to come.

"Correct," Gregor confirmed. "There are roughly thirty thousand droids and eighty thousand more Kveet clones on board."

Closing his eyes for a few moments, the general shook his head at the bad news. He then spoke into his radio. "Hart, are you there?"

"I'm here," the other general replied. "Congratulations on your victory, Sanderson."

"You might want to hold off on the congratulations," Sanderson warned his colleague. "There are still more of these things on the alien ship."

"How many more?"

Sanderson gave him the numbers and Hart couldn't quite stifle his groan. "The ship is on the move," Sanderson continued. "It's heading to the southwest."

Putting aside his disappointment that the war had only just begun, Hart surged into action. "I'll send a ferry to pick you up. A jet is already waiting at JFK. It'll be ready to fly as soon as we know which city the aliens are going to target next."

"Roger that. We'll head for the ferry asap," Sanderson replied. He signalled for us to follow him and his men fell in behind us automatically as we trotted southward.

By the time we reached the southern tip of Manhattan, a ferry was waiting for us. Whatever the submersibles were, they hadn't arrived in time to bring the reinforcements that we'd been promised. I hoped the extra soldiers were somewhere close by, because we were going to need them.

We piled onto the ferry and it immediately took off and headed towards Brooklyn. I tracked the Viltaran ship as it moved slowly across the US ever to the southwest. It almost seemed to be searching for something. I figured it had found whatever it was looking for when it finally halted.

"The ship has stopped," I told Gregor. Sitting across from me, he nodded, but remained deep in thought.

"What do you think their next move will be?" Luc asked from his seat beside Gregor. Once, he'd sat by my side, but now Geordie and Ishida were my constant companions. Now that Kokoro and Gregor were an item, it seemed I had adopted the former child king. He didn't cling to my side like Geordie tended to, but it appeared he was coming to rely on me as well. It had been unnerving enough having a two hundred year old vampire looking to me for guidance. Ishida was far, far older than that and he'd been a ruler for his entire unlife. To say I felt unqualified to be in charge of the pair was an understatement.

"I think the attack on Manhattan was just a test," Gregor said. "They now know that the American's defence capabilities are no match for their technology. They are aware that their ship is able to hide from their missiles. They have probably guessed that the humans won't fire a nuclear weapon at their own people. If I were the Viltarans, I'd target an isolated city. I would ring the city in toxic gas at a distance most of the inhabitants won't be affected by. Then I would send in the clones to round up the humans and take them to the droids to be converted."

"It doesn't make sense for them to surround the city with gas," Geordie said. "Wouldn't they all be trapped inside forever?"

Gregor shook his head. "I think we will soon discover that the gas to the north of Manhattan is already beginning to dissipate. After seeing their own planet become all but uninhabitable, they won't make the same mistake again. Their fuel supply will be almost gone by now and they have no way to return to Viltar. Remember, they want Earth to become their new home. They would no doubt prefer for it to remain intact."

"Over my undead body," I muttered. Both Geordie and Ishida sniggered, but I wasn't trying to be funny. I might not particularly care about the earthlings, but I didn't want our planet to be overrun with droids and imps.

Uldar wouldn't be happy with anything but total subservience from every living, or unliving, being and I would never bend my knee to him. It might sound arrogant, but I didn't particularly relish the idea of bowing down to anyone.

Transportation had been arranged during our short ferry ride. A convoy of army trucks waited as we disembarked. We squished into the vehicles and took off without fanfare. Horrified spectators lined the river, staring at the destruction of the Brooklyn Bridge.

The citizens of Manhattan had been extremely lucky. We'd managed to avert both of the disasters my dreams had predicted. They'd lost nearly eight hundred thousand souls to clone conversion or from the deadly blast from the ship, but the rest had survived. It was a far better outcome than all of them being turned into clones, food or their entire city being reduced to a ruin. On the downside, I now had no idea what would happen next. My dreams had only shown me a glimpse of the Viltarans' plans.

What do you think they're going to do, my alter ego asked dourly. *Throw a party and invite you all along?* It didn't wait for me to reply and inflicted its opinion on me. *They're going to continue to turn the flesh bags into imps until they have enough of them to take over the whole country.* It wasn't telling me anything I didn't already know. What I wanted to know was where the aliens would strike next. We'd managed to enter Manhattan before the Viltarans had attacked, but we weren't going to be so lucky next time.

Presumably heading for the JFK airport, we listened in as a report came through Sergeant Wesley's radio. As Gregor predicted, the aliens had created a ring of toxic gas around a large, but isolated city somewhere in Texas. Several airplanes had been spotted dropping out of the sky after being hit with an electromagnetic pulse. If the pilots had flown through the gas cloud, they would have died anyway. The passengers and crew had been doomed either way.

"The whole town is surrounded by that yellow vapour and there's no way in or out," Wesley summarized.

"Does anyone have a hazmat suit handy?" one of the soldiers asked sourly. A few chuckles sounded, but most of the soldiers were too concerned to find any humour in the situation.

Entering the airport grounds, we were driven directly out onto the tarmac and over to a waiting army jet. It was far larger than any aircraft I'd seen before and could easily carry a couple of thousand soldiers. There were no seats and comfort obviously wasn't an important factor.

Sanderson's original team, of which there were still six hundred or so men and women left, boarded first. Fresh troops squeezed on next and my friends and I were last. More planes would meet us in Texas with several thousand more soldiers on board. They'd be bringing enough weapons and ammunition along to invade a small country.

In less time than I'd expected, we were airborne and were heading towards the latest disaster zone. We landed a few miles away from the city that had come under attack. The private airstrip was tiny. Only one plane at a time could land and offload its cargo of soldiers. The other planes circled above, being careful not to approach the city and risk being zapped by the spacecraft.

A plane that had been carrying a few civilians and special equipment had arrived before us. A large, camouflaged command tent had been erected by several industrious soldiers. Neat rows of hazmat suits waited for the soldiers to claim them. There wouldn't be anywhere near enough for the tens of thousands of troopers who were on their way, but there were enough for several thousand at least.

Sanderson's soldiers donned them in resignation. Sweat popped out on their brows almost immediately. No one bothered to put their helmets on yet. That would have to wait until crunch time, or they'd risk passing out from the heat. I imagined they'd also have a limited amount of oxygen per suit and would have to use it sparingly.

Gregor waved away a frazzled civilian when he offered us a suit each. The man gave us sidelong looks as he handed the suits to some nearby soldiers instead. Going by his white lab coat, I figured he was a scientist. My friends gave the lab coated men and women unfriendly stares as they distributed the bright yellow outfits. They hadn't forgotten their torture sessions in Colorado. Their terror, agony and helplessness would most likely linger for many centuries. I knew my rage wouldn't dissipate any time soon.

We watched Sanderson and several other high ranking officers as they gathered in the command tent. At the general's order, a sleek, heavily armoured army jeep was readied. Another white coated civilian bustled over to it and disappeared inside for a few minutes. He eventually climbed out, shut the door and gave the command tent the thumbs up.

"The soldiers do not think the Viltarans will just allow them to drive into the city, do they?" Luc asked no one in particular.

"The driver will be stranded once the electromagnetic pulse disables the vehicle," Igor added.

Hovering close by as always, Higgins replied to both men. "No one will be inside the jeep. It will be controlled remotely by a scientist. He'll be able to steer it using a camera mounted on the dashboard. It was just fitted with a device that will hopefully be able to test just how deadly the vapour is. If we're lucky, it will tell us if we can make it through the toxic ring wearing these suits." Sweat trickled from his brow to his jaw and he armed it away. All of the people wearing the bright suits drank water to remain hydrated as they sweated inside their thick protective layer.

My friends and I moved closer to the tent to watch the proceedings. Sanderson and two colonels gathered around the scientist as he operated the remote control device. The jeep lurched into motion and we watched the action on a large monitor. It quickly approached the yellow cloud of gas and disappeared into it. For a couple of minutes, the screen was a whirling mass of dust and a golden fog. Then the monitor lit up with bright light as the vehicle was hit with a pulse ray. The screen went dark, but they'd managed to get some readings on the toxicity of the gas.

"Your suits should keep you safe," the scientist decided after studying the readouts. "But it would be a good idea to test them to be certain."

"We can each escort a pair of soldiers into the city," Luc offered.

"I would like to volunteer to test the suits, sir," Higgins said to his commanding officer from right behind me. Sergeant Wesley stepped up beside him, also offering his services

Geordie threw them both a scowl. "What a surprise," he muttered.

Sanderson chose twelve more soldiers to test their suits and the men donned their helmets. They would have enough air for an hour, but it wouldn't take us that long to reach the city. Slow and clumsy in their oversized outfits, the fourteen volunteers each chose a vampire to be their escort and stood beside us uncertainly.

Since it had been his idea, Luc took his test subjects firmly by the arm and sprinted towards the billowing yellow wall. The rest of us were right behind him. We ran so quickly that the soldiers' feet left the ground and they probably felt like they were flying. I glanced at Higgins to see him wearing a huge grin behind the helmet. Sergeant Wesley had his eyes squeezed shut. He was rapidly mumbling a fervent prayer.

Reaching the far side of the danger zone, we continued our sprint until we were well clear of the toxic fumes. Releasing his soldiers, Geordie waved a hand in front of his face and wrinkled his nose in disgust. We were coated in the smell of rotten eggs. I knew from experience that it wasn't going to fade any time soon.

Higgins cautiously removed his helmet and took a tentative breath of air. At his thumbs up, the others took their helmets off as well. Sergeant Wesley radioed Sanderson that it was safe to enter the city.

"Stay where you are," was the general's order. "I'll join you shortly."

From what I'd seen of the map of the city, we had entered from the west. There were no signs of panic in the suburban neighbourhood. We were too far from the centre of town to hear the battle that was raging away. No one in this suburb even knew they were under attack yet.

"How many enemies are we facing this time, Natalie?" Gregor asked.

Sending my senses eastward, I tallied the numbers and frowned. "Not many. There are only two thousand robots and five thousand imps on the ground." I didn't include the growing number of humans that were rapidly being converted into clones in the total.

Igor's shaggy head turned to take in the quiet streets. "I do not like this. Something feels very wrong."

Things had felt wrong for so long now that I didn't know what 'right' felt like anymore. I had to agree with Igor, though. Why would the Viltarans send in such a small group to subdue and convert a population of several hundred thousand people?

Wesley quietly updated the general about how many enemies we were facing.

Twenty minutes later, Sanderson and a small group of his soldiers arrived. Bright yellow hazmat suits soon lay strewn on the streets as the men gratefully stripped down to their uniforms. Most had to catch their breath from their efforts of jogging while wearing the bulky suits.

"My soldiers have encircled the city and are waiting to move in on my signal," the general informed us. He'd changed out of his officer's suit into the fatigues that suited him more. "We should have more than enough firepower to take down these droids and clones. Have you pinpointed where they are?" He directed the question at me.

My answer was to point eastward. "They're that way." I would have preferred not to interact with him directly, but now wasn't the time to be childish. While I hadn't verbally agreed to call a halt to our mutual hostilities, it made sense to utilize the resources that were available. His forces were crucial to battle the invaders and that meant I had to get along with him.

"Let's move out." At the general's order, we began jogging quietly through the suburban streets.

Chapter Sixteen

Drawing closer to the centre of the city, I detected the sounds of battle long before the soldiers did. I wasn't surprised to hear gunshots ringing out. Guns had been outlawed in my home country of Australia, but Americans had different laws and they still had the right to bear arms.

Bear them these townsfolk did and they weren't shy about using them. Many of the civilians had opted to defend their city. They weren't about to cower inside their homes and allow themselves to be invaded without putting up a fight.

The soldiers hurried their pace when they drew close enough to hear the defiant screams and civilian gunfire. Piping cries from the Kveet imps added to the cacophony, creating fear in even the stoutest of human hearts. For most of the soldiers, this was their first encounter with extra-terrestrials. Only Sanderson's diminished team of six hundred men and women recognized the sounds that they were hearing.

Sanderson remained in constant contact with his men. In a well-choreographed manoeuvre, ten thousand soldiers moved in to eradicate the enemy. More hazmat suits must have arrived along with the extra troopers for our force to have grown that much.

We reached the outskirts of a large park where most of the civilians had gathered to fight the enemy. Sensing movement from the Viltaran ship overhead, I tilted my head back, but it remained hidden from view. Dropping lower and lower, it halted only a few streets away. The camouflage was switched off and the black hull became visible as it disgorged more automatons and Kveet imps. Hovering just above the rooftops and moving in a wide circle, it continued to drop its payload of clones and imps.

"We are about to be in serious trouble," I said to my friends. Before they could ask me what I'd meant, I hurried over to Sanderson. "The Viltarans have just dropped off another eight thousand droids and twenty thousand clones."

The general seemed to age ten years right before my eyes at the grave news. "Where are they?"

"They're mimicking our attack and are encircling the town." I wasn't much of a strategist, but even I understood that we would now be under attack from two sides. It wasn't a position any of us wanted to be caught in.

"How far behind us are they?"

"They're a few streets away and they're closing in fast."

Reaching for his radio, Sanderson changed his orders. "We're about to be attacked by a large force from behind. They don't know that we are aware of their presence yet, so use this to your advantage. They'll be here in a couple of minutes. Take cover and look sharp." He signed off and cast a look at the beleaguered civilians. We didn't have enough people to fight both forces at the same time. For now, the townsfolk would have to battle their foes alone.

Obeying the general's hand signals, we scattered to find shelter. Some of the soldiers ducked down behind cars that had been parked on the street. Several hundred readied death rays. They might have a short range, but they were highly effective against both the clones and the droids. It was a pity they couldn't destroy both at the same time.

Leaping over a fence, I dropped down out of sight. I was surprised when Luc landed beside me. My smile died when he merely glanced at me coolly then made room for Geordie. The teen sent me a sympathetic glance, then turned to peer between the wooden palings. I wasn't sure if the fence would be able to protect us from the death rays. At least they would keep us out of sight as the automatons approached.

The pitter-patter of tiny, clawed feet alerted us that the clones had arrived. They were eerily silent this time instead of moaning pitifully for food. This was an ambush and they'd been cautioned by their masters to be silent. Unfortunately for them, their ambush was about to be turned against them. Several units of androids followed just behind the imps. Their silver faces were blank, but their red eyes were alert.

"Now!" At Sanderson's shout, we opened fire.

A burst of bullets sent the first wave of imps flying backwards in a spray of fluorescent yellow blood. The droids reacted immediately and began firing their death rays at the soldiers. Two men scrambled for fresh cover when the car that had been shielding them turned to dust motes beneath several beams of violet light. They weren't quite quick enough and turned into tiny piles of minute particles a second later as another droid targeted them.

Some of the soldiers were hit by nanobot darts and became the very creatures they were trying to destroy. Higgins threw himself sideways, narrowly avoiding one of the syringes. It hit the man who had been standing beside him instead, instantly transforming him into a hulking, heavily muscled monster. Higgins fired an explosive round into the new imp's face and dived over a fence to safety a bare second before his former teammate exploded.

Punching a hole in the fence, Luc fired his death ray at the killbots. Geordie and I copied him, sharing a sheepish look that neither of us had thought to make a murder hole of our own. On the far side of the street, Igor, Gregor, Kokoro and Ishida had also taken cover behind a fence. Igor took careful aim through a gap where a paling was missing. The others also made holes that they could fire through. We might be superior supernatural creatures, but we weren't above using sneak tactics.

We were slowly whittling down their numbers, but they would be on us shortly and we would be forced to retreat. The civilians in the park had rallied and were making a concerted effort to destroy the robots and imps at our backs. It was a never ending battle. Their friends, family and neighbours were converted into monsters when they were hit with nanobot darts, adding to the enemy's ranks.

The tide turned in our favour when several thousand more armed townsfolk arrived, drawn by the noise of battle. Now it was the droid's turn to be caught between two forces. They changed to their nanobot guns and started firing darts wildly into the crowd.

Sanderson bellowed an order to close in and we surged out of hiding to converge on the enemy. Imps and bots crumpled beneath our barrage of firepower. The earthling's guns might not be as technologically advanced as the alien weapons, but they tore through both flesh and metal easily enough.

It was almost dawn by the time the soldiers finished off the last of our enemies. Each fallen droid was stripped of their weapons and the death rays were distributed amongst the remaining troops. Most were shell shocked and would require therapy after the things they had witnessed. War was never pretty, no matter who or what you were fighting. I should know, I'd been in my fair share of them by now.

Gregor stood in a contemplative silence as he watched the soldiers scrounging through the wreckage for alien weapons.

Knowing his old friend well, Luc voiced a question. "What are you thinking, Gregor?"

"Nothing comforting, I am afraid. This battle seemed almost too easy."

Geordie made a sound of disagreement. "We lost hundreds of soldiers and thousands of civilians." Their bodies lay everywhere and reminded me of confetti that had yet to be cleaned up after a New Year's Eve party. Some had been torn apart and eaten by newly converted imps. Gory skeletons that had been almost completely stripped of their meat stood out from the rest of the carnage. The Kveet clones might be tiny, but their appetites were prodigious.

I hated to admit it, but Gregor was right. "I don't understand why they didn't just send all of their droids and clones out to take over the town. Surely they'd have a much better chance of success that way?"

Gregor nodded, still studying the fallen. "I have a theory." *Of course he does,* I thought with a mixture of amusement and admiration. "I believe the Viltarans have become almost too cautious."

"What do you mean?" Ishida asked.

"Before they decimated their own planet, they numbered in the millions," Gregor explained. He'd either been told this by M'narl, or he'd deduced it through the number of broken cities he'd observed on the alien monitors. "Their tactic when invading other worlds was to use overwhelming numbers. Their adversaries simply couldn't withstand the barrage of firepower and most succumbed with little resistance."

Kokoro backed up his theory. "Now there are a mere twenty-one of their kind left and their forces are minimal. They are facing over seven billion humans. I imagine that must be a daunting prospect, even for the Viltarans."

"If they weren't hiding on their ship, we would crush them like bugs," Igor said. He clenched a meaty fist to illustrate his point.

"Do you think we'll be able to defeat them?" Geordie asked Gregor.

"We will, eventually," was Gregor's response. "But I fear they will cause a great deal of damage before we can destroy them all."

He'd been right, again. His theory wasn't very comforting at all.

Tired and coated in a layer of dust and the lingering smell of sulphur, Sanderson called Corporal Higgins to his side. After a short conversation, he sent the young soldier to speak to us.

While he didn't make the offer in person, Sanderson showed he still had the capacity for decency. "The General has had some rooms set aside in a hotel where you can get cleaned up," Higgins told me.

I wasn't about to turn down the offer of a shower. "Lead the way," I replied.

"New clothing would also be very welcome," Kokoro added. All of my friend's modified Viltaran clothing was torn and stained. My borrowed jeans and red sweater weren't quite as bad. I'd managed to take one shower since landing back on our home world, but the others hadn't even had that. Even Geordie perked up a bit at the offer. His hair was in matted clumps that smelled like rotten eggs. Unfortunately, mine reeked almost as badly.

The sun was dangerously close to rising as Higgins escorted us towards a small hotel. There were no skyscrapers to block the killing rays this time and we hurried through the doors into a tiny foyer. The décor was dated and the dark brown carpet was worn and in need of replacement. A few garish prints did their best to brighten the beige walls. It wasn't exactly a five star establishment, but at least it was clean.

Still white faced and trembling from the battle, a clerk stood behind the counter. Higgins didn't bat an eyelid at the sight of a shotgun lying on the counter. The clerk already had a row of key cards lined up, ready for us. We all took one, except for Kokoro. Naturally, she and Gregor would be sharing a room.

It hit me then that this was the first time Luc and I wouldn't be sharing the same room. His expression was as serene as always and gave no indication that he felt any pain at the demise of our relationship. Meanwhile, I felt as though a rusty sword was stabbing me repeatedly in the heart.

Higgins also took a key card, making sure he had one of the rooms next to mine. The clerk raised his eyebrows suggestively, but wisely remained silent. Geordie opened his mouth to voice his displeasure, but Igor frowned at him in warning. The teen swallowed his jealous tirade, but shot the soldier a narrow eyed glare. Oblivious to the byplay, the corporal nodded his thanks at the clerk.

Our rooms were all on the first floor and we followed Higgins upstairs. He stopped at his door and addressed me. "I'll request some new clothing for you all and have them delivered asap." He waited for my nod of acknowledgement before disappearing into his room.

Geordie had the room to my left and pouted as he unlocked the door. He sent one final glare at me before stepping inside. I was pretty sure his jealousy was unfounded. Higgins wasn't interested in me, he was just following orders. He was staying close so he could report back to his boss if he thought Sanderson needed to be appraised of any developments. I was under no illusions that the soldier was anything but a spy.

The rest of my friends entered their rooms and I noticed that Luc had made sure his was as far away from mine as possible. He closed his door without a backward glance. I desperately wished Kokoro could still read minds so she could tell me what Luc was thinking.

Surely he can't stay mad at me forever. My thought held more than a hint of desperation. He'd *beheaded* me and I'd managed to forgive him. *Yeah, but what you did was much worse. You told him your love wasn't real,* my inner voice pointed out. *That was your fault!* My subconscious fled at my internal shriek.

Becoming conscious of the fact that I was still standing in the doorway, I stepped inside and locked the door. My room was as bland and inoffensive as most hotel rooms tended to be. Beige was the main theme, with a few splashes of colour in more cheap prints on the walls.

Stripping off, I left my filthy clothes on the floor and took a long shower that left my skin pink and prune-like. The wrinkles smoothed out as soon as I shut the water off. The pinkness faded quickly enough until I was back to being corpse pale again. I dried my hair with the cheap blow dryer the hotel provided, then sat on the bed to wait for my new clothes to turn up.

When a knock came at my door a few minutes later, I opened it to find a soldier holding a bulging bag in one hand and a small bundle in the other. His eyes met mine then flicked down to the towel that rested just above my breasts. His cheeks turned bright red as he handed over some underwear, jeans, a fresh t-shirt and a dark purple sweater with a picture of a flaming skull on it. He mumbled a response at my thanks, then turned to knock on Ishida's door directly across the hall.

My new outfit fit well enough, except for the bra, which was one cup size too large. I shook my head at man's inability to successfully gauge a woman's boob size. At least the panties fit and they came with a tag, which indicated that they were new. My sneakers were stained and scuffed, but they would have to do for now since new footwear hadn't been provided.

I wasn't sure why someone had chosen a sweater with a flaming skull on it. I wondered if it was supposed to be an insult. Strangely, the picture of a grinning skull cheerily blazing with fire appealed to me. I'd definitely stand out from the crowd while wearing it.

I was neither tired, nor hungry and there was little to do but watch TV or pace. I opted to pace and trudged up and down the worn carpet while the others settled down to sleep, or to at least pretend to sleep.

When I couldn't take the solitude anymore, I left my room and headed to the end of the hallway. I could sense Luc inside and knew he would have heard me approaching. At first, I thought he was going to ignore me when I knocked softly. He roused himself when I knocked again and he finally opened the door.

Looking up into his model handsome face, I was reminded of the first time we'd met. He had been intimidatingly sophisticated and elegant then and had worn expensive cashmere. I'd felt decidedly shabby and insignificant in his presence.

He'd been provided with plain black jeans and a black fake leather jacket this time, but I still felt insignificant beneath his distant gaze. His eyes dropped to the skull on my chest and he almost looked amused for a second.

"Can we talk?" I asked him, knowing our friends were listening in.

Luc's lips thinned as he considered my request. I figured the answer was affirmative when he stepped out into the hall and closed his door. I followed him up the stairs to the third floor and then into a tiny maintenance closet. The door was heavy and made of metal, which would help to keep our conversation private. The fact that he was going to such lengths for the others not to overhear us didn't escape my notice. I had the distinct feeling that this talk wasn't going to go as well as I hoped.

Leaning against the wall, Luc crossed his arms. It was an intentional sign that he was closing me out. "What did you want to discuss?" His tone wasn't exactly cold. At best, it could be called neutral.

"The depletion of Earth's natural resources," I said sarcastically. "What do you think I want to talk about?"

Annoyance flashed across his face before he schooled his features to serenity again. "It was your choice to end our relationship. I do not understand what there is to discuss."

Crossing my own arms, I held onto my biceps tightly. "I didn't choose to end anything. I just had a brief moment where I doubted that you really loved me."

"Your brief moment of doubt was enough to convince me that your feelings for me do not run as deeply as you claim," he fired back. "You told me that what I feel for you has been fabricated by fate and that you weren't sure that your love for me was true."

Rubbing my face with both hands to keep in a frustrated scream, I clasped my fingers together to stop myself from strangling him. "I know what I said. It was just a theory and I realized how stupid it was almost right away."

A hint of sadness crept into Luc's dark eyes as he stared down at me. "The fact that you doubted me at all tells me that you do not love me as I love you."

Hope blossomed within my shrivelled heart. "So, you still love me then?"

"I do not know." My hopes were shattered at his response and silence reigned after he threw my own words back at me. Not quite done yet, he crushed my heart even more. "You are not the same woman I fell in love with. The Ladybug I knew is gone."

My stomach fluttered at hearing the nickname I'd previously found so annoying. Now I wished he would use it with the same teasing affection he'd once felt for me. "If I'm not your Ladybug anymore, then who am I?" I asked in a small voice.

His sadness became more apparent as he answered my question. "You have become Mortis in deed as well as in name." He paused before making a final observation. A hint of red light began to glow in his eyes. "It would take a very strong man to love Death itself."

Inside my chest, my heart didn't just break. It withered and crumbled to dust. Any last hope that Luc could find it within himself to forgive me dissipated, gone forever. He'd voiced my greatest fear, that no one could ever truly love a creature like me.

Chapter Seventeen

Waiting for Luc to retreat down the stairs to his room, I stumbled out of the closet. An unbearable weight settled on my shoulders as I slowly shambled down the stairs.

My subconscious had been trying to tell me that I would end up alone one day. I'd assumed that meant my friends would all die. Now it seemed that we would all live forever, but I was doomed to eternal solitude anyway. On some level, I'd known that I wasn't the same person anymore, but I hadn't realized how much I'd changed until it had been pointed out to me so brutally.

Back on the first floor, I entered my room, gathered my swords and stripped the coverlet off the bed. Once my friends saw how heartbroken I was, they would know that Luc had broken up with me for good. They would undoubtedly shower me with sympathy and I didn't need that right now. I needed to be alone so I could wallow in self-pity in private.

I knocked on Higgins' door. He opened it immediately, almost as if he'd been waiting for me. Fully dressed, his light brown hair was still wet from his shower, but he was ready to move at a moment's notice. His eyes dropped to the coverlet that was draped over my arm. "Are we going somewhere?"

"Yes," I replied and he needed no further urging.

"Nat?" Geordie asked as he heard us leaving. "Are you ok?"

"I'm fine," I lied in a falsely cheerful tone. "I just have to check on something."

"Be careful," Ishida said from within his own room.

Hastening down the stairs to the lobby, I paused long enough to pull the coverlet over my head before stepping outside.

Higgins grabbed my arm to guide me as I took off at a fast trot. "Where are we going?"

"I don't care. Just take me somewhere dark and private." I struggled not to cry and managed it, just.

Altering our trajectory, the soldier increased his pace. "You look like you're about to burst into flames," he observed. I didn't feel any pain, but if the coverlet was beginning to give off steam, then the sun was burning through it and would soon touch my skin. The heat wasn't as overwhelming as I'd once found it to be, but it was still unpleasant.

We entered a cool, dark room seconds before the coverlet was about to disintegrate and leave me exposed to the sun. Higgins had led me into a store that appeared to have gone out of business several years ago. Most of the windows had been boarded over. Dust caked the carpet that may once have been dark blue and was now black.

There was no furniture or signs to indicate what sort of business had once been conducted here.

I turned to my escort and his obvious concern made my bottom lip quiver slightly. "I'll be fine here on my own." Being alone was a state I was going to have to get used to eventually. I might as well start practicing it now. "Come and get me when it's time to leave." My escort was reluctant to obey me, but turned and left anyway, closing the door behind him. He didn't go far and I sensed him joining a group of his fellow troops half a block away.

Alone at last, I covered my face with my hands and sobbed out my anguish. My hands muffled most of the wails and none of the humans were close enough to hear me, thankfully. Leaning back against the wall, I slid to the floor and wrapped my arms around my legs. No tears dampened my new jeans. I'd left tears behind a long time ago, along with my humanity and the ability to eat solid food.

An ache settled in my chest when my dry sobs finally petered out. I'd never been in love before and this was the first time I'd ever had my heart broken. I desperately wanted to take my anguish out on someone else, but I only had myself to blame.

If Luc really loved you he wouldn't let something like a little bit of doubt pull you apart, my inner voice ventured almost timidly. My response was immediate and vicious. *You can cram your opinion where the sun doesn't shine! If you'd kept your mouth shut in the first place, he never would have dumped me!* My alter ego quailed at my anger and slunk off without another word.

Squeezing my eyes shut, I wondered if I'd lost my mind at some stage since being kicked off our planet. I'd woken up in space to find myself a frozen block of ice along with the rest of my friends and allies. We'd been captured by a Viltaran spaceship and had been taken to their planet. We'd lost all but seven of our number. I'd been shot with around fifty nanobot darts and I still wasn't sure if all of the side effects had made themselves known.

All of that, plus the rest of the awful things that had happened to me since I'd been turned into the living dead, was bound to strain most people. I hoped this was just stress I was feeling because I'd just had a mental screaming match with myself. As far as I knew, only crazy people had arguments like that with themselves.

Eventually growing tired of feeling sorry for myself, I spread the coverlet out on the carpet. I curled up on my side, facing away from the door. My back would suffer the worst of the rays if someone opened the door and let the sun in, but at least my face wouldn't melt off. That had happened to me once already and I didn't want to suffer that type of pain again. Then again, compared to the mental anguish I was now feeling, a little physical pain probably wouldn't bother me.

On the edge of dozing off, I found myself thinking about the Viltarans. Gregor's theory that they were going to cause untold damage before we could put an end to their invasion was more of a concern than I'd thought it would be. Fate had brought us home so we could save the earthlings. I wished I could figure out what they were planning to do next, so I could do the job that I'd been destined for.

Opening my eyes, I found myself floating in a dark hallway. The walls, floor and ceiling were made of metal. It might be black instead of dull silver, but I recognized it as being Viltaran in origin.

Just thinking of the Viltarans set me in motion. Like the visions I'd had of the First's cavern of doom so long ago, I drifted along without being able to direct my movements. I floated past a doorway and glanced inside to see Kveet imps. They were crammed in side by side with barely any room to move.

It was daylight, so most of them were sleeping. Those that were still awake were on their feet, struggling to remain alert. Their scarlet eyes kept sliding shut, only to snap open and blink owlishly before immediately sliding shut again. I passed room after room and all contained dozens of the creatures. Many more cells spread throughout the ship. They all had the same cargo stored away for use against the humans.

My stomach tried to flop over when I was suddenly whisked upward through several levels of metal. My suspicion that I had dreamed myself onto the Viltaran ship was confirmed when I ghosted through a door and into a large room.

Consoles in different shapes and sizes were covered in lights, buttons and levers. Over a dozen wafer thin monitors hung in mid-air. Each one showed a view of the Texan city that had just been attacked. None of the aliens in the command centre looked in my direction when I coasted to a stop beside them. I figured that meant I was invisible.

Out of the twenty-one aliens on board, only fifteen were actually present. The shortest Viltaran was just over ten feet tall. He cringed whenever one of the others glanced in his direction. Staying at the back of the group, he made himself as unobtrusive as possible. Instead of a nose, he had a protuberance that almost looked like a beak. A light fuzz of hair coated his grey scalp. Compared to the others, he was almost handsome. He lacked any visible scars, which meant he'd never engaged in the hand to hand combat that most of them were so fond of. If there was a weak link amongst the aliens, I was pretty sure I was looking at it.

"The humans are proving to be harder to subdue than we'd anticipated," a female Viltaran said. She backed away a step when her leader's gaze fell on her.

Self-appointed ruler of the remaining Viltarans, Uldar clenched fists that were almost the same size as my head. "It is useless to send in small forces of our droids and servants," he grudgingly conceded. "We have wasted our resources and have gained little in the process."

"What do you propose we do next?" the female asked. Her hand dropped to her belly in a very human gesture. It drew my attention to the fact that she was about six months pregnant, by human standards. I had no idea how long her gestation period was.

The imps that had been made by the First had given birth after only a nine or ten day pregnancy. All had been former vampires that had become alive again after being converted into clones. Maybe the transformation had kick started their ability to conceive. The bad batch of nanobots might have caused the incubation process to become much faster than was natural.

Natural? There's nothing natural about any of the clones, my alter ego scoffed.

There were seven females among the group of aliens. None of the others were showing signs that they were carrying offspring. Considering how few of them had been left when we'd arrived on their planet, they probably had trouble conceiving. They were a dying race, which made it all the more important for them to find a healthy home so they could attempt to rebuild their numbers again. They were already discovering that the earthlings weren't going to fold easily.

"We will target a larger city and send in our remaining droids and clones," Uldar stated in a tone that brooked no argument. "This time, we will not allow any human soldiers to intervene." Several doubtful glances were exchanged behind his back, but no one was brave enough to voice an objection to his plan.

"Which city are we going to target next?" the pregnant female asked.

Tapping one of the screens, Uldar brought up the picture of a city that I'd seen in dozens of movies. Their alien camera zoomed in on a dazzling array of neon lights that blazed blindingly even during the heat of the day. "Once darkness falls, we will make this city ours!"

His cohorts chortled in glee as the dream faded.

Waking with the sound of guttural alien chuckles still resounding in my head, I was standing before I'd fully formed the intention to move. It was mid-afternoon now, which meant we only had a few hours left to attempt to avert the coming attack.

The sun had moved to the far side of the building, leaving the front in shadow. It was still painfully bright when I yanked the door open. "Higgins!"

Startled by my shout, the soldier sprinted towards me. "What's wrong?" he asked when he reached me.

"Get Sanderson on the radio. I need to speak to him urgently."

Not wasting time with further questions, Higgins unclipped his radio from his belt. "General Sanderson, this is Corporal Higgins. Do you copy?"

Sounding groggy, as if he'd just woken up, Sanderson responded. "Go ahead, Corporal."

Feeling time weighing on me, I snatched the radio out of Higgins' hand. "You have to gather as many soldiers as you can and head for Las Vegas," I said without preamble. The dazzling casinos lining the world famous Glitter Strip had been unmistakable.

"You're positive that they're attacking there next?" The general sounded fully awake now.

"Yes and they're sending all of their droids and clones in to attack this time."

"How many of each?"

"Twenty thousand robots and fifty-five thousand Kveet clones." We'd whittled their numbers down during the last two attacks, but the odds were still stacked against us. The soldiers who'd gathered around to listen in knew just how poor our chances of winning were. Higgins wasn't the only one to turn pale at the news that I'd just divulged.

Sanderson's palm scraped against a cheek that needed to be shaved as he digested the warning then he galvanized himself into action. "I'll alert the President and General Hart immediately. I just hope we've learned of their intentions in time to act."

Still emotional from being so recently dumped, a lump formed in my throat at the hint of accusation in his tone. The Viltarans had only reached their decision moments ago, but I was somehow supposed to know what they were planning before they'd even planned it.

"We appreciate your warning, Natalie," Higgins said as I handed his radio back. He'd accurately read my expression. Some of the other soldiers, mostly from the original crew who had arrived with Sanderson, murmured their agreement. Some seemed to have lost their suspicion of my kind after working with us to defeat the enemy.

Unable to speak for fear that I'd begin sobbing again, I nodded. It seemed ironic that the humans I despised so much were rallying around me. Of course, it could just be my vampire mojo at work. All vampires had a dark magnetism that drew humans to them. Mine just happened to be stronger than most.

Chapter Eighteen

It was late afternoon by the time the arrangements had been finalized. I kept my distance from my friends as trucks arrived to ferry us to the closest airport. It would take us an hour to get there. That would give the planes that would be transporting us to Vegas time to arrive.

Peeking out from beneath the coverlet that I'd draped over my head again, I saw Geordie craning his head from the shadows to search for me. Dark sunglasses protected his eyes from the painful glare. Each of my friends wore what seemed to be standard issue army sunglasses.

Spying me, Geordie waved frantically, but Igor put a hand on his shoulder when the teen took a step in my direction. They might not know exactly what had happened between Luc and me, but they had probably figured out that we hadn't managed to reconcile during our brief talk.

The troopers had enough time to retrieve their hazmat suits, return to the centre of the city and don the protective gear before our transportation arrived. Crammed into the back of a truck with soldiers wearing the yellow suits, my misery was so overwhelming that I barely smelled the toxic gas as we sped through it.

Once we were safely out of range of the gas again, the men struggled to strip their suits off. It was an amusing sight, but I'd momentarily lost the capacity to laugh. I managed a ghost of a smile when a soldier bent to free his feet and knocked heads with another man. Both cursed bitterly in pain, but they were separated before any punches could be thrown.

A row of planes was waiting at the tiny private airport to carry us to Las Vegas. President Rivers had decided against trying to evacuate the city. To do so would tip off the aliens that we were aware of their plans. They would then simply choose a different target, one that we wouldn't be able to guess the identity of until after they'd struck. The ship hadn't moved yet and still hovered high above Texas. I'd know we were running out of time once it finally began to travel.

Boarding seemed to take forever and the sun was sinking when I took my seat and closed the shutter on the window. Higgins took the seat beside me. His gun was nestled in the crook of his arm and my swords were across my knees. We were both tense as our airplane became airborne.

Sanderson and my friends were on another plane that had left long before ours. I sent out my senses and found them already well on their way to Las Vegas. Both of my hands were clamped on the armrests and I had to force myself to switch my attention to the Viltaran ship.

We were halfway to Vegas when I finally sensed the spaceship moving. Reading the apprehension in my stiff shoulders, Higgins advised Sanderson that our time was running out.

"Roger that, Corporal. Let me know when the ship nears its destination." The general signed off and I realized all conversation on our plane had ceased. We were in a race to try to beat the spaceship and it could move a lot faster than us, if it wanted to.

Picking up speed, the ship veered away from the course that I'd expected it to take. "That's weird," I murmured.

Turning an anxious gaze on me, Higgins readied his radio again. "What's weird?"

"The ship is heading northeast."

"But, Las Vegas is to the northwest." He was as bewildered as me and I didn't have an explanation for him. His uncertainty came through loud and clear when he updated Sanderson.

"Put Natalie on," the general ordered.

I took the radio, expecting to be blasted for being wrong. "I'm here."

"How certain are you that Las Vegas is their intended target?" Sanderson's tone wasn't exactly friendly, but it wasn't as hostile as I'd expected either.

"My dreams have never been wrong so far," I said by way of a reply. My certainty became more fragile as I sensed the ship coming to a stop. I had a sinking sensation as it began to lower. "But, I might be wrong this time," I amended.

A tense silence descended as we waited for news.

Minutes later, General Hart's voice came over Higgins' radio. "Sanderson, do you copy?"

"I'm here."

"I've just received word that a city in Arizona has just been surrounded by the yellow vapour. It appears that the vampire's dream was a false lead."

Hearing the sneer in his voice, I bristled. Sweeping my senses towards the city that had just been ringed by a deadly layer of gas, I went still as tens of thousands of lives were snuffed out.

"I'll redirect the planes towards Arizona," Sanderson said wearily. "Hopefully, we'll arrive before the aliens can convert the entire town."

I grabbed for my companion's radio and spoke. "Don't bother," I cut in before he could make any further plans. "I'm pretty sure they just blasted the town to pieces. The ship is already on the move again, heading north this time."

"Are you saying they killed everyone instead of converting them into clones?" General Hart demanded. "Why would they do that?"

Gregor spoke to General Sanderson. He came through loud and clear to me, but probably not loudly enough for the humans to hear him. "This could be a ploy to divide our forces. By attacking several cities and forming a ring of poison around them, they could be attempting to make it seem as though the citizens are under attack."

Sanderson relayed the information to all who hadn't heard Gregor. "They'll expect us to send soldiers to assist the civilians who, according to Natalie, are already dead," he concluded.

"It would be a waste of both your resources and your time," Gregor added, this time directly into the radio. "By using this tactic, there is no way for us to know which city is their actual intended target. Fortunately for us, Natalie was sent an early warning."

General Hart snorted loudly enough to make me wince. "You'll have to excuse me if I don't put much faith in a monster's dreams. The ship isn't heading anywhere near Vegas and we have no way of knowing whether the civilians in Arizona are really dead or not."

"Are you completely stupid?" Geordie yelled. His voice was several pitches higher than usual from his outrage. "You're going to fall for the Viltarans' ruse!"

"That's a chance we'll have to take," Hart said coldly. "I'm redirecting the troops to Arizona until we receive advice that another city has been targeted."

"I believe that would be a mistake," Sanderson said. His tone was also cool, but towards his fellow officer rather than the undead.

"I don't answer to you, Sanderson. President Rivers has given me her backing and I am in control of our troops," Hart said, ending the discussion.

We listened in as orders were given to turn the planes around. While I wasn't absolutely positive that my dream was going to come true, I'd learned to trust my instincts. The fact that the population of the latest city to come under attack had been destroyed backed my gut feeling. The Viltarans were already lowering their ship to launch another cloud of gas. I waited for the sensation of over two hundred thousand human lives winking out before telling Higgins what I'd sensed.

The corporal hastily updated his boss. Our plane began to angle back the way we'd come and I was suddenly standing in the aisle. Blinking at me in astonishment,

Higgins opened his mouth, but I was already on the move before he could ask me how I'd gotten past him.

The cockpit door opened at my knock and the co-pilot backed away warily. "What are you doing in here?" he asked. His voice quavered slightly.

"Ignore General Hart's orders and head for Las Vegas," I instructed the pilot.

Glancing over his shoulder, he was immediately caught in my snare. "Yes, ma'am."

Before the co-pilot could protest, I bamboozled him as well. He took his seat as the pilot corrected our course. Angry questions were fired through the headset from whoever was in charge of air traffic. Both of my minions ignored them.

Suspicious stares from the closest soldiers met me when I closed the cockpit door and turned to face the passengers. "The Viltarans are trying to lead us on a wild goose chase by attacking random cities," I explained. "They're not leaving anyone alive, so it would be a waste of time to try to save them."

Sergeant Wesley's radio squawked and news came through of the second city somewhere to the north being surrounded by the toxic gas. "So, I take it we're heading for Vegas?" Wesley asked when the radio went silent again.

"That's the plan. Does anyone have a problem with it?"

"I don't," General Sanderson replied through Wesley's radio after the sergeant relayed my message. "I agree that we should stick to the original plan and continue on towards Vegas."

"Roger that, General," Wesley replied.

Higgins politely stood to allow me access to my seat. "How did you get past me?" he asked when I was settled in again. "I didn't even see you move."

"You'd be surprised how fast I can move when I want to." The truth was, I didn't know how I'd gotten past him either. It had almost seemed like I hadn't moved at all and had just appeared in the aisle.

During the time it took us to swing back around and cross the country to Nevada, the alien spacecraft vaporized half a dozen more cities. All up, several million lives were extinguished without a single loss on their side.

Feeling slightly ill that I'd been unable to stop the carnage, I wondered if fate was going to blame me for their deaths. If it did, I could only imagine how horrible my punishment would be.

"Are you all right?" Higgins asked. He kept his voice low to avoid being overheard.

"Not really." He impatiently nudged my arm with his elbow when I didn't elaborate further. "The Viltarans just finished off an eighth city," I told him quietly.

"How many civilians have they killed now?" He strove to keep his tone even, but it was a struggle. I imagined he felt almost as impotent as I did.

"Around five million, give or take a few thousand."

The corporal went rigid in shock and an expletive escaped him. Flushing at his momentary lack of control, he mumbled an apology. I waved it away, then concentrated on the ship when it began to move again. Finished with placing its decoys, it headed directly towards the city my dreams had warned me about.

A sinking feeling settled in the pit of my stomach when I suspected we weren't going to make it to Vegas in time.

The spacecraft was moving far faster than us and we were still fifteen minutes away from the airport. Not all of the soldiers had obeyed General Hart's orders and several pilots had continued on towards their original goal. The planes at the front of our small aerial convoy began to land with precise choreography. I'd overheard a soldier say that a military air force base towards the north end of Vegas was our intended destination.

"The spaceship has picked up speed and it'll reach the city in a few minutes," I said to my escort.

Higgins relayed the information to his commanding officer. Sanderson's reply was heavy. "Roger that, Corporal."

We'd almost made it to Vegas then the alien craft began to sink lower in the sky in preparation to shoot toxic gas around its true target. "They're about to fire their gas gun," I said to Higgins. "You'd better tell the pilot to abort." I'd been holding the mental reigns of my hypnotism over both pilots. I released my control enough for them to be able to respond quickly to the warning.

Leaping out of his seat, the soldier used his radio to warn his comrades to veer away from the city and to find an alternative landing site. Pounding down the aisle, he burst into the cockpit to alert our captain. Our plane immediately swerved away from the coming disaster.

Moments later, the sky darkened even further as a yellow cloud of vapour formed right before our eyes. The spaceship momentarily became visible during the process. Awed soldiers pressed their faces up against the glass to view the gigantic black spacecraft before it disappeared again.

Despite my warning, one of the pilots wasn't able to veer away in time and flew directly through the gas. The plane went into a nosedive as the pilots, and everyone else on board, expired. Even through the billowing cloud of deadly haze, we saw the explosion as the plane collided with some buildings. Dozens of citizens and tourists died instantly in the collision, but maybe they were the lucky ones. At least they'd be spared from the terror that was about to rain down on the city.

I was almost afraid to search for my friends. While they could conceivably survive being mangled in a crash, I quailed at the thought of any of them suffering such a horrible ordeal. Taking a mental breath, I sent out my senses and found all six vampires safe and sound on the ground. I sagged in my seat in relief. My only regret was that Sanderson was probably also still alive and well.

My relief was short lived. It disappeared completely when the spacecraft finished firing its ring of death then shifted towards the centre of Vegas. It lowered and began to disgorge its passengers. My dream proved to be accurate as every killbot and Kveet imp on board hit the streets and began to spread out in search of victims. The ravenous clones would feed very well this night. The surviving humans would quickly be transformed into a clone army.

Only two thousand soldiers had managed to land safely in Vegas before the ring of death had sealed them inside. Sanderson and my friends were cut off and the Viltarans weren't about to let any more soldiers into the city this time. The odds were definitely not in our favour.

Chapter Nineteen

Staying well clear of the billowing cloud of fumes, our pilot landed on the highway to the south of the city. Two more planeloads of soldiers had opted to trust my information that Vegas was the intended target and they landed behind us. Instead of the ten thousand troopers that had been on their way to assist us, we numbered just over three thousand. A third of our small force was trapped outside the city that we'd been sent to defend.

The emergency ramps were activated and the passengers lined up to slide down the steep chutes. Higgins went first, then turned to catch me when I rocketed down after him. He pulled me to my feet and I moved aside to allow the next soldier to disembark.

I was surprised at how quickly the heat was already fading from the desert now that night held sway. Australia had vast deserts of its own, but I'd never had the misfortune of visiting any of them. I was a city girl at heart and always would be.

The myriad lights of Vegas had almost disappeared behind the curtain of yellow gas. A whiff of rotten eggs drifted to us on a breeze and most of the soldiers dry heaved. Higgins peered at the toxic cloud almost forlornly. "Our people are confined inside the city and we have no way of reaching them," he said softly. "They're going to be annihilated if we can't get inside and help them."

His radio buzzed and he unclipped it from his belt. "This is General Sanderson," the general said and Higgins waved his fellow soldiers to silence. "I need a status update. I saw one plane go down somewhere in Vegas. How many more landed safely?"

Sergeant Wesley responded to the question. "The rest of us made it, sir. We've landed on the highway to the south of Vegas. What are your orders, General?"

"Find a way into this city," was Sanderson's succinct reply. "I will contact General Hart and advise him that Natalie's intel was correct. The aliens have sent in thousands of robots and clones, too many to count with any accuracy. I'll get him to redirect the troops and send them to assist us."

Instead of drawing back high above the clouds to watch the carnage from afar, the Viltaran ship hovered just above the city. I wasn't a mind reader, but I had a hunch that they were staying close so they could guard against human invasion.

We'd managed to use hazmat suits to enter the town in Texas, but that wasn't going to happen this time. The scarlet eyed extra-terrestrials weren't going to allow us to come to the rescue again. If they spotted anyone trying to enter by foot or in vehicles, they'd blast them into nothingness. We had to find a way into the city that would keep the humans safe from the deadly gas and also somehow sneak past the watchful eye of the patrolling aliens.

Panicked soldiers milled around in confusion. None were willing to step up and take charge. Moving away from the plane, I crossed the highway. If we didn't do something to help Sanderson's men kill off the robots, Vegas would soon be lost. It wouldn't take long for the entire country to be overrun with freshly minted human imps once the vapour evaporated.

Standing with my back to the once bright and now obscured city in the distance, I stopped at the edge of the road. Soldiers had blocked the traffic in both directions. A long line of vehicles was already beginning to build up. Motorists honked their frustration, but they were going to be in for a long wait.

A guardrail had been erected to stop the unwary from leaving the road and from driving into a deep gully. Leaning against it, I kicked a stone and tracked its progress to the ground below. It echoed strangely when it landed and I leaned further over the railing to peer downwards.

Directly below my feet, twin concrete pipes sat side by side and protruded slightly into the gully. A runnel of dirty water sluggishly oozed from the one on the right. Turning around, I followed the direction they took and saw the billowing yellow cloud in the distance. Chance had led me to this exact spot. I had little choice but to believe that the conduits would lead us safely to our destination.

Sprinting back to the plane, I grabbed Higgins by the shoulder to get his attention. "I think I just found a way to get your soldiers safely into Vegas."

"Show me," he demanded eagerly.

Taking the lead, I jogged back to the side of the highway and pointed down at the pipes. He leaned over the railing to examine my find. They weren't exactly large and anyone who climbed inside would have to hunch over. It would be better than trying to hold your breath and sprinting through the deadly cloud.

Higgins called several more soldiers over and they examined the proposed route. "What the hell?" Sergeant Wesley said with a shrug. "We all gotta die some time. I'd rather go out choking on poison than have my legs gnawed off by an ugly little alien gremlin."

Taking Higgins' handgun from the holster on his waist, I fired a shot into the air. Soldiers whirled around with their weapons raised, but they were too well trained to open fire on me. Higgins took his gun back, shaking his head at my risky move.

My shot had the desired effect and everyone gathered around to hear what I had to say. "I know I'm the last person any of you wants to trust right now, but we need to get into Vegas asap. These storm drains should be safe and if we hurry, we might arrive in time to stop everyone in the city from being turned into clones."

I'd never been particularly persuasive before, but every man and woman who met my eyes nodded in agreement. Higgins was right behind me when I jumped down into the gulch. He would have broken both legs if he'd attempted the leap and instead slid down the steep incline. His flashlight came to life and pierced the darkness of the tunnels. "Which one should we use?" he queried.

Following my instincts, I chose the left tunnel and leaped inside. It was bone dry and I doubted any runoff water had travelled down this chute in years. The pipe was smaller than it appeared from the outside. I was only average in height, but I still had to duck to avoid banging my head. It was going to be a miserable journey for anyone who was over six feet tall. I just hoped the tunnels would lead us deeply enough into the city that the soldiers wouldn't be poisoned when we eventually emerged on the other side.

Rats fled from our approach with squeaks of annoyance, scurrying into pipes that were too tiny for us to enter. Our force of a thousand humans and one lone vampire traversed down the main tunnel.

It ran in a fairly straight line until it eventually opened up into a wide chamber. I'd known by the increasingly noisome smells that we were closing in on the sewage channels. It came as no surprise to see a small river of brown water rushing by several feet beneath us.

A narrow walkway ran alongside the waterway and I jumped down and edged my way along it. We were almost beneath the outskirts of the city now, but the route had just become far more complicated. I wished I had one of the handy monitors from Viltar, not that it would have had access to a map of this world's sewage systems.

Allowing my instincts to take over, I continued down the walkway. Up above, I sensed a plane approaching. Sending out my senses in a wide sweep, I picked up on several more planes heading in our direction. General Hart had apparently seen reason and had ordered his soldiers to change course for their original target.

Once the planes landed, more troopers would follow behind us. Even when they were added to our ranks, we'd still be badly outnumbered. Even a few thousand reinforcements would help to make a difference in the coming war.

"How do you know you're going the right way?" Higgins whispered, interrupting my train of thought. There was enough space between us and the others that they couldn't overhear us.

"I don't," I told him. "I'm just following my gut."

Higgins wasn't reassured by my answer. "Well, I hope your gut knows where it's going."

So do I, I thought, but kept my uncertainty to myself.

Chapter Twenty

One of the soldiers had the foresight to mark our route with a strip of black tape on the grey concrete walls. Large black arrows would point the way for those about to land and who would shortly be following us.

My instincts proved to be true. They unerringly led us beneath the toxic cloud and into the outskirts of Vegas. I figured it would be safe enough for us to surface when I sensed live humans up above.

Stopping at a rusty ladder, I cautioned the others to wait and climbed up to the top. There were no droids or imps nearby, so I lifted the manhole cover and set it down gently on the road. A faint whiff of gas washed over me in a sluggish breeze.

"Eww, what is that stench?" a teenage girl in a house across the road complained. The smell spread and humans in the houses around me made retching sounds. While they were stricken with nausea, at least none of them fell over dead. We were far enough away from the ring of death for it to no longer be lethal.

Higgins climbed up the ladder first when I motioned that it was safe to leave the tunnel. Reaching the surface, he covered his nose and mouth with one hand and held his gun ready in the other. Filled with both bullets and explosive rounds, it was too heavy for him to be able to hold one handed for long.

Curtains were drawn aside and faces peeked out at us as more and more soldiers emerged from beneath the ground. One civilian was brave enough to open his door. "What's going on? Are we under attack?" His face was pale and I detected a faint hint of vomit on his clothes.

"The alien ship that attacked Manhattan has now targeted Las Vegas," Higgins informed the civilian. "It would be safest for you to stay in your home and barricade the door." That wouldn't stop the droids from kicking their way in, or the Kveet from eating their way in for that matter. I had a feeling that nowhere in this town would be safe for long.

"Screw that," the civilian replied and pushed his door open to reveal a shotgun in his hand. "Consider me to be your newest recruit." Somewhere between thirty and forty, he had a paunch and a week's worth of stubble on his face. Wearing a stained white singlet and torn cargo pants, he didn't look particularly fit or healthy. He was putting on a brave face, but the slight tremor in his voice gave away his fright.

Higgins slanted a glance at me and I nodded. We would need all the help we could get if we wanted to win this war. "Fine. Grab as much spare ammo as you can carry as well as food and water," the soldier instructed the civilian.

More doors opened and people were given the choice of joining us, or remaining in their homes. Most people with weapons decided to join our hunt. Each was sent back inside to retrieve ammo and supplies. This war wasn't going to be won overnight. It was going to drag on for days, if not weeks, depending on how many reinforcements were sent to our aid.

What happens if you do manage to kill all of the droids and imps? I paused at the question my inner voice raised. *Do you think the Viltarans will just give up and go away?* They'd most likely blast our planet with toxic gas in a fit of rage.

If Gregor's hunch was right then the vapour would dissipate over time. The aliens could always hide out on their ship until the air became breathable again. Of course, all of the humans and most of the birds, insects and animals would die. The aliens would be able to rule over whatever life remained, which would probably only be cockroaches.

If they did unleash their deadly stink bombs and killed off all animal life, they'd be left with nothing to eat. *Unless they like fish,* I mused. I wasn't sure if any of our aquatic life would be affected by the airborne toxins or not.

More and more civilians opted to stand and fight when they saw us marching quietly towards the battle. Each one that joined us gave us a greater chance of success. It amazed me to see so many people carrying anything from handguns to assault rifles. I felt a chill at the thought of my countrymen coming under alien attack. It was against the law for Australians to own guns, except in a few instances. While we had a low rate of deaths by gunshots, the average Aussie would be defenceless against the droids and clones.

Our force quickly increased to around ten thousand, most of whom were civilians. Undisciplined and untrained, the townsfolk were a noisy, unruly mob. Halting the crowd, the soldiers gathered to discuss our options. General Sanderson and his people had engaged the enemy and he was too busy trying to survive to organize our troops for us.

Sergeant Wesley stepped up to take charge. Not much taller than me, he was wide through the shoulders, which made him seem shorter than he actually was. The other soldiers were willing to obey his orders, which meant they respected him.

"I suggest we break into ten teams of a thousand," he said. "We should have enough people per group to take on large numbers of either droids or clones without sustaining too many casualties."

No one disagreed with his decision, so he chose a team leader for each group. Higgins was momentarily surprised when he was picked to lead a team. He ranked far lower than some of the other men and women in uniform, but again no one argued with Wesley's decision. Higgins had participated in both battles against the aliens and he'd comported himself well so far.

It was decided that our teams would stay close so we could come to each other's aide if necessary. Our ten groups moved through the suburban streets, staying mostly parallel when the streets allowed us to.

Keeping my senses on a constant sweep of the area, I picked up on a group of adversaries. "There's a herd of Kveet imps ahead," I warned Higgins. While small, they were highly dangerous and shouldn't be underestimated. Anyone who'd witnessed them in a feeding frenzy knew just how quickly they could strip a human down to a twitching skeleton.

"How many are we facing?" Higgins had become a seasoned warrior since I'd first met him in Manhattan. He could almost have been mistaken for being in his thirties instead of his mid-twenties now. Responsibility had settled around him in an invisible weight that he bore stoically.

"Five hundred." It wasn't an exact number, but it was close enough. "I can also sense a couple of units of droids. They're only a couple of blocks away from us. As soon as we start shooting the clones, we'll draw the robots straight to us."

"That sounds like an opportunity to set a trap to me," he mused. The team leaders all listened in when Higgins called them over his radio. Everyone in our group quietened down while the corporal explained the situation. "We have five hundred Kveet clones and forty droids just ahead. If we play our cards right, we should be able to take them all down relatively easily."

I hid my snigger at his card analogy. I wasn't sure if it had been said on purpose or unintentionally. We were still in the suburbs rather than the Glitter Strip, yet gambling was probably on everyone's mind. We were in Las Vegas after all.

My mind tried to wander as the soldiers discussed our options. I preferred action to long, drawn out planning, but there were too many creatures to just attack them head on. To my relief, it didn't take them long to agree on a plan. "Do you mind being the bait?" my pet human asked after they'd hammered out the details.

My attention was drawn back to their discussion. "Better me than any of you," I decided. I was far quicker than a human and I had recently learned a new trick that could rapidly carry me out of harm's way, if needed.

Everyone moved into position as stealthily as was possible for hundreds of humans. When they were all hidden, Higgins gave me the nod that it was time to bait the trap. With my swords held nonchalantly under one arm, I strode down the street and around the corner. Whistling tunelessly, I pretended that I had no idea that I was walking into danger.

Small grey shapes that were just vague blobs in the darkness turned when they heard me. Scarlet eyes illuminated their faces almost too well. "Food?" one of the tiny monsters queried hopefully. It didn't wait for a reply and scampered towards me. The rest of the mob quickly scrambled after it.

Running back the way I'd come, I made sure I stayed in sight of the pursuing monsters. With their low level of intelligence, they might forget about me if I moved out of their line of sight.

As planned, the street I turned into ended in a cul-de-sac. Piping shrieks of glee rebounded from the houses as the tiny terrors closed in on what they thought was helplessly trapped prey.

I waited until the small horde of clones had almost reached me before employing my new talent. One second I was about to be chewed to pieces and the next instant I was standing on the roof of a car parked in a nearby driveway.

I fired my death ray into the mass of milling, ravenous imps and half a dozen of the creatures instantly disintegrated. It was the signal the humans had been waiting for. They stood up from behind the cover of fences, cars and even rooftops and opened fire on the enemy.

Even the soldiers who were seeing the aliens for the first time were well disciplined. They'd been warned of what they'd be facing and fired single shots into the heads or chests of the Kveet imps. Sanderson's people opted to use their guns instead of death rays in order to lure the droids into the second part of their trap.

The noise was horrendous and my ears rang painfully. Their tactic worked and I sensed the murderbots heading towards us. "The droids have taken the bait," I shouted to Higgins. He nodded and spoke into his radio.

Gun smoke drowned out the vague smell of rotten eggs for a few moments after the last bullet was fired. Not all of the imps were dead. One crawled towards a human who'd jumped over a fence to take a closer look at the enemy. A large hole had been blasted in its back and yellow blood spurted from the wound. Its piping cries sounded pitiful and birdlike to the soldier. "Poor thing," the female soldier said as she put a bullet into its skull.

"Do you want to know what it was saying?" I asked her as I leaped to the ground. My sneakers skidded in the alien blood and gore, but I managed to stay on my feet. Unlike Geordie, I did possess catlike reflexes.

"You could understand it?" Her scepticism was heavy, but I nodded anyway. "Ok, what was it saying?"

"It was asking if you were food."

"How can you possibly know that?"

I didn't feel like explaining my miraculous ability to understand and speak foreign as well as alien languages. "A translator robot on Viltar taught me a few of their words," I said instead.

"Oh." Looking down at the imp she'd made the mistake of feeling pity for, her gaze hardened. I doubted that particular soldier would have any qualms about mowing down any more clones, no matter how pathetic they appeared to be.

Higgins waved for silence as a report came through his radio. Even a hundred yards away I could hear the report clearly. "We've just spotted the droids," Sergeant Wesley advised. "We're about to go radio silent."

"Copy that," Higgins replied and was echoed by the other team leaders. "The droids are almost in position," he said to the rest of us. We had played our part and now it was up to the other teams to demolish the two approaching units of automatons. There were only forty of the metal men, so the humans shouldn't encounter too many problems. The civilians in Wesley's team had been cautioned to keep quiet. So far, they were obeying orders and hadn't given their trap away.

I couldn't actually view the battle remotely with my eyes, but the scene lit up for me as coloured dots on a black background in my mind. The dull silver spots of droids walked between two far larger groups of yellow dots that were humans. More yellow dots penned them in from behind then we heard the sounds of gunfire a couple of blocks away.

We converged on the droids just in case the other teams required assistance, but the skirmish was already over by the time we arrived. Death rays were stripped from the fallen robots and were handed over to those without. None of the civilians were given access to the alien technology. A death ray in the wrong hands would be a disaster.

While the civilians let out cheers that our trap had worked so well, the soldiers remained impassive. We'd only made a tiny dent in the overall number of our adversaries. We hadn't lost any of our people yet, but our luck couldn't hold out forever. Casualties were a given when it came to war and this one was going to be brutal.

Chapter Twenty-One

Since it had worked so well the first time, we kept up the tactic of luring imps or droids into traps, then overwhelming them with superior numbers. Our plan ran smoothly for several hours before disaster struck and one of our traps backfired. The soldiers were beginning to flag and civilians were weaving on their feet in exhaustion. It was only a matter of time before things went pear shaped.

The soldiers had grown complacent with their steady run of victories. They'd split up into smaller teams so they could target more than one group of enemies at a time. My warning that they would be safer to stay in larger groups had been ignored. It had seemed obvious to me that the more spread out we became, the larger the risks we'd face.

My hunch came true and I sensed several units of killbots converging on one of our groups. They'd drawn too far away from the others and were quickly isolated and surrounded by droids.

Warning Higgins about our people's plight, we hurried to their location. We arrived in time to see the last few humans being shot by nanobot guns. Horrified mutters were uttered as naked, hugely muscled grey monsters were born.

"Cut them down!" Higgins screamed as the newly made clones lumbered towards us. Dozens of droids followed behind their newly made servants. They fired their dart guns with the intention of reducing our numbers and increasing the size of their imp army.

Sliding my death ray into my pocket, I caught a flicker of motion from the corner of my eye and saw a dart flying straight towards Higgins. Moving lightning fast, my hand flashed out and caught the tiny syringe when it was a mere inch from his face. I grimaced as the tiny dart pierced my flesh and more micro-robots were released into my bloodstream.

Eyes wide, the soldier gave me a shaky nod of thanks. "Tell everyone to retreat and form into ten groups again," I told him. "I'll take care of the droids and imps."

Knowing his teammates would be eaten or transformed if they remained to fight, Higgins bellowed for his people to retreat. No one needed to be told twice and they turned to flee. Already ravenous despite being created only moments ago, the imps went on the chase.

I ran to intercept them and my swords went into motion. Droids fired their nanobot guns and death rays at me, but I used the imps as cover as I sliced my way through their ranks. Battle lust took over, making me as close to happy as I was ever likely to get now that Luc and I were no longer a couple.

Spearing hearts, slicing throats and stabbing deep into eye sockets to reach the brain, I hunted down every last imp before turning my attention to the droids. A wave of violet light speared towards me, but I disappeared before it could hit me.

I found myself standing in a well-maintained yard with a high fence and a very angry guard dog growling at me. Mostly black with a few brown markings on its face, I was pretty sure it was a Doberman. White teeth gleamed as its lips drew back and its growl intensified.

Distracted by the sound of splintering wood, I glanced over my shoulder to see a droid punching its way through the fence. I turned back as the dog lunged forward and sank its teeth into my upper thigh.

A second droid appeared in the robot sized hole in the fence and aimed its death ray at me as the dog savaged my leg. I shifted out of harm's way, leaving behind a confused and angry dog.

"Toby!" The alarmed shout came from the bushes beside the house as a teenage boy burst out of hiding a moment after I shifted. The darts that had been intended for me hit the dog and his owner instead.

Screams and howls of agony pierced the night as the pair began to transform. I'd seen hundreds, if not thousands of adults converted into clones before, but I'd never witnessed a teen turning into one. As always, the morphing process took only seconds. The end result was a stunted, six foot imp that was much less muscular than usual. I would have to ask Gregor why this was the case. I suspected it was because the boy hadn't finished growing to his full potential yet.

The dog's transformation was far less smooth. I watched it writhe and howl in horrified fascination. Black fur disappeared as its body bulged, swelled and turned ashen. The howls turned deeper and became almost guttural as it voiced its agony as its entire skeleton seemed to change subtly. It's already pointed ears grew longer and curled at the ends while long, sharp claws sprouted from its paws. The process took only a few seconds longer than usual and the beast struggled to its feet as its master spied me.

"Food!" the former teen declared and loped towards me. Red light glowed from the dog imp's eyes and it bared teeth that were now much longer and sharper at its master. On closer inspection, they weren't teeth at all. In fact, they looked a lot like vampire fangs.

I wasn't alone as I watched the battle between the pair. More of the fence was torn away as several droids came in search of me. They viewed the biting, clawing imps with a detachment that I wished I could share. Yellow blood flew as grey flesh was torn open to expose meat and bone.

Roaring in rage, the stunted imp batted at the doberclone's head. He shrieked in agony when the vampirelike fangs sheared through his wrist. Spitting out the hand of its former master, the doberclone lunged upwards and closed its teeth around the stunted imp's throat. With a grisly wet tearing sound, the imp's head toppled to the ground.

Turning to me, the doberclone's head was on a level with mine. It had doubled in height and more than quadrupled in bulk. Hate and rage blazed from its scarlet eyes and I prepared myself to leap to safety. Instead of attacking me as it clearly wanted to, the dog imp turned to face the droids. It almost seemed to be guarding me.

"Interesting," one of the droids remarked. Plain silver and with only rudimentary facial features, it didn't look anything like Robert the traitorous robot, but it sounded eerily like him.

"This is a strange anomaly," another remarked.

"Shall we initiate the Third Protocol?" the first droid asked the others.

"Agreed," they all replied and levelled their death rays.

The glare of violet light blasted the doberclone to dust motes, but sailed harmlessly through the spot where I'd been standing. My handy new talent had shifted me behind the robots so quickly that they hadn't been able to detect my movement. My swords were a blur of motion again as I hacked them to death.

Programmed by their Viltaran masters not to retreat, the remaining droids continued to attack me despite it being obvious that they were all going to die. Slicing the head off the final robot, I watched it sail over a fence into a front yard then gathered up the dropped death rays. I picked up a shirt that had been torn from a human as he'd transformed into an imp and used it as a crude carrying bag.

Still slightly freaked out about what had just happened with the doberclone, I jogged back to my team. Higgins, Sergeant Wesley and the other team leaders had followed my suggestion and had organized the soldiers and civilians back into our original groups again.

Maybe they'll listen to my advice from now on. My thought was wry because humans always thought they knew best. I should know, I'd been one for twenty-eight years before

I'd become a vampire. With a start, I realized that I would have turned forty this year. I'd lost an entire decade when we had drifted as frozen lumps through space. It was a small comfort that I would never look my age, not even if I lived to be a million. It scared me that there was a distinct possibility that I might live far longer than that.

I was in a gloomy mood as I located Higgins and handed over the cache of weapons. "Did you kill them all?" he asked and was relieved when I nodded. "Can you tell how General Sanderson and his men are doing?"

It was impossible to tell who was who when using my senses remotely, but I could at least sense that the majority of soldiers were still alive. Six bright white dots still showed up clearly, so I knew my friends were intact. "Most of them are fine. I think they're using a similar tactic to ours."

The team leaders had switched to a different frequency so their orders wouldn't get mixed up with Sanderson's. The last thing we needed was the confusion of conflicting orders.

Sweeping my senses back through the city, I gave a mental shudder at how many humans had already been converted into imps. Las Vegas had a far larger population than the town that had been attacked in Texas. Thousands of civilians had already been turned into monsters. Hundreds more were being converted with every passing minute.

The droids were ignoring our attacks against their flanks. They were concentrating on the centre of the city where the vast bulk of people had congregated. If the Viltaran ship hadn't been hovering right above us, I would have urged the Americans to bomb the city in a desperate attempt to contain the threat. It would be a useless venture, since the spaceship would simply zap any bombs that came its way out of the air.

At least relief would come once the sun rose and the imps were forced to take shelter. The droids would have to search the casinos and hotels for fresh victims rather than shooting them down in the streets if they wanted them to survive. Our best tactic would be to keep chipping away at their edges, then move in and destroy as many robots as possible once dawn arrived. I didn't need to check the watch I didn't own to know nightfall would give way to daylight in less than an hour.

We'd worked our way from the suburban areas to a local shopping district when the sun peeked over the horizon and my time ran out. My helpfulness at stopping the droids had just come to an end for the day, unless I found protective clothing.

Spying a motorcycle store, I crossed the road for a better look. A female mannequin wearing a full leather outfit and helmet caught my eye. I tested the door and found it securely locked.

"Stand aside, ma'am," a voice said from right behind me. "Let me help you with that."

Glancing over my shoulder, I saw one of my team members ready to lend assistance. With a shrug, I gave the soldier some room. Taking a step back, he launched a kick at the door and sent it crashing back against the wall. I cringed in anticipation of the alarm blaring in warning, but none sounded. If it had, it would have drawn some nearby droids straight to us. I could easily have broken the door open myself, but it was nice to be treated like a lady instead of a leper for once.

The store was crammed with all types of clothing and accessories for those who liked to thumb their nose at death and ride motorcycles. I spent a few minutes browsing through the range of female clothing before deciding on an outfit. My reflection in the changing room mirror made me smile for a second before it withered and died.

Midnight black, the leather pants were tight and clung to me like a second skin. The matching jacket was a perfect fit and was tailored to make my waist look small and my bust bigger than it actually was.

A picture of a dark haired angel was on the back. She held a sparkly red trident and horns sprouted from her forehead. A long tail with an arrow shaped tip was wrapped around one of her legs. It was as red as the horns and trident. A fingertip was caught between her teeth, giving the impression that she was trying to decide whether to be good or bad. I knew Geordie would get a kick out of it when he saw it.

I found gloves and knee high boots to match the outfit, then chose a plain black helmet with a heavily tinted visor to finish off my new look. It fit snugly enough that I might have become claustrophobic if I'd still been alive. My vision was sharp enough to see clearly through the dark visor. Now I just had to test the outfit in the sun.

My hearing was slightly muffled, but wolf whistles rang out when I stepped outside. I flipped the offending group of soldiers the bird and moved out of the shadows and into the weak dawn light. Apart from needing to squint slightly against the brightness, I felt no adverse effects of being bathed in sunlight. As long as I stayed mostly in the shadows, the leather would be thick enough to keep me from boiling down to the bone.

Higgins gave me a grin of approval when I stepped up beside him. "I assume that's you inside there, Natalie?"

"It's me," was my muffled response.

Rummaging around in his backpack, he held out two items. "One of the guys found these in a store that sells all kinds of weapons and accessories. He thought you might find them useful."

A pair of black sheaths rested in his hands. They were far plainer than the white pair I'd once owned. They'd been decorated with a lion and a dragon to match the blades that had belonged inside them. The swords I now owned were as plain as these new sheaths, so they were a good match.

Taking his offering, I slid both samurai swords inside. They were slightly too long, but I could wear them crisscrossed on my back for easy access. "They're perfect. Tell your guy I said thanks." One of the soldiers nearby ducked his head and studied his feet bashfully.

"I'll do that," Higgins said dryly, subtly nodding at the bright red soldier who obviously wanted to remain anonymous.

"The clones will have taken shelter by now," I said to my temporary right hand man. "You should contact Sanderson so we can coordinate an attack against the droids. They'll still use their death rays on us, but they won't be able to use their nanobot guns." Not unless they wanted their newly made clones to instantly be burned to death by the sun.

"Are you sure you don't want to speak to him yourself?" He couldn't see my upper lip curling at the offer, so I shook my head. After changing his frequency, he spoke into his radio. "General Sanderson, do you copy?"

"Is that you, Corporal Higgins?" Sanderson's voice was gravelly from fatigue.

"Yes, sir."

"How the hell did you make it into the city through the gas?"

"We went under it, sir, through drainage tunnels."

"I bet that was Nat's idea," I heard Geordie say from somewhere in the background. My chest tightened at the sound of his voice. We'd only been apart for a short time, yet I missed my friends already.

"Give me a status update," Sanderson demanded.

"We have about ten thousand soldiers and civilians in our group and several thousand more behind us, General." Higgins gave his report in a crisp manner, seeking no praise. He was just doing his job and was trying to live up to the expectations of his commander.

"What is your current location?"

"We're in the suburbs to the south, sir."

There was a rustle of paper as Sanderson consulted a map. "We're to the north of the Strip. We haven't been able to make much headway so far, but now that the clones have gone underground, we should be able to concentrate on the droids."

"That was our thought as well, General."

The pair spoke for a few more minutes about their strategy with Sergeant Wesley and the other team leaders occasionally chiming in. They rapidly came to the conclusion that we'd been following the same rough plan. Since it was working so well so far, it was decided that we would remain in our current teams. We'd move in on the centre of the city to start taking down the automatons. By the time the rest of our troops arrived, we would have equal numbers to the droids.

My hope that we would easily be able to wipe them out came to a halt when I sensed the Viltaran ship descending. "Hold on for a second," I told Higgins as he was about to sign off. "The ship is moving again."

"What's going on?" Sanderson asked.

The ship didn't quite land, but it dropped down low enough for the robot army to pile inside. "The droids have just boarded their mothership and are already heading back into the clouds," I told Higgins. I half expected the ship to leave and find another city to torment, but it stayed in position high above us. "It looks like they're staying put, but we're going to have to rethink our plan."

Sanderson cursed when he heard the report from his subordinate and I heard the rasp of his palm across his cheek again. "We'll have to start targeting the clones instead. Can Natalie give us an idea of where they are located?"

I shrugged at Higgins helplessly. "They're pretty much everywhere." The soldier's shoulders slumped at that news. "There are still over fifty thousand Kveet imps and an additional thirty thousand human clones as well now," I reported. "Most are underground, but some are hiding in the buildings."

There was silence on the airwaves as Sanderson consulted with someone, probably Gregor. The general had a plan ready when he came back. "Break your people down into smaller teams of five hundred and distribute them around the centre of the city. Wait for my signal, then we'll send two thirds into the sewers and the rest into the buildings."

"I want to talk to-" Geordie's strident voice was cut off before he could finish his request to speak to me. I told myself it was for the best as I trotted after Higgins.

Fresh troops had just arrived. They would be sent to the frontlines to give the others a rest. Many of the humans who had joined our fight looked as if they were regretting their decision. Filthy and bedraggled, most were half asleep from exhaustion. Army medics tended those with injuries, mostly people who had been bitten or clawed by the Kveet imps. Anyone who came into close contact with the human hell spawn tended not to survive the encounter.

I doubted that any of the civilians would be happy to hear that we would shortly descend into the bowels of the city. We'd have to fight the imps in the dark and no doubt noisome tunnels. I was a creature of the night and even I wasn't a fan of fighting in the cramped and lightless depths.

Chapter Twenty-Two

At night, Las Vegas was a breathtaking sight of ever changing colours from the millions of neon lights. During the day it was still impressive, but far less dazzling. We jogged along the world famous strip and I craned my head back to take in the famous casinos.

One in the shape of the Eiffel Tower caught my eye. I'd driven through Paris once and had seen the real thing briefly as I'd driven by. Again, I had no time for sightseeing. A quick glimpse here and there was all I had time for.

A feature I couldn't help but notice was the fountains and mini lakes. There was far more water than I'd expected to see this close to a desert. Some of the more impressive fountains intermittently spewed jets of water high into the air. They appeared to be dancing to a tune that I couldn't hear.

I spent a few moments gawping like a country bumpkin. I was glad no one could see me goggling in wonder behind the dark visor as we trotted past one casino after the other.

Even through the visor, I smelled the smoke from a fire that had been caused by the plane crash. It had taken out the top half of a hotel, as well as one of the smaller casinos behind it. The plane had broken in half after impact and the back half was still lodged in the hotel. The upper half was buried in the casino, which was still smouldering in places. Sprinklers had stopped the fire from spreading, but firefighters weren't going to turn up to attend one disaster when their entire city was under attack.

A few bodies lay strewn on the ground around the hotel. Some were soldiers that had fallen from the plane. The rest were civilians that had been in the wrong place at the wrong time. Smears of blood left a trail where some of the deceased had been dragged off to be eaten by human clones. Several stripped skeletons had been left behind by the Kveet imps.

Higgins scanned the dead, but made no move to check to see if they were still alive. Their bodies were torn, tattered and shattered from the collision. A glance was enough to know they were beyond help.

After splitting into the groups of five hundred that Sanderson had recommended, we spread out to find access to the sewer system beneath the streets. Even with my protective layers of leather, the sun became uncomfortably hot when I moved out from beneath the shade for more than a minute. It was a big improvement from instantly melting as soon as the light touched me.

I probably had the Viltarans to thank for my new resilience. Drinking their blood had strengthened all seven of us who had survived our unplanned trip to Viltar.

Corporal Higgins had proven himself to be competent as a team leader and remained in charge of our group. Gesturing for everyone to crowd around, he cautioned the mixture of soldiers, civilians and me to use our ammunition wisely. We weren't to shoot unless we could be fairly certain we'd kill our targets.

We were standing beside a manhole without any shade nearby. The sun quickly grew unpleasantly warm on my back. I interrupted the soldier's speech before my flesh could begin to melt. "Can we hurry this up? Some of us are allergic to the sun, you know." A spattering of laughter rippled through our team.

Thrown off his stride, Higgins couldn't tell if I was joking or not since the helmet hid my face completely.

"Your clothes are starting to give off steam," someone told me helpfully.

"Move," I instructed the corporal. He shifted aside and I bent, flipped the manhole cover away with one hand and dropped through the opening. I landed in calf deep, foul water and was glad for the protection of the knee high boots.

Moving away from the ladder, I took the helmet off and tucked it beneath my arm. It wouldn't serve much purpose while we were beneath the ground. Cries, moans and screams echoed throughout the underground tunnel system. I barely needed to send out my senses to find the Kveet and human imps in the conduits around us.

I hadn't been exaggerating when I'd told Higgins that they were everywhere. Most were in much smaller groups than ours, but some were in much larger herds. The larger groups had brought live snacks along. I tried to imagine how terrifying it would be for a fragile human to be dragged off into the sewers by a creature that looked like it had come from the depths of hell. The night I'd been captured by Silvius came back to me and I shivered. That event had been traumatic enough and he'd been human looking, until his fangs had descended.

I counted seven small groups of Kveet imps. They were standing between us and a force of nearly a thousand human imps and their two hundred or so captives. Higgins slid down the ladder and landed with a splash that narrowly missed me. He winced as a bloodcurdling shriek sounded in a distant tunnel. I felt a human life end a few seconds later.

"I take it the clones have brought hostages into the tunnels?" the soldier asked shakily.

"They aren't hostages," I corrected him. "They're food." The imps wouldn't be interested in negotiating a swap with their meals to save their own lives. They weren't intelligent enough to even grasp the concept.

Higgins gave me a pained look. "Do you think we have any chance of saving any of them?"

More and more of our teammates descended the ladder. They were making enough noise to alert every imp within a few miles of our presence. "What do you think?" I asked him wryly. "Keep everyone here and try not to make any noise. I'm going to sneak up and take down the small groups of clones that are between us and the captives." It would give us a far better chance of closing in on the larger group without being detected. It was doubtful we'd be able to rescue the captives, but we had to at least try.

"Give Natalie your radio," my right hand man said to one of the soldiers. He handed it over and I slipped it into a pocket of my trendy new jacket. "Let us know when you're in position and we'll join you and help you to free the prisoners."

My helmet would be a hindrance so I tossed it to a civilian. "Can you look after this for me?"

Fumbling the catch, she almost dropped it into the murky water and clutched it to her stomach. In her early twenties, she was short, plump and looked like I'd just handed her a treasure chest full of gold and jewels. "I'd be honoured to, ma'am!"

With a nod at Higgins, I quietly sloshed my way down the tunnel. There were no handy walkways to keep me above the disgusting muck this time. At least my boots were tall enough to stop anything from getting inside and squishing between my toes.

Been there, done that and I don't want to do it again. I distinctly remembered chasing after the Second and his brothers in the sewers beneath a city in Africa. It had been in even worse shape than this one. Come to think of it, I'd been in far too many sewers for my liking.

Soft cries from hungry Kveet imps floated to me as I closed in on them. Reaching an intersection, I peeked around the corner to see thirty clones standing waist deep in sewage. Huddled together, they blinked scarlet eyes sleepily. Red light illuminated the tunnel softly, ruining their night vision and helping to keep me hidden.

"Wet!" one said disgustedly and glared down at the water, as if wishing it could take a bite out of the flowing stream.

"Food?" another said hopefully as a wad of toilet paper drifted by. A clawed hand reached out and stuffed the pulpy mass into its mouth. The wad was spat out a second later and the imp's face scrunched up in disgust. "Not food," it decided mournfully. It was interesting to see they were smart enough to make that distinction. It was also something of a surprise to see their vocabulary extended beyond a couple of words.

A dead rat floated towards them and their interest perked up again. "Food!" several declared and began racing towards it. They were hampered by the flow of water, but three imps reached the rodent at the same time. They immediately began to squabble about who the tasty treat belonged to. They became a viciously clawing mass of tiny grey bodies all intent on devouring the rat.

My death ray cut a swathe through their ranks and also zapped the rat. Holding a tail that was the only remnant left of the rodent, a surviving clone turned on me with accusing scarlet eyes. It threw the tail down with a cry of rage and started towards me. It was easy to pick it and the rest of them off as they struggled against the flow of water. The screams of the human captives helped to muffle the slaughter that I doled out.

The next group I came across were just as miserable as the first. They should have been asleep by now, but would either drown or drift downstream if they tried to lie down in the water. There were only fifteen this time and I sent several bursts of violet light in their direction. They probably would have thanked me for ending their torment, if I'd given them the chance to speak.

Moving as quietly as possible, I knew the next group were former humans even before I saw them. My senses could easily make the distinction. All forty-three were sitting shoulder to shoulder with their backs to the slimy walls as I crept to within a few yards of them. Snores reverberated around me, sounding vaguely like a small avalanche tumbling down a mountainside.

They were so deeply asleep that they didn't hear me as I snuck in close enough to tickle them. Water covered their legs and pooled in their laps. My swords did their duty and snuffed out their lives one by one. Conscious that some of my teammates were normal everyday civilians, I merely stabbed the imps through their hearts instead of hacking them limb from limb. There was no need to cause anyone worse nightmares than they would already have, if any of them were lucky enough to live through this ordeal.

I wasn't sure when my concern towards the mental health of humans had reasserted itself, but it was difficult to ignore. While I wanted to hate all of humanity for what a few of them had done to my people, I couldn't quite bring myself to do it.

It was impossible to be completely noiseless when walking through water, even for me. An alert Kveet imp heard me approaching the next group. Probably hoping I was food, it headed towards me. The tunnel curved, hiding me from view. I waited for the clone to round the bend, then leaped forward and stabbed it through the chest.

The sword speared straight through it and the imp hung from my weapon like a piece of meat on a skewer. It slid off, plopped into the water and floated back towards its comrades. The rest came to investigate and I used my death ray to annihilate them all.

Finishing off the last few groups that barred the way from the much larger herd, I resisted the temptation to rush to the rescue as yet another captive was pulled to pieces. Slobbering sounds of imps chewing with their mouths open made my stomach want to flop over.

The red glow from my eyes intensified as my rage increased. Holding onto my anger tightly, I edged to the corner of another intersection. My right eye popped out of its socket and I cautiously held it out into the tunnel to see what I was up against. It was unnerving to see it still glowing softly even when it was no longer attached to my face.

Several tunnels had converged to create a large open space. It was packed wall to wall with newly made seven foot imps. Their captives were gathered in the centre of the small lake of human waste. Many of the clones were asleep on their feet, but were scrunched in so tightly that they were in no danger of falling over.

If all of the monsters had been asleep, I might have tried using my holy marks to destroy them. If I attempted it when they were awake, they'd most likely kill their captives in their rush to get to me. Like it or not, I'd have to call my teammates to help.

Backtracking for a few tunnels, I used the radio. "Are you there, Higgins?" I whispered.

"I'm here," he responded.

"The way is clear."

"Did you leave marks for us to follow?"

I hadn't and it had been a stupid oversight. "I didn't, sorry. I'll have to guide you to me."

"You can remember the way you took?"

I couldn't blame him for his scepticism, but he had no idea of what my mind was capable of now. Just by closing my eyes, I could bring up a map of the route I'd taken. "I remember it well enough. You'll know you're on the right track when you come across blood splattered walls."

"Go ahead. I'm ready when you are."

It took precious time that we didn't have to move the whole team through the tunnels. More humans were slaughtered while I waited for my allies to turn up. Finally, I heard the splashing of hundreds of footsteps sloshing through the water.

Higgins came into view a few minutes later. Relief smoothed out the frown he'd been wearing when he reached me. As quietly as possible, the rest of our team gathered around. I described what we were facing and word was passed back to those who were too far away to hear me.

"Our priority is to rescue the captives," Higgins whispered. "Unfortunately, it sounds like they are surrounded by the enemy. I propose we split into three groups and try to lure the clones into an ambush using these three tunnels." He pointed at the tunnel to our right and one directly opposite from us. That meant two groups would have to try to sneak across the fourth tunnel opening without being spotted by the imps.

"It's a pity we don't have a blanket," I said quietly.

"Why?" my faithful right hand man asked.

"We could hold it up across the opening while everyone moves into position. The imps are so stupid I doubt they'll even notice they can't see down the tunnel any longer."

"I have a blanket you can borrow," a woman said. "I thought it might be cold down here so I grabbed it just in case," she explained when she received several strange looks.

At my impatient gesture, the blanket was passed up the line and into my hands. I'd been hoping for a dark fabric, but instead was faced with a hot pink one. Even worse, it had pictures of fluffy cats all over it. Higgins looked at it doubtfully, then shrugged and took one end. I leaped across the tunnel opening so quickly that I was barely a flash of movement. Landing lightly on the other side, I held my end of the cat blanket up. No startled sounds came from the horde of imps, so I motioned the first group to start moving.

Creeping as quietly as possible, two groups of soldiers and civilians splashed quietly down the intersecting tunnels. The more experienced warriors were in the front ranks. Once the clones began to attack, they would drop down and shoot from a kneeling position while the ranks behind them fired over their heads. Everyone in the front row would use their death rays to disintegrate the enemy's bodies and stop them from piling up and hampering our shots.

Once everyone was in place, I tossed my end of the blanket to Higgins. It might come in handy later, so he quickly folded it up and handed it back to its owner. She scurried down the tunnel to hide behind the soldiers.

Higgins and I stood in plain sight in the middle of the four-way intersection and waited to be spotted. Most of the imps closest to us were deeply asleep. The rest were too stupefied with weariness to notice us. Growing tired of waiting, I used my death ray to blast a full dozen monsters into nothingness before they realized they were under attack.

With a gurgling cry of anger, an imp pointed at us with a clawed hand. "Kill!" he bellowed and his kin began to wake. The captives screamed at us to save them, waking even more of the creatures with their desperate pleas. They were buffeted by their captors as the clones stampeded towards us. Some went down beneath their feet and didn't rise again.

Higgins fired more violet rays into the crowd, creating a small pocket of death. The enraged clones surged towards us and we put our plan into action. Higgins raced into the left tunnel and I went straight ahead. Reaching my small team of sixty civilians, I took up a position in the second row and fired at the imps as they reached the intersection.

Dazzling violet light that was even brighter than the neon on the surface blazed from three directions as we cut down hundreds of creatures that were intent on murder. Their rage and hunger were so intense that they ran directly into our beams in their determination to end our existence.

The Viltarans may have made a grievous error when altering their nanobot formula. They'd stripped too much of their slaves' will away and had taken their sense of self-preservation with it. What use was an army of servants that were so stupid that they would allow themselves to be slaughtered without putting up even a token defence?

A heavy cloud of particles hung in the air when the last imp winked out of existence. At first, there was silence as my teammates waited for more clones to burst into sight. "That's all of them," I said and someone cheered. He was immediately shushed by the others.

We had annihilated only a fraction of the monsters that hunkered within the tunnels. Making too much noise could draw them straight to us. Even now, I could sense another group of Kveet hell spawn slogging their way in our direction. No doubt drawn by the battle cries of their far larger contemporaries.

Still huddled together, standing knee deep in polluted water, the captives didn't realize they'd been rescued at first. Their screams and sobs drowned out Higgins when he tried to get their attention by shouting. Firing a bullet into the carcass of a dead Kveet imp silenced them to whimpers. "The clones that were guarding you are all dead and you're safe now," he said to the cringing prisoners.

"Safe?" a woman in her fifties croaked. "These monsters tore my husband apart and ate him right in front of me! We won't be safe until every last one of them is dead." Her voice had been bordering on hysterical at the beginning of her short speech, but she ended in a dull whisper.

"We're working on it, ma'am," one of the soldiers said wearily. "I'm sorry for your loss." His sympathy cut through her shock and she started to cry in great, wracking sobs.

"Let's get these people out of here," Higgins said to his fellow troopers.

A small contingent of two soldiers and a dozen civilian recruits escorted the survivors back through the winding tunnels and up to the surface. We'd saved most of the captives, but there were many more humans under siege all throughout the city and sewers. Despite our best efforts, we weren't going to be able to rescue them all. Their lives would be added to the tally that I would no doubt have to answer for to the being that had arranged for me to be created.

Chapter Twenty-Three

I kept track of our overall progress as the day wore on. By late afternoon, we'd eradicated a total of seventeen thousand imps. There were still forty-six thousand Kveet clones and twenty-two thousand human clones in hiding. They'd wake up as soon as the sun set. They'd eat before rounding up more victims for the droids to convert.

Speaking of the murderbots, the Viltaran ship began to lower as the sun faded from the sky. Sanderson had recalled his troops from the sewers an hour before dusk. Almost all of his troops were crouched behind cover. All were ready to spring into action the instant the ship dropped off its bipedal cargo.

A particularly foul curse escaped me when I sensed the ship swinging wide of the area it had used as a drop off point last time. "Tell Sanderson the Viltarans aren't going to fall for our trap," I told Higgins. "They're moving towards the south instead."

Thousands more soldiers had landed a short while ago and were making their way towards the drainage tunnels to bolster our numbers. Apparently, my senses weren't the only ones to detect them. The Viltaran ship didn't stop to set down the droids, but instead continued southward. It passed high over the toxic cloud to avoid being gassed and hovered over the only entry point to the city.

Choked screams came through Higgins' radio as the aliens blasted a fresh wave of noxious poison at what was supposed to have been our backup teams. It seemed there would be no more fresh troops entering the city to bolster our flagging numbers.

"What just happened?" Sanderson asked. He and my friends were on the far side of a parking lot, hidden behind the ornate fence of a gigantic casino.

"The drainage tunnels have just been cut off by the Viltarans," I said to my pet human. Higgins relayed the information to his commanding officer. I turned to follow the ship's course as it stopped to offload some of the droids. It moved in a circular pattern, stopping briefly until every last robot had been released from its hold. It then returned to its position high above Vegas.

With the vast bulk of our forces gathered in the centre of Las Vegas, any civilians who had chosen to remain in their homes were about to be hunted down. We'd never be able to reach them in time to stop them from being converted into clones. Our enemies would grow in number while we would slowly but surely be worn down with each sortie onto the battlefield.

"You'd better tell Sanderson that our plan just went out the window." I tried to keep my tone neutral, but some of my despair came through. "The droids have the city surrounded and are working their way towards the centre. They're converting every human they come across into imps."

While I could function for an unknown length of time without sleep, the soldiers and civilians were exhausted. They'd only managed to snatch a few minutes of rest while we'd waited in vain for the spaceship to descend into our failed trap.

The general uttered an even worse expletive than I'd used when Higgins updated him. "I suggest we all find transportation and attempt to head the droids off," Gregor said calmly, presumably from right beside Sanderson.

We were going to have a long night ahead. It would be followed by another long day of hunting down the freshly made imps. *This isn't looking good for our side,* my inner voice said. *There's a good chance you're going to lose this time.* I wished it was wrong, but I was very much afraid that it might be right.

Utterly cut off from help, the city was doomed unless we could destroy the androids. Sheer numbers had worked for us in Manhattan, but we only had a fraction of the civilian population behind us this time. It wasn't that the city lacked warm bodies, they just didn't seem to have the same drive to survive as the Manhattanites.

I could sense hundreds of thousands of humans cowering inside the casinos and hotels. Most would be tourists and the rest employees of the hotels and casinos. It was doubtful that many were armed. We had gathered enough death rays to arm several thousand more people, but the soldiers were reluctant to hand them over to the townsfolk.

"We need to convince the civilians to help us again," I told Higgins. "They need to know that they will all either be eaten, or turned into monsters if they don't get off their arses and start fighting."

"We don't have enough weapons for all of them," he said with a helpless shrug.

"Give them your guns if you don't trust them with the death rays."

I didn't realize my words were being broadcasted until Luc spoke through Higgins' radio. "Natalie is right. You have to put your mistrust aside if you wish to save not just your country, but the entire world." I felt a small tingle of happiness that he'd agreed with me. Then I felt depressed that something so small could make me feel happy at all.

Sanderson had little choice but to succumb to common sense. "Agreed," he said heavily. Higgins looked relieved at his commander's capitulation and so did his comrades. "Head for the most densely populated hotels and casinos and start recruiting help," Sanderson ordered. "When you've handed out all of your spare weapons, find transportation and make your way to the suburbs and start taking down the droids. I'll contact the President and ask her to send out a message to everyone in the city asking them to rally and help us fight." It had worked last time and hopefully it would work again.

The team leaders acknowledged their orders then, still in teams of five hundred or so, we scattered. I pointed at one of the smaller hotels, where I could sense several hundred humans hiding. The lobby doors were locked, but a booted foot sent them crashing open. Muffled screams came from the staircase, followed by fleeing footsteps and slamming doors.

Pairing up, soldiers headed for each floor while our civilian team members waited in the foyer. Some took the opportunity to pilfer bottled water from a vending machine. A couple of hungry men were prying open the snack machines when I followed Higgins upstairs.

Most of the survivors were relieved when they realized it was soldiers rather than monsters knocking on their doors. We eventually coaxed everyone downstairs and out onto the street.

Higgins launched into the speech he'd prepared. "Some of you may have heard of the attack on Manhattan several days ago." Nods and murmurs of agreement sounded. "As you've probably guessed by now, Las Vegas has now been targeted by that same spaceship. The city has been cut off by a cloud of toxic gas. This means no one can get in or out."

"You mean no one is coming to rescue us?" a woman in her seventies or eighties asked timidly. She was dressed in a worn pink robe with matching slippers. For reasons I couldn't define, my heart went out to her. She was just a harmless little old lady who'd probably never hurt anyone in her entire life. Now she was being hunted for her meat as if she was nothing more than a mindless animal.

"I'm afraid not," Higgins replied gravely. "We're outnumbered and the enemy ranks are growing every hour. We need your help to fight the droids and clones, or we'll be overwhelmed within days."

His statement was met with incredulous stares. "You want *us* to fight the aliens?" someone asked. "You've got to be kidding."

Higgins' expression remained serious as he replied. "I wish I was kidding. We simply don't have enough manpower to destroy all of the droids."

A man somewhere in his late forties pushed his way through the crowd to confront the soldiers. Glasses perched on the end of his nose and he peered through them at my companion. "You cannot seriously expect us to do your job for you." His accent was English and bordered on haughty.

Lifting my hand, I stopped the corporal from giving the man a polite answer. "I'll give you two choices," I said to the crowd, raising my voice so they could hear me. "Either take a weapon and prove yourselves to be useful, or I'll bite your face off and save the imps from doing it."

Screwing his face up in derision, the English guy crossed his arms. "That is the most ridiculous threat I've ever heard…" His words trailed off as my fangs descended and my eyes began to glow.

"I suggest you decide now," I said around fangs that felt far longer than normal. "I'm getting hungry."

Screams were squelched and the soldiers prevented anyone from fleeing. "What are you?" someone in the crowd asked.

"She's Natalie, the vampire that was imprisoned a decade ago for going nuts and trying to kill General Sanderson and his men," someone else answered.

"Things have to be going to hell if they dug *her* up from wherever they buried her," yet another civilian muttered. Her thoughts were echoed by several others.

I didn't bother to tell my side of the story. We didn't have the time and I hadn't exactly helped my image with that little stunt. My presence, or the threat of having their faces bitten off, worked and most agreed to join our group.

Only the elderly and children were exempt. Someone suggested they should hide inside the vault of a casino, or wherever it was that the money was stored. The suggestion was seconded and they went in search of food, water and other supplies that they'd need. I had no idea what they'd use for a toilet inside the strongroom, or how long their air would last if the room was sealed after the door was shut. Whatever measures they took, their protection wouldn't last long if we lost this war. The droids would root them out and turn them into clones regardless of where they hid.

Several soldiers went in search of transportation. They returned minutes later in tour buses that were large enough to carry our entire crew of nearly one thousand people. Most of the new recruits held their borrowed weapons gingerly. I wasn't sure what use they would be when we clashed with the droids and imp clones. Maybe we'd get lucky and a few stray bullets would hit their marks. If we were really lucky, they might not accidentally kill each other.

In the lead bus, I guided our driver towards the outskirts of the city where scores of humans had already been turned into clones. We didn't head directly towards the murderbots, but circled around behind them before disembarking from the buses.

Every house we passed was devoid of life. Doors had been kicked in, sometimes knocked completely off their hinges. Screams of terror and pain came seemingly from everywhere as the automatons mercilessly continued their search through the streets around us.

Higgins split our group into two, choosing another soldier to be the new team leader. Our teams separated and we commenced our own hunt of the enemy.

Shots rang out as the second group encountered a unit of droids. Our team came under attack at the same time. Two units of robots and a small mob of newly minted human imps raced towards us. Higgins and I fired our death rays, which prompted the rest of our team to start shooting.

A mixture of bullets, explosives and violet bursts of light rained down on our adversaries. An imp came galloping out of the shadows and I spitted her on my sword. It was going to be tricky fighting creatures of both metal and flesh. I hoped the civilians would have the sense to use their guns on the clones while the soldiers targeted the droids with their death rays.

Our next skirmish was with another mob of imps, but there were no droids this time. They'd probably been ordered by Uldar to ignore us. Their task was to root out helpless civilians and turn them into an army of slaves. It was a clever tactic. The Viltarans had been warring for millions of years and had had a lot of practice with subduing alien species.

"I'm going after the droids," I told Higgins. I could fight more effectively on my own if I didn't have to worry about saving anyone's butt.

"Be careful," he said then turned to shoot an imp in the face.

Putting my death ray in a pocket, I slipped my swords free from my new sheaths and sprinted towards the nearest unit of droids. They didn't know I was hunting them until I cut the first few down. Most continued to fire their nanobot darts at the humans that were fleeing through the streets or hiding behind cover.

Only two of the robots turned to confront me. My swords flashed out and took them both through an eye. With a distressed buzzing sound, they fell. I stepped over their metal corpses and cut the rest of the droids down.

Newly converted imps that had been human mere seconds ago, watched me through eyes that matched mine in colour and ferocity. Naked, grey skinned and bulging with muscle, they came at me in a rush. Limbs fell, yellow blood spurted and death cries gurgled out. When they were no longer breathing, I wiped my swords on a tattered piece of cloth, then went on the hunt for more victims.

I was in my element, doling out death to the damned and saving the humans from woe. In the back of my mind, I wondered not for the first time why I'd been picked for this job. I'd never wanted fame or notoriety. It had been thrust upon me and I feared there would never be an escape from it.

Chapter Twenty-Four

As I'd predicted, it was a long and harrowing night. My worst moment by far was when I'd sensed a small family uselessly attempting to hide from a ravenous imp. Five lives became four as the clone infiltrated their residence. Four became three as I came in sight of the small, neat house. Three became two as I leaped through the entryway and stepped over the destroyed door. Two narrowed down to one as I sped down a hallway, passing the mangled bodies of the mother, father and two children.

A shrill, high pitched scream of torment pierced me through to whatever soul I had left as I stepped through the doorway of a bedroom. A little girl of maybe three or four was in the clutches of a blood stained monster. I leaped forward to attack, but I was already too late. The child's scream went up several octaves as the imp tore both of her arms off.

Screaming in rage, I watched her tiny body fall to the floor as one of her arms disappeared into the creature's maw. My sword lashed out and the head of the former human bounced to the floor to land beside the girl. His body stayed upright for a few seconds before toppling backwards.

Inordinately glad that Geordie wasn't with me to witness this horror, I picked the little girl's body up and placed her on her bed. I put her intact arm beside her and retrieved her chewed arm from the dead imp's mouth. Pulling the pink coverlet up to her chin, she almost looked like she was sleeping peacefully. Only the splashes of blood on her cheek and in her blonde curls spoiled the effect.

My chest ached with sorrow as I left the house. Belatedly, I realized I should have used my new talent to move at blinding speed to save her. Hers would be just one more death that I would have to answer for once this was all over.

I'd personally killed off over three hundred droids and clones before the night waned, but it wasn't nearly enough to stop the tide of new imps that were being created. My steps dragged as I re-joined what was left of our team.

We'd lost a third of the newly recruited civilians, but not all had been killed in battle. Some had snuck away to cower in the homes that had recently been searched by the droids and imps. I could feel them hiding inside, but there was no use alerting the soldiers to their desertion. Cowards would be of little use to us anyway.

The young woman who had been looking after my helmet shyly handed it to me when I sat on the curb beside Higgins. I nodded my thanks and spent a few minutes cleaning my swords. Most of the soldiers were taking the opportunity to sleep now that the droids had broken off their attack and had rushed off towards the east.

Already, their mothership was moving into position to pick them up. Instead of them all gathering in the same spot, they'd chosen several different locations to be evacuated from this time. We didn't have enough people in the area to attempt to wipe them all out. I tried to contain my frustration when they slipped out of our reach and retreated back into the heavens again.

Higgins had fallen into a sound sleep. Lying on his side, he breathed quietly, but deeply. Dawn was only a few short minutes away and I savoured the quiet as most of our team rested. All up, we'd managed to destroy another three thousand droids, but there were still fifteen thousand automatons safe and sound on the Viltaran ship.

I dreaded updating Sanderson about how many new imps were roaming the streets looking for somewhere safe to hide from the sun. Our odds of survival had increased since forcing more civilians into duty as recruits, but it still wasn't going to be enough.

I wish Gregor was here so I could pick his brain for ideas, I thought wistfully as I slid my now clean swords into their sheaths. An instant later, the world blurred around me and I was sitting on a dark grey marble floor looking at the very vampire I'd wished to speak to. Gregor and the rest of my friends sat on chocolate brown leather couches in an elegant foyer of a high priced hotel.

Geordie was the first to spot me and he leaped to his feet. "Nat! Where did you come from?" Without waiting for my answer, he scurried over, dropped to his knees beside me and wrapped his skinny arms around my neck. "I've missed you, *chérie.*"

"I've missed you, too," I admitted. I didn't realize just how badly I'd needed a hug after witnessing the little girl's death. I wished I hadn't killed the imp so quickly and painlessly. It had deserved to suffer for murdering the family of five. *All of the alien spawn deserve to suffer,* my alter ego pointed out. *But there's not enough time to torture all of them to death.*

Igor hauled his apprentice out of the way and offered me his hand to help me to my feet. "It is good to see you." He gave me a brief squeeze on the arm then stepped aside to let Ishida hug me. Kokoro gave me a wide smile and a peck on the cheek, then Gregor enveloped me in a rib creaking hug.

Luc stayed in his seat on the couch. He deigned to give me a cool nod that was more suitable for a stranger rather than a former girlfriend. I came very close to bursting into dry sobs and had to bite down hard on my tongue to stop myself. My blood tasted far less rank than usual as I swallowed it down. My tongue healed instantly, presumably without a scar.

"Do you realize you just materialized out of thin air?" Gregor asked me.

Tearing my eyes away from Luc, I stared at him dully. "I did?"

"Yes. I believe you now have the power to-"

He was interrupted by General Sanderson as the soldier stepped into the plush foyer. "Good, you're all here. We need to talk about our strategy." His eyes swept across me and were almost as cool as Luc's.

Ugh, he's the last person I want to see right now. At that thought, the foyer was gone and I was standing beside

Higgins again. Staggering a step, I looked around wildly, but no one seemed to have noticed my arrival.

"What the hell just happened?" I asked myself. My new trick of moving rapidly from one spot to another had just taken a huge leap. I'd somehow transported myself halfway across the city. *Unless that was just a dream.* It was possible I'd fallen asleep for a few moments and had only imagined that I'd seen my friends.

My helmet was still sitting on the road and the sun was about to rise. I scooped it up, donned it and moved into the shadows. Sunrise was a sight I thought I'd never be able to witness again. I stared in silent wonder at the beautiful, delicate pastel colours as they spread across the sky.

I wasn't particularly tired, yet my eyelids slid shut. I settled into a light doze that quickly became a deep slumber.

I found myself standing in front of a building that every Australian recognized on sight. The Sydney Opera House stood in bright sunlight that should have caused me tremendous pain. The multiple white sails of the building caught the light and reflected it straight at me. Since it was just a dream and not real life, I barely had to squint against the brightness.

I'd lived in Sydney for a short time after my parents died, but had opted to head north to Queensland rather than stay in New South Wales. I'd visited the Sydney Opera House a couple of times and it had been packed with tourists both times. It was no different this time. People from all over the world stood on the steps of the iconic building, asking fellow tourists to take their photo.

The sky darkened with shocking suddenness. I tilted my head back, expecting to see clouds. The sky was clear and without a blemish, yet I sensed danger coming. Turning in a slow circle, I saw no threats in Circular Quay, or in the harbour that sported boats of all sizes and descriptions.

Coming to a stop at the vast metal archway of the Sydney Harbour Bridge, I concentrated on it and was suddenly standing high on top of the structure. I stood among a group of brave souls who were in the middle of the bridge climb.

One of the tourists pointed towards the sea. "What is that?" she asked with a strong Japanese accent.

Shading their faces with their hands, the rest of the group squinted into the distance. My eyesight was far better than theirs, but even I couldn't tell what it was that was coming towards us. It was just a dark, vague shape that gave off a sense of profound doom.

"Is it a cruise ship?" another of the tourists asked doubtfully.

"I don't think so," replied their tour guide. "Whatever it is, it's moving really fast."

The sun was still shining, but gloom covered the city It spread out its dark wings to encompass every living soul. I understood that it was a metaphorical darkness that only I could see. Fate was warning me of coming danger and I had no way of knowing when it would strike.

In the short pause between closing my eyes to blink, everything changed. The bridge that had been beneath my feet only a moment ago was now a twisted wreck that had fallen into the harbour. Every building within my sight had been razed to the ground. Some seemed to have been uprooted and cast aside. The Opera House had been reduced to a crumbled ruin. Smoke darkened the sky from fires that had been left to rage out of control.

The city that had been teeming with humans was now a ghost town, devoid of the living. The trail of destruction didn't stop at Sydney and continued northwards. Whatever it was that had decimated one of the largest cities in Australia wasn't finished yet. It was on a rampage that left devastation unlike anything I'd ever seen in its wake.

Snapping awake, I mulled over the warning I'd just been sent. I was pretty sure the ruin hadn't been caused by the Viltarans, which was something of a relief. Unfortunately, I had no idea what would cause the devastation.

The fact that I'd been sent several dreams now that didn't seem to have anything to do with our current crisis was both a relief and a concern. On one hand, it appeared we might have a shot at living through the Viltaran invasion. On the other hand, if we did survive, it seemed we would be facing something even worse than the aliens.

Higgins woke, sat up and looked around. Groggy and ill tempered, he spied me, struggled to his feet and ambled over. I was glad to be distracted from my worried thoughts as he sank down to the grass beside me. Leaning back against the house, he searched through his backpack. Taking out an energy bar, he offered it to me.

I flipped up my visor so he could see my incredulous expression. "Are you kidding?"

Flushing, he withdrew the food. "I forgot about your liquid only diet." Tearing the bar open with his teeth, he gestured towards my stomach. "Speaking of which, do you need to feed yet?"

I gave him a small shrug. "I guess I could use a snack."

"You can have some of my blood, if you want," he offered with a show of nonchalance. The pulse beating in his throat sped up, either from fear or excitement. He gave off no vibes that he wanted to jump my bones, so I doubted it was sexual excitement he was feeling. I'd been very careful not to let any of the soldiers fall too deeply beneath my spell. The last thing I needed was several hundred mindless slaves following me around and telling me how beautiful I was. They needed to be sharp and able to think for themselves rather than be deeply beneath my thrall.

"I appreciate the offer," I said by way of acceptance.

I wasn't a fan of eating in public, so waited for him to finish his energy bar. When he was done, I gestured towards the kicked in front door of the house we were leaning against. His pulse increased even more and he trembled slightly as he climbed to his feet. "Is this going to hurt?" His voice had gone up a couple of octaves in nervousness.

"Nope. You'll barely feel a thing," I reassured him after taking my helmet off.

I stepped into the wreckage of the living room first, glad not to see any dismembered bodies lying around. Higgins took hold of his courage then tilted his head to the side and closed his eyes. Accepting the invitation, I moved in closer and bit his neck gently. Salty, sweet blood flooded into my mouth. I drank only a few mouthfuls before pulling away. I hadn't been anywhere near starving and I was instantly energized by the quick meal.

Opening his eyes, the corporal looked at me in surprise. "Is that it?"

"Yep. It makes you wonder why people make such a fuss about it, huh?"

He nodded at my wry question. "We'd better round everyone up. There must be thousands more clones to eradicate now."

"Try a hundred and twenty-six thousand," I told him. "Seventy thousand humans have been converted now. Plus, there are still forty-six thousand Kveet clones roaming the sewers and buildings."

He shook his head dolefully then passed on the bad news to Sanderson. The other team leaders listened in on the short conversation.

"Tell Natalie that I need to see her," Gregor said into the silence.

I shook my head at Higgins, pulled my helmet on again and left the house. One instance of being treated like a distant acquaintance by Luc had been enough. I wasn't sure I could bear to go through that again just now.

My mood was decidedly fragile after the death of the little girl and the disturbing dream I'd just had. Miserable and not in the mood to be a team player at the moment, I figured the humans had learned enough to be able to tackle the imps without my help. I could move a lot faster and kill far more clones if I was on my own.

With my decision made, I sent out my senses and found imps hidden all throughout the neighbourhood. Some were in houses and others had made their way into the sewers and other dark places where they would be safe from the sun. I debated whether to hunt down small groups, or head straight for the larger herds of monsters.

Higgins emerged from the house and headed towards me. His expression was anxious and I guessed he had orders for me from Sanderson. I spoke before he could. "There are a lot of clones inside the houses in this area as well as in the sewers. You should send in small groups of three or four to each house and eradicate them. I'm going after the larger groups to see if I can cut down their numbers."

The corporal stretched out a hand to stop me. "Wait! I have a message for you!"

He sounded urgent, but I sprinted away before he could burden me with whatever plan Sanderson wanted me to follow. I stuck to the shadows whenever possible as I headed back towards the centre of Vegas. Humans were still hiding in the hotels and casinos, but imps had also taken refuge inside many of the tall buildings. If they weren't dispatched before nightfall, they wouldn't have to go very far in search of their next meal.

Picking a hotel at random, I entered the foyer and headed straight for the stairs without stopping to admire the expensive décor. Picking my way around the seven foot imps that were slumbering in the stairwells, I paused to run my swords through each one until I reached the top floor. Doors had been kicked open all up and down the hallway. Most had cracked under the blows and hung askew.

Turning left, I systematically entered each room and slaughtered its occupants. Blood was already thick in the air from the humans that had been eaten by the clones. Some had been pulled apart. Their intestines had been torn from their bodies from the sheer joy of destruction. Bright yellow blood joined the darker maroon stains on the carpet as I turned the tables on the imps and sent them to their deaths.

It took time to search every room and murder the sleeping giants. I used my new talent to zip to each hotel suite and room instead of wasting time running up and down the hallways. It was a much faster mode of travel, even if I didn't fully understand how I was managing it.

Finishing off the last imp, I concentrated on the floor below me and was instantly standing one level lower. Even with this much faster method of travel, it would take weeks to eradicate all of the imps. New ones would be created as soon as the Viltaran ship descended and dropped off its robot passengers again.

It took me nearly an hour to clean out the hotel. Both the casino to my left and the hotel to my right were chock full of clones. I picked the casino to be my next target and zapped myself into the lobby.

There were no humans lined up to play the slot machines that were loudly and fruitlessly trying to entice customers through an archway to my right. They whistled, jingled, gave off musical bursts of sound and generally made a racket. *Maybe that's why there aren't any hell spawn down here.* It seemed the slot machines were too noisy for the alien offspring.

Although the ground floor was deserted, the rooms above weren't. I didn't bother with the stairs this time, but transported myself directly up to the highest level. Hundreds of imps lay on the floors in the hallways and inside the suites.

None of the clones in the immediate vicinity were awake, so there was no need for stealth. Using an unstained coverlet to clean my swords, I slid them back into their sheaths. Picking my way over to two imps, I knelt and put a hand on their heads. Neither stirred as the holy marks went to work.

The power built, but this time something was different. Usually, I just blanketed the area and hoped the monsters were touching so they would be caught up in the blast of power. This time, I felt the marks seeking out individual victims.

Using my senses to pinpoint each target, I encompassed every grey skinned clone on my floor. Extending the search, I picked up the imps on the floor below and snared them in my net as well. Faster and faster, the power jumped from one monster to the next and from floor to floor until every alien spawn in the building was caught in my mental snare.

The floor was shaking and ominous creaking noises were coming from the walls when I unleashed the holy marks. I didn't wait around for my new clothes and helmet to be splattered with goo, but shifted myself into the lobby. I kept track of the imps as they exploded. They disappeared from my senses like hundreds of balloons being popped by gleeful children.

Previously, the power had only been able to target more than one monster if they'd been touching. It now seemed that I could use it to destroy every creature in an entire building, as long as they showed up on my senses.

A grim smile appeared behind my dark visor as I used my handy new talent to shift into the next imp infested building. I'd just discovered a way to wield my dark mojo far more effectively than I'd ever dreamed was possible.

Chapter Twenty-Five

Several hours later, I'd cleared dozens of hotels and casinos of their alien invaders. Captive humans fled screaming as the imps exploded around them. I didn't waste time trying to calm them down. They were alive, so my job was done. It wasn't my task to look after their mental health, especially since my own was so fragile at the moment.

I fostered some hope that if we managed to destroy the aliens and their minions and then averted the next threat that was looming, fate might finally leave me alone so I could live out the rest of my life in peace.

When battle lust was upon me, my misery faded, but when the fight was over my woes always returned. So did the depression that was trying to creep up and smother me. I didn't kid myself that I might actually one day be happy again. Right now, I'd settle for having a break from constantly coming to the rescue of the hapless earthlings.

When I'd cleared out the last casino, I paused for a moment to check on my friends. Alarm shot through me when I found them in a precarious situation in the sewers. They were surrounded by imps, both human and Kveet. Their teammates were being decimated and their entire group of soldiers and civilians would shortly be entirely wiped out.

I left my helmet in the casino lobby, since I wouldn't need it where I was going. Pulling my swords free, I used my strange new ability and was suddenly beneath the ground. My feet went into action and I sprinted through foul water towards the ravenous group of clones. It would be dark soon. They'd either woken up early, or they'd been woken by the humans who'd been hunting them.

Reaching the tail end of the imps, I cut my way through the throng. My friends were only a few tunnels away now. Almost at the same moment, Geordie screeched in pain and Kokoro let out a shrill scream.

Zeroing in on her, I appeared beside her as she was torn in half by two human imps. She was a grown up version of the little girl that had been dismembered right in front of me. Again, I was a second too late to save her. Guts, black blood, intestines and other things that I wished I could unsee splattered into the water.

I stabbed one imp in the eye and Gregor dispatched the other one with a death ray as Kokoro dropped into the water in two separate pieces. Geordie had also been injured. His shirt and jacket had been shredded when an imp had punched a hole through the teen's chest. For a moment, I imagined I could see the kid's spine, then the wound began to heal. Igor steadied him with a hand on his narrow shoulder when his legs wobbled.

Born from rage, the power of the holy marks began to build without me consciously calling it. My friends sensed the power gathering and glanced around uneasily. "What is happening?" Igor asked as he fired his death ray into the oncoming mass of small Kveet and far larger human clones.

Carving the closest imp's chest open, I threw a desperate glance back at the others. "It's the holy marks and I don't think I can control them!"

Gregor grasped the implications immediately. Snatching Kokoro's two halves up beneath both arms, he shouted for the others to run. Igor pushed Geordie into action and bolted after him. Ishida hesitated for a second, then followed them. Luc took up the rear without acknowledging my presence at all. I hadn't even been worthy of a distant nod this time.

Unsure why their vampire allies were fleeing in terror, the surviving humans also stampeded towards the exit. The tunnel was narrow enough that my whirling blades stopped the imps from chasing after them, but the strain of containing my dark power was making my hands shake. The instant I sensed Luc reach the surface, I dropped my swords into the filthy water.

Soldiers and civilians were still exiting the tunnels when the ground began to shake. "Earthquake!" someone screamed in panic.

Taking a step forward, I reached up and grabbed hold of the closest imp by the chin. Dragging her face down to my level, I unleashed the power on her, then shoved her backwards. With her body swelling alarmingly, she crashed into several of her brethren, knocking them to the ground.

Bending to scoop up my weapons, I escaped a millisecond before she exploded.

Geordie made a startled sound when I appeared beside him. My friends had moved out of the rapidly fading sunlight into the shade of a hotel. I maintained my contact with the imps, feeling the power rapidly jump from one to the next as their lives were extinguished. Ignoring the pandemonium that had broken out from what the humans mistakenly thought was an earthquake, I kept my attention on the imps that I could sense below.

The clones in the immediate area had been evaporated by the force of the dark power that resided within me. Instead of petering out, the holy marks jumped to the next group of imps and then the next. Spreading my senses out wider, I included every clone that was slinking through the sewers and guided the deadly power to them all. A strange exultation filled me as the power thrummed in my veins.

When the last imp winked out of existence, I staggered a step, drained of energy. Geordie put an arm around my waist and Ishida moved to my other side and offered me his arm as well. The pair guided me over to Kokoro and I collapsed to the ground beside her. Gregor, Luc and Igor were shielding the severity of her injuries from the humans who were calming down now that the ground was no longer shaking.

Kokoro's panicked eyes met mine and I took her hand to calm her. She'd managed to reattach her severed hand and I knew she'd heal from this injury as well.

A tingle shot from my hand up my arm when her lower body began to tremble. The tiny gap between her upper and lower halves disappeared as her flesh melded. Her injury disappeared and only a jagged, thin red line remained. Some of my fatigue was washed away with the residual effects of her body healing itself. I didn't even want to know what had happened to the bits of her that had fallen out. Her body had replicated them, so maybe the originals had broken down into the usual slushy remains that occurred when our kind died.

"How do you feel?" Gregor asked her anxiously.

Taking his hand, Kokoro sat up and gifted him with a smile. "I feel fine."

I swung my gaze to Geordie to see the hole in his chest had almost closed. He looked down at his flesh as it became smooth and unmarred again and gave me a sickly smile. "I felt the imp destroy my heart when it punched its fist through me," he said quietly. "Then it just grew right back."

Now that his ladylove was whole again, Gregor turned his attention to me. "How many clones did you just destroy?"

Sweeping the entire town, I counted the number of enemies that were left. "Almost all of them," I replied and came close to giggling giddily. I was still feeling the effects of using up most of my reserves. "All of the imps that were hiding in the sewers are gone. There are still seventeen thousand or so left spread throughout the houses in the suburbs." I'd already polished off the ones that had been holed up in the casinos and hotels, but it would feel like boasting if I mentioned them.

"Out of one hundred and sixteen thousand imps infesting the city, there are now only seventeen thousand left?" Igor asked incredulously. "How is that possible?"

Raising my hands, I showed him the crosses. "I guess I finally worked out how to use these properly."

Ishida shook his head in wonder. "Incredible. If only you could use them to destroy the droids, our fight could be over within hours!"

"I wish," I said in heartfelt agreement. "Unfortunately, they only seem to work on imps and vampires."

"Did you get the message that I gave to Corporal Higgins?" Gregor asked me. In dire need of a nice long nap, I shook my head wearily. Glancing around to make sure none of the humans were close, he leaned in. "I believe that this new talent of yours will be the key to defeating the Viltarans."

"Maybe," I replied doubtfully. "But they're up on their ship so I'm not going to be able to unleash the holy marks on them in a hurry."

Making an impatient gesture, Gregor checked over his shoulder again and stiffened when he saw Sanderson striding towards us. Putting his hand on my arm, he gave me an urgent command. "Take us somewhere else! Quickly!"

In the blink of an eye, we were in a hallway on the third floor of a hotel across the road. Gregor lost his balance and went down to one knee. My balance was fine since I was already sitting down. "Just as I suspected," he said cryptically. At my ignorant look, he explained further. "You have gained the ability to teleport yourself."

I grinned at the joke, but he remained solemn. "Are you serious?" I asked and he nodded. "I just thought I was moving really, really quickly." Now that I had time to think about it, I realized none of my limbs had actually gone into motion each time I'd used my new talent. It seemed that Gregor was right and I'd physically willed myself from one location to another.

"Have you tested how far you are able to transport yourself?" Gregor asked.

"The biggest jump I've made so far was from one side of the city to the other."

His fist came to rest beneath his chin as he worked on a plan. I had an inkling of what he would ask me to do and I hoped I would be up to it. I'd depleted my stores while annihilating the vast majority of clones in the sewers. I would need to feed before attempting to take on any more enemies.

When Gregor began to smile, I figured he'd worked out a plan that he was fairly certain would succeed. When he finished explaining it to me, I was also smiling. "It will be dark in a few minutes," I pointed out. "I'd better go and round up some humans to feed from. Using my holy marks to destroy so many imps at once has left me drained."

I took his arm and teleported us to the lobby then we walked out into the lingering dusk. Pretending they weren't freaked out that we'd disappeared without warning, the others ambled over to join us. "General Sanderson was not happy that you weren't available to discuss strategy with him," Luc said to Gregor.

Unperturbed, Gregor shrugged off the warning. "Natalie and I have come up with our own strategy. I am fairly certain that it will resolve this conflict once and for all."

Almost dancing on the spot with excitement, Geordie gave an exaggerated glance around to make sure no one was listening in. "What is your plan?" he asked. His mouth dropped open in shock once it was outlined for him. He turned to me in apprehension. "This sounds very dangerous, *chérie*. Are you sure it will work?"

There was no way to be sure about the plan until I attempted it, but I wasn't about to admit that out loud. "It'll work." I sounded far more certain than I felt.

"I take it we're not going to advise General Sanderson of this plan?" Igor said. His tone was curious rather than accusatory. He might be practical about the necessity to work with the general but, like me, he wasn't particularly happy about it.

"I'd prefer it if the humans didn't discover Natalie's new talent just yet," Gregor answered. "The less they know about the extent of our abilities, the safer we'll all be."

He met my eyes and I read the knowledge that he suspected none of us would be safe once we managed to eliminate the Viltaran threat. I'd warned him that this would be the case, but I had to concede that we hadn't really had a choice. I might now be able to rapidly eradicate mass numbers of imps, but my mojo was useless against the robots. We needed the soldiers' firepower. That meant we'd have to remain their allies until the last automaton was neutralised.

"Good luck fighting the droids," I said to the group. "I'll see you all when I've taken care of Uldar and his buddies."

Geordie and Ishida gave me a combined hug, then the others also stepped up to wrap their arms around me and each other. Luc took a step towards us then stopped. I caught a hint of sadness in his dark eyes before he turned away. Thanks to me, he now felt like an outsider amongst his own friends. Soon, they would have to choose between us and I knew who I'd pick if I were them. Their friendship was all I had and it would shortly be taken away from me. I would be left with nothing but the duty to save humankind, which frankly wasn't all that important to me.

Too weary to bother teleporting after our huddle broke up, I walked over to the closest group of soldiers. All were from Sanderson's original crew and each soldier knew me on sight. "I need blood," I told them with my usual lack of tact. "Does anyone want to volunteer to be my snack?"

Half a dozen men stepped forward. I knew it would be necessary for me to recharge fully, so I drank a few mouthfuls from each of them. The teeth marks on the first soldier had already mostly healed by the time I was done with the last man.

Nodding my thanks, I walked away as they were ordered to vacate the area by their team leader. My tiredness was gone. I felt strong and powerful as the mothership slowly began to descend once more. If all went according to Gregor's plan, I would shortly have my final showdown with the Viltarans.

Chapter Twenty-Six

Gregor launched his sly scheme into action by lying to Sanderson. He advised the general that the ship was heading northward to offload its cargo of droids this time. Sanderson immediately ordered his people into motion. In reality, the ship was descending towards the southern end of the strip. I would be the only one waiting for it when it touched down.

Zapping myself into the fancy lobby of a casino, I peeked out through the door and watched the ship descend. The ramp lowered and neat ranks of shiny metal men disembarked. I waited for the tail end of the droids to appear before I went on the move.

Materializing beside an abandoned van, I used it for cover as I moved in closer to observe the robots. They marched in orderly rows of five abreast as they exited from the spaceship. They were going to have to hunt far and wide to find humans to turn into clones. As ordered by the soldiers, most of the townsfolk were stampeding towards the eastern and western suburbs.

Gregor would shortly advise Sanderson that the ship had changed course. The soldiers would then be redirected to the strip to battle the droids. If our plan worked, the mothership wouldn't be returning to pick them up when dawn next rolled around.

When the last droid stepped onto the road, the ramp immediately began to close. I teleported myself inside just before it snapped shut. Just like in my dream, the hold was dark and the walls were a uniform black. It took a few moments for my eyes to adjust to the gloom then I trotted silently down a hallway.

I couldn't feel the ship moving, but I knew it had taken off when I sensed my friends and allies rapidly receding. My senses picked up most of the Viltarans gathered together in a small clump. The rest were spread throughout the gigantic vessel, performing tasks that I neither knew, nor cared about.

Picking one of the aliens at random, I willed myself to appear a few feet away from him. Surprise briefly registered on his misshapen, familiar face. I recognized him to be the runt of the litter, the weakest link in the Viltaran chain of command. He was the perfect subject for an experiment that Gregor suggested I should try.

Snarling, he leaped at me and I allowed myself to be caught in his crushing grip. He lifted me up to his level and his head reared back as he readied himself to bite my face off.

Our eyes met and his rage slowly turned to puzzlement as my vampire mojo went to work. Caught in my dark snare, he lacked the will to free himself and became mine.

I hadn't been sure that my hypnotism would work on our distant ancestors, but Gregor had been confident that I would succeed. I was glad he was right because my task had just become a lot easier.

"Put me down," I ordered my new slave. He did so, then waited for further instructions. "Are there any escape pods on this ship?" I now spoke fluent Viltaran and I was almost grateful to have been shot with the nanobot darts. It'd hurt like hell, but they'd given me a couple of cool new abilities. One of which meant that we wouldn't need a robot to translate our conversation.

"Yes," he intoned. His scarlet eyes stared blankly over my head.

"Do you know how to disable them?" He nodded again. "Where can this be done?"

"In the engine room, or in the command centre."

"Is anyone in the engine room at the moment?"

Turning jerkily, he touched a small monitor. A picture of a room full of high tech equipment appeared. A lone Viltaran female was tinkering with something. Concentrating on her, I took my captive by the wrist and willed us both to her side. She started back at our sudden arrival and I didn't give her time to react. "Kill her," I ordered my slave.

Obeying me instantly, he calmly took out his death ray and shot his colleague. She disappeared in a whirl of particles. "Disable the escape pods so no one can leave the ship," I ordered. Several minutes later, he completed the job and went still again. "Can you control the direction of the ship from here?"

"No," he said with a shake of his head. His grey scalp shone through his light fuzz of hair. "The ship can only be controlled from the command centre."

I had one final question for the alien. "What is the Third Protocol?"

"Any accidentally cloned unintelligent species must be destroyed," he replied by rote.

"Why?"

"Because their intellect is not advanced enough to accept our nanobot technology. Without a certain level of intelligence, clones become uncontrollable, mindless monsters." That had certainly described the doberclone fairly accurately. "They will attack any creature that is not of their species, including their creators." That explained why the dog imp had turned on the droids, but I was still at a loss as to why it hadn't attacked me.

I had no further use for my lackey and held out my hand for his death ray. He handed it to me and became another small pile of particles on the smooth black floor when I shot him with it. I pocketed the extra weapon instead of discarding it.

Uldar was somewhere on this vessel and I was willing to bet he would be in the command centre. I could have hunted each alien down one by one, but destroying them all in one fell swoop would be much quicker.

Gregor had advised me to do my best to make sure the ship couldn't be salvaged by the humans. He'd made a suggestion of how to destroy both the ship and its crew. It involved leaving Earth's atmosphere. I only hoped the vessel had enough fuel to reach the destination I had in mind.

Flying a spaceship was far beyond my capabilities. That meant one of the Viltarans would have to do it for me. Zeroing in on the cluster of extra-terrestrials several levels above me, I teleported closer then walked the rest of the way. Soft lights lit the hallways that were most frequently used by the aliens. The black walls, ceiling and floor seemed to absorb the light, as if they were perpetually hungry.

Glad I'd had the foresight to keep the extra death ray, I held one in each hand and stepped up to the command centre door. It whooshed aside to reveal an array of monitors and consoles from my dream. The Viltarans were clustered around the largest monitor, discussing the war that raged far below. I simultaneously zapped two of them to get the attention of the others.

Uldar whirled around and his scarlet eyes came to rest on me. "You!" he spat in disbelief.

"Me," I agreed in his native language.

He didn't waste time asking me stupid questions such as 'how the hell did you get onto my ship' and reached for his death ray. I eradicated two more of his people in warning. The heavily pregnant female took a shot at me, but I teleported to safety before the bar of light could reach me.

Using Uldar as a shield, I pressed one of the death rays into his back. He stiffened in shock to find me standing right behind him. "Tell everyone to leave the room," I commanded. "You and I are going to have a private chat."

Breathing hard, enraged at being captured so easily by a creature that he considered to be far inferior to him, Uldar tried to spin around. I jammed the other death ray into his side. "I don't need to keep you alive," I warned him. "I'm sure one of your minions here will be only too happy to answer my questions."

Debating about his chances of besting me, he reached his decision. "Get out!" he snarled at his kin. They fled, but only as far as the next hallway. I didn't really care where they went, just as long as they didn't try to interfere with my plan.

Taking a few steps back, I allowed Uldar to turn around. Fully eleven feet tall, he towered over me, bristling with an almost uncontrollable rage. I silently marvelled at just how hideous he was. The fangs in his upper and lower jaws were almost thick enough to be tusks. His nose wasn't quite as flat as a bat's, but the nostrils were like small caverns in his face. Long, filthy black hair fell to his waist. Chunks of Kveet meat were still tangled up in the strands. Not only was he far from pretty, he also stank very badly. He could almost have used his stench to render his enemies unconscious.

I caught his gaze and we had a staring match that lasted far longer than any I'd ever instigated. It took several minutes before his hands unclenched. His shoulders slumped as he finally fell beneath my spell. I didn't waste any time and got straight to business. "I want you to change course," I told him.

With a faint hint of unhappiness, Uldar trudged over to the largest console and waited for my command. He stiffened when I told him where I wanted him to point the ship. "We will all die," he told me woodenly, as if I couldn't figure that out for myself. Uldar's will was far stronger than the runty Viltaran I'd bamboozled. He'd retained enough control to argue with me.

"Yeah, that's pretty much the plan. Do it anyway," I ordered. He keyed in the new coordinates, but I had no way of knowing if they were correct or not. I'd hoped to strip him of his will, get him to set the course that Gregor had suggested then leave. Now I was going to have to ride along to make sure he didn't regain his senses in time to save the ship.

I'd only get one shot at this and I wanted to get it right. Even if I failed, the vessel would shortly run out of fuel. The crew wouldn't be able to return the relatively short distance to Earth, let alone make their way back to Viltar. The possibility that they might be discovered and rescued by yet another alien species was too great a risk to take now that I knew aliens really did exist. One way or another, the ship and its crew had to be destroyed.

Grey fingers flew over the alien console. They hesitated, then pushed a final button. This time, I felt the ship move slightly as it changed course and presumably picked up speed. "I have done as you ordered," Uldar said with heavy reluctance.

"Good. Now back away." I wasn't going to make the mistake of ending his life until I knew without a doubt that he'd followed my orders. He backed away until he reached the far wall and crossed his arms. His biceps bulged as he clenched his fists again. I had a feeling the hypnotism wasn't going to last much longer, unless I remained vigilant. I could almost feel him prying at the mental hands that I'd clasped around his brain. Every now and then, I caught his eye to reinforce my hold over him.

We travelled for over three hours before a voice blared through a set of unseen speakers. "Warning! The current trajectory will result in complete destruction of this ship.

The emergency fuel tanks are now dangerously low. I suggest an immediate course correction." The voice was robotic, male and sounded like Robert the treacherous droid. Uldar flinched slightly at the message and clenched his fists even tighter.

The warning came again about half an hour later. Bright red lights began to flash, accompanying the message. "Warning! The emergency fuel has now been depleted and the ship will reach the point of no return in fifteen minutes. I suggest immediate evacuation." The robot voice didn't actually use the word 'minutes', but that was how my mind translated it.

Waiting for the countdown to end was agony. Each minute seemed more like an hour. Uldar's top lip drew back to reveal his fangs as he fought against the hold I had over his mind. Relief came as the final warning sounded. "The ship has now passed the point of no return. Escape may still be possible if the pods are activated within the next sixty seconds."

While I was momentarily distracted by the message, Uldar broke free from the hypnotism and lunged towards me with a bellow of rage. My own battle lust took control, pushing aside my common sense as his hands closed around my throat. My neck dissolved into particles, leaving my head floating in mid-air for a brief moment. Uldar shifted his grip to my arms and tried to pull them off like the wings of a fly. At my mental command, both arms became a whirling mass of molecules. Clasping air, the leader of the all but extinct Viltaran race gaped at my empty sleeves.

Concentrating, I ordered Lefty and Righty to remain apart while the rest of my cells returned to my body. Uldar caught sight of the swirling molecules and tried to bat them out of the air. Righty re-formed and tapped him on the shoulder. The alien whirled around with a belligerent roar and lunged at thin air as my hand became minute particles again.

My hands tormented him, whipping him into a frenzy until the robot voice broke into my amusement. "Warning! Thirty seconds remain until the ship will be destroyed."

Alarmed by the reminder, I'd almost forgotten that I'd ordered Uldar to fly his ship towards the sun. I became aware of an immense heat enveloping the vessel. The ship might have run out of fuel, but it was moving at an extremely high rate of speed and it wasn't slowing down. I only had seconds to reach safety, but I had one final task to perform first.

Uldar had managed to capture both of my hands while I'd been distracted once again by the robot voice. His hands sprang open when Lefty and Righty disappeared. He didn't see them re-form on either side of his face and stared at his empty palms incomprehensively. His scarlet eyes shifted to mine when my hands settled on his cheeks.

I didn't have enough time to make a smartass speech. In fact, I was almost completely out of time if I wanted to avoid being burned to a crisp. Far more rapidly than ever before, the power of the holy marks built up inside me. I released it through my hands, feeling the rush of dark magic passing through my palms. Uldar's eyes bulged then burst in a scarlet splatter. His head and body swelled rapidly, like a balloon being filled with helium. I teleported to the far side of the room as he exploded, raining body parts all over the consoles and monitors.

"Warning! Five seconds remain until the ship is destroyed," the urgent, yet almost bored robot voice informed me.

I'd distantly heard and sensed the rest of the Viltarans fleeing towards the escape pods. They were several levels below us and they'd never reach them in time. They wouldn't have been able to escape from the ship anyway, since all but one of the pods had been disabled. With a final smirk at the remains of my nemesis, I recalled my hands, then teleported myself directly inside the only still functioning pod.

My runty Viltaran minion had given me a tutorial on how to operate the escape pods before I'd evaporated him. He'd already prepped the pod for me, so all I had to do was push a button on the console. Doing so, I was thrown off my feet as the craft was violently ejected away from the mothership. It trembled as powerful engines propelled it away from the much larger doomed spacecraft.

Built for an emergency getaway, the pod was almost simple compared to the two other alien ships that I'd ridden inside. A single long window stretched along the wall above the console. A thick shutter kept the sun out, but it couldn't block the overwhelming heat that was slowly beginning to fade as I zoomed to safety. The hull was softly glowing red and the floor was hot even through the soles of my boots.

There was only enough room for four seats, two on each side of the rectangular vessel. Choosing one, I climbed up and buckled myself in with the oversized harness. I sent out my senses and latched onto the remaining Viltarans as their ship was unavoidably sucked towards the sun. It would burn up long before it could crash land. One by one, the evil alien overlords fizzed out of existence. I could almost hear them screaming in agony as the walls of their ship melted and they were instantly vaporized.

My escape pod was small, but fast and followed the coordinates my slave had keyed in via the console in the engine room. All had gone according to Gregor's carefully thought out plan. I believed he was going to be proud of me when I returned. They all would, except for Luc. Once we finished mopping up the killbots and the new imps that had undoubtedly been created during my absence, I wasn't sure what would happen. It would be awkward to stay with the others with the constant tension that would be between Luc and me.

First things first, I had to make it back to Earth safely. I'd instructed the Viltaran to take the pod close to my home planet. It would slow down briefly, allowing me to exit before zooming off into space again. It was going to take some serious concentration to make my way back safely. If I missed the chance to escape while I was close to home, I wasn't sure what would happen to me. I didn't know what my teleporting limits were, but I doubted I'd be able to shift myself across hundreds of thousands of miles.

Sending out my senses in a wide net, I knew I was drawing close to home when I detected the presence of billions of human lives. When I felt the faint sensation of the pod slowing down, I teleported myself outside. I was close enough to Earth that it seemed to fill the entire universe. A mixture of green and brown land, blue water and white clouds, it was the most beautiful sight I'd ever beheld. Then I was caught in its atmosphere and began to fall.

Zooming downwards at a terrific speed, the ground was hurtling at me in a dizzying rush. Breaking my body down into microscopic cells, I came to a sudden and almost shocking halt. My clothes and weapons continued to fall, since they no longer had anything to support their weight. Walking around naked until I could steal some more clothes held zero appeal for me, so I sent my particles after my belongings. I formed my eyes and hands to catch the items before they could scatter far and wide.

Just as I'd planned, the US was spread out beneath me. I knew the geography well enough to know roughly where Las Vegas was located. Teleporting closer in fits and spurts, I finally spied the gas cloud. It was already beginning to look tattered and would soon dissipate and become harmless. Behind it were the sparkling lights of the strip.

I drifted high above the noxious vapour to avoid the smell, then angled downwards. By the time my feet hit the ground, I was whole and fully dressed again. I had to admit that being Mortis wasn't all bad. At times like this, it was pretty freaking awesome.

My first order of business was to track my friends down. I sensed them deep in battle with several units of Murderbots. Geordie started so hard he almost fell over when I suddenly appeared beside him. I pushed him out of the way of a death ray blast and decapitated the offending droid. The teen sent me a quick grin of thanks, then concentrated on killing the enemy.

"I take it your mission was successful?" Gregor called out over the noise of battle. He and Kokoro had taken cover behind a low fence.

"The Viltarans have all been crispy fried and their ship is toast," I confirmed, then simultaneously sliced the arms off two different droids with my twin swords.

Crouched down out of sight behind a car, Sanderson suddenly stood and revealed himself. "Did I just hear you correctly? You have destroyed both the aliens *and* their ship?" He flinched when a blast of violet light came close to obliterating him. His distress momentarily overrode his sense of self-preservation.

Gregor and I exchanged a brief, knowing look. Our suspicions that the humans had been planning on nabbing the alien ship had been confirmed. They'd probably been planning on studying it in the hopes of advancing their technology.

"The Viltarans flew it directly into the sun when they realized I was about to take control," I lied blandly and speared a droid that lurched into view.

Sanderson didn't know whether to believe my story or not, but he had more pressing matters to deal with right now. There were still over fourteen thousand robots to eradicate, as well as the thousands of imps that'd been created while I'd been otherwise occupied.

"We'll discuss this further once we've finished dealing with the remaining enemies," he grated. Pointing his gun at the droids, he blew four of them away in rapid succession with his explosive rounds.

Something told me he wished I'd been the one within his sights.

Chapter Twenty-Seven

Our battle seemed to be without end as we hunted down our foes. Each droid we took down had already created hundreds of new clones. Word began to spread that the Viltaran ship had been destroyed, which gave the civilians new hope. More and more people left the safety of their hotel rooms to come to our aid. The war could have come to an end far sooner if they'd taken hold of their courage when the aliens had first attacked, but it was better late than never.

When dawn neared, the robots milled in confusion as they waited in vain for the mothership to descend and pick them up. Rescue wouldn't be forthcoming, but it took them a while to figure that out.

Sanderson ordered his soldiers and raw recruits to move in and surround the killbots. Taking cover behind anything that wasn't made of metal, we sent barrage after barrage of bullets, explosives and violet blasts from death rays towards them. Exposed and left with nowhere to hide, the droids finally realized they were on their own. They abandoned their nanobot guns in exchange for their death rays. They were going to die, but they would take as many of us down with them as they could.

Moments before the sun made its appearance, I retrieved my motorcycle helmet from the lobby of the hotel where I'd left it. As long as I didn't stay out in the direct sunlight for too long, I'd be able to continue to fight the metal men. The thousands of newly made imps fled beneath the ground and into the sewer system. They could wait for now. Taking down the droids before nightfall was our main priority.

Doing what they could to help from the shadows, my friends donned their sunglasses and fired their death rays into the crowd of droids. Gregor caught my attention and waved me over. "I have an idea that I'd like you to try," he said when I jogged over and flipped my visor up. I'd taken his advice not to let the humans know that I could transport myself at will. They'd probably find out about it eventually, but I would try to keep my new talent a secret for as long as I could.

"It is a very good idea," Ishida said with a smile at the vampire who looked nearly four times his mortal age, but was seven thousand years younger than him. Ishida had lost a lot of his reserve since abdicating from his throne. He was becoming more comfortable with being a teenager instead of a revered ruler. Wearing trendy clothes and dark glasses, he could almost have passed for human. Only his ultra-pale skin and the hint of red light shining through his sunglasses gave his true nature away.

"Only the droids in the outer ring can fire at the humans," Gregor explained. "Those in the middle can do little but wait for someone to fall so they can take their place. I propose you start thinning their numbers by teleporting into their midst and setting off explosives." He handed me a small bag of the bombs that could be activated by pressing a red button on the top. They had a short timer of only three seconds before they would explode.

Geordie clapped his hands together in glee. "That sounds like fun! I wish I could go with you."

The danger of him being zapped by a death ray was far too high to grant his wish. The damage from the blast would almost certainly be too catastrophic for anyone but me to repair. "I'll give it a try," I said. Igor and Gregor stood shoulder to shoulder to shield me from view as I teleported away.

When I reappeared, I was in the centre of the droid army. None of the robots even noticed me when I suddenly appeared amongst them. I was much shorter than any of them and they were focussed on the ring of attacking humans. Taking half a dozen of the small devices out, I depressed the red button on the first one and threw it far into the crowd. The other five followed suit, then six explosions ripped through the automatons' ranks.

A robot looked down, saw me and shouted a warning, but I disappeared before it could lift its death ray. Materializing in a small pocket that had been created by an explosive, I sent more bombs flying. In a short time, the bag was empty and several hundred droids had been destroyed.

I appeared behind Geordie and he gave a shriek of fright when I tapped him on the shoulder. "You were right," I told him as he clutched his unbeating heart, "that was fun." I didn't find it strange that his hand rested on the right side of his chest instead of the left. Geordie had been born with his heart on the wrong side of his body. It was just one of the many things about him that I found strangely endearing. Luc might have been my lover, but Geordie was probably my best friend. I didn't want to examine why I got along so well with a teenager. My mother had always despaired that I might never grow up. Sadly, it seemed that she'd been right. Some part of me would always be an adolescent.

"Can you gather as many explosives as possible?" I asked Gregor. "There's something else I want to try."

Everyone scattered to scrounge up more of the explosive devices from the soldiers. They came back with several small bags this time. Taking the bags with both hands, I ordered the rest of my body to become tiny particles. Only my eyes and hands remained intact. My weapons, helmet and empty clothes fell to the ground. My gloves would protect my hands from the late afternoon sun, but my eyes were exposed and were already burning from the glare.

"How are you doing that, Natalie?" Kokoro asked me as my hands and eyes floated in mid-air. The particles that formed the rest of my body were holding them up. They were so tiny they were almost invisible even to our eyes. I didn't have a mouth to answer her at the moment so I made a helpless gesture with one hand. Ishida politely gathered my belongings into a neat pile before any curious civilians could trip over them.

Lighter than the air itself, my particles carried my eyes and hands as well as the explosives above the crowd of robots. I formed a dense, protective shield over my eyes so

I could see where I was going. They acted like the sunglasses my friends had been given and the burning sensation faded. Holding all of the bags with one hand, the other delved inside and pulled out an explosive. Righty depressed the button, then dropped the small bomb. It exploded in the centre of the group, sending shards of metal spraying in all directions. The droids couldn't figure out who or what was attacking them. None thought to look upwards.

Like a malevolent sprite spreading toxic fairy dust, I dropped bomb after bomb on the robot army. When the bags were finally empty, great holes had been torn in their ranks. The soldiers and civilians moved in, forcing the droids into a smaller and tighter group.

Thousands of humans had already died and more would suffer the same consequence before our war would end. The droids' programming wouldn't allow them to give up. Each human that fell was replaced by more soldiers or civilians. They were all eager to eradicate their adversaries once and for all.

Now aware why they'd been asked to hand over their explosives, even if they had no idea who was actually dispensing them, the soldiers were happy to relinquish more of the devices. I teleported back to my friends, silently amazed that I could do so when I was still mostly in particle form. Without a word, since I still didn't have a mouth, I held out my hands for more bags. Igor handed them over, gave me a salute and I teleported back over the vastly diminished robot army.

Half an hour before nightfall, less than a thousand droids were left. The humans would have to finish them off now. I had another urgent task to take care of. Shifting back to my friends, I handed the not quite empty bags to Igor, then poured my particles back into my clothes.

"That is so cool," Geordie said in awe as I became whole again, miraculously fully dressed.

"I know," I said with a small smirk. "I'm just going to pop down into the sewers and destroy the imps. I'll be back in a minute."

Igor was shaking his head in disbelief at my strange abilities when I disappeared. I didn't have to go far, just into the tunnels directly beneath where the battle was raging. Thousands of newly made imps were currently asleep. They would shortly wake up and would immediately seek out food. My goal was to eradicate them before any more humans could become tasty treats.

Kneeling, I placed my hands on two of the slumbering giants. I let the power of the holy marks build until I was thrumming with it. My senses sought out every cloned monster that had taken refuge beneath the ground. Releasing the power, I teleported into an empty tunnel to avoid being covered in ooze. I concentrated on maintaining the wave of deadly power until it had reached out to destroy every last imp in the city.

I staggered when I appeared amongst my friends. Luc was closest and steadied me with a hand on my shoulder. I smiled my thanks, but he released me and stepped away as if he was afraid of catching Mortis cooties.

Geordie gave Luc a filthy look and put his arm around my waist. Highly attuned to emotions, he knew I was close to tears. "Are they all gone, Nat?"

I nodded, unwilling to speak in case my voice betrayed my devastation at Luc's continued rejection.

It took another couple of hours to pick off the rest of the droids. When the last robot went down in a shower of flying metal shards, silence descended. Soldiers and civilians alike looked around wildly for their next target, but none presented themselves.

Higgins spied me standing between Geordie and Ishida and loped over. The bite marks on his neck had faded to mere dots, but Geordie spotted them and gave me an accusing glare. "What?" I asked him crankily. "It's not like I tore his pants off and had sex with him." Both teens giggled and Higgins gave me an uncertain look. I waved him over and he closed the distance.

"I heard a rumour that you destroyed the Viltaran ship," he said. "Is that true?"

"I had a hand in it," I replied modestly. "They crashed it into the sun so I couldn't steal it from them." That was the lie I'd told Sanderson and I was sticking with it. He already loathed and feared us. It made sense not to give him another reason to want us dead. Knowing I'd purposefully destroyed the alien vessel wouldn't exactly endear us to him.

"The Viltarans are gone and the droids have all been destroyed," the soldier summed up. "What about the clones? How many of them are running loose in the city?"

"None. They're all gone," I assured him. "The threat of alien invasion is over. We won."

Higgins stared at me in incomprehension, then my final two words sank in. "We won?" I nodded and he grinned in dazed amazement. "We won!" With a whoop of glee, he darted forward, picked me up and whirled me around in a circle. Geordie gave a squawk of protest, but the corporal dropped me and ran off to spread the news before the teen could react. Within minutes, the survivors were dancing in the streets and cheering themselves hoarse.

My friends and I stood in a small pool of aloneness and watched the creatures we had all once been celebrate their victory. Under Sanderson's direction, soldiers were gathering up the alien weapons that had been dropped. They were also retrieving any the curious civilians had picked up. They'd never be able to find them all. Some would be kept as souvenirs and would eventually be worth a lot of money on the black market.

Remembering something I hadn't yet had the chance to tell the others, I turned to break the news to them. "There's something you should know." Gregor lifted a brow in silent query. "We aren't the only vampires left," I told them and received the reactions I'd expected.

Kokoro's hand went to her mouth in shock. Ishida and Geordie immediately started babbling questions. Igor and Luc exchanged surprised looks and Gregor nodded as if I'd confirmed his suspicions. "How many are left?" he asked. The teens went quiet to listen in.

"I sensed fifteen of them in Europe. I think they're somewhere near Romania, so they might be the Prophet and his guards."

Kokoro nodded in agreement. "The seer may have received a warning in time to have escaped from General Sanderson's purge."

"There are others," I went on. "About twenty of them scattered around the world." A dozen had formed another group and were also somewhere in Europe.

"So, we aren't the only remnant then?" Geordie asked. "The others are as well?"

I hadn't written the prophecy, I'd just acted it out, so I shrugged. "I guess so."

Igor made a shushing motion with his hand and we ceased our conversation as Sanderson made an appearance. Filthy and exhausted, he was barely able to remain on his feet. He took us all in with a long look. "I would like to extend my thanks to you all for your assistance in eradicating this threat."

"Again," Geordie said sourly. "That's three times we've saved your butts now."

The general nodded gravely. "I am aware of that and so is our President. She would like to honour you all with a parade, once the gas has dissipated and it is safe for us to leave Las Vegas."

Gregor glanced at me to judge my reaction and I shook my head surreptitiously. He knew I would never be able to trust the general after what he had done to us all. He opened his mouth to decline the invitation, but Kokoro beat him to it. "We would be delighted to attend the parade, General."

With a nod, Sanderson strode off to arrange medical attention for the surviving civilians and his soldiers.

Chapter Twenty-Eight

From Kokoro's surprised expression, she hadn't meant to accept Sanderson's invitation. "I do not know where that came from," she stammered. "I did not intend to say anything at all!"

I had a feeling I knew exactly where her words had come from and my heart tried to sink. It seemed that fate still wasn't done with us. It would continue to twist and turn us to suit its ultimate purpose, whatever that may be.

"I could use a shower and a change of clothes," Luc said to break the silence. A picture of him naked and wet popped into my head.

"You can pretty much take your pick of any hotel room," Geordie said. "By the way," he turned and gave me an approving grin. "I like your new outfit. I especially like the naughty angel on the back of your jacket."

The leather gear was surprisingly comfortable, despite it being skin tight. "It saved me from being boiled down to a skeleton," I said with a half-hearted smile.

My pitiful smile faded quickly. I didn't know what form it would take, but I had the sudden and horrible sensation that time was running out again. I didn't need a crystal ball or a vision to know that doom was coming for us. Kokoro had been used as a conduit to ensure that we would be in the right place at the right time for whatever horror was in store for us next.

Before heading to a hotel, we split up to search for a change of clothes. There were plenty of stores with broken windows to browse through. I escorted the teens to a store that caught Geordie's eye. I nodded to Igor that I would take care of his protégé. He inclined his head to indicate he trusted me with his care.

Several minutes later, the boys had picked jeans, t-shirts and a hooded sweater for Geordie and a jacket for Ishida. They'd chosen identical sneakers and compared them with grins before we headed to the hotel Kokoro had chosen.

The power was still running and bright neon in all shades of the rainbow glittered down on us, turning night into day again. The lobby was marbled, luxurious and familiar. I realized it was the same foyer where I'd unexpectedly paid them a visit earlier.

Igor disappeared behind the counter and came back with enough key cards for everyone. Unsurprisingly, he'd chosen plain black pants and a white long sleeved shirt to wear.

Luc wore similar clothing, but a black shirt instead of white. He'd upgraded to a real leather jacket that matched mine, but lacked a picture on the back.

Kokoro had donned a pair of tight jeans and a fitted black jacket. Gregor surprised me by sticking with casual clothes instead of choosing a suit. He seemed slightly uncomfortable in his jeans and dark green sweater, but maybe he was trying to remain unobtrusive. He tended to stand out when he wore one of his beloved tweed suits.

Igor chose rooms on the first floor and I had a flashback to being dumped by Luc again. I clamped down hard on my urge to start sobbing. *You're supposed to be Mortis, mistress of death,* my inner voice said derisively. *Not a pathetic, lovesick human.* My alter ego had been silent for a while now and I wished it had remained so.

During my long, boiling hot shower, I pondered on the nature of mankind and the encounters I'd had with them since becoming one of the undead. I knew all the way through to my bones that they would never trust vampires. They had already tried to eradicate us and when that had failed, they'd booted us off the planet. There was no doubt in my mind that they would stab us in the back once more. The only question was how they would double cross us this time.

My friends had gathered in Gregor and Kokoro's room to chat. Too tired and heartsick to mingle with them, I slid between the luxurious sheets of the queen-size bed and pulled the blankets up to my chin. I no longer felt the chill like I used to, but I was still comforted by the thin coverlet.

Still exhausted from expending so much energy exterminating the imps, I slid into a deep sleep.

From the rocking motion, I knew I was on a boat before I opened my eyes. My nose wrinkled at the nauseating odour that permeated the room. It wasn't fish that I smelled this time, but something far more horrible.

The top bunk was empty this time. That meant butt fog couldn't be to blame for the stench.

I rolled to my feet and saw I was on a different vessel from my previous dream. The sleeping quarters were much larger and could have held twenty sailors. A couple of inches of water covered the floor. I sloshed over to the hatch and it opened with a reluctant squeal. An incredible reek rolled over me and I doubled over, gagging. I wasn't actually able to vomit, but the urge to still struck me sometimes.

An ominous silence had settled over the boat. Apart from groaning metal and lapping water, there were no other sounds. I couldn't sense any humans on board and wondered if I was on a ghost ship that was doomed to sail the ocean for all eternity.

I climbed a set of stairs and stepped through a hatch into darkness. Skeletons were strewn all over the deck. Maybe my crazy idea that I was on a ghost ship might actually be correct. Hunkering beside one of the corpses, I studied its deterioration.

The flesh had been eaten away by some sort of acid. Even the metal deck was rusting and holes had begun to form. My skin was starting to sting as if it, too, were being eaten by something that I couldn't see.

Standing, I walked to the railing and squinted into the night sky. My eyes widened when I saw another boat nearby. Its crew were also dead and the vessel was beginning to break down. Moving over to the other side of the ship, I saw something that made me blink to make sure my eyes were working properly.

A wooden building bobbed on its side. The roof and one of the walls was missing, exposing shabby furniture and fixtures. It was a dilapidated mess, but it had definitely been a dwelling of some kind. Squinting into the distance, I saw more wooden shacks and boats. I had the distinct feeling that I'd stumbled into an oceanic graveyard.

Glancing up, I saw no stars, but I also didn't see any clouds. In my last dream, the boat had drifted into a gigantic cave. Maybe this boat was in the same cave. If so, it had to be the biggest one on the planet because I couldn't see the top or the sides.

If this dream was a warning of danger, it was a poor one. I failed to see how a cave could impact on humanity in a detrimental way, not even one that had become a resting place for boats and shacks.

"This dream is so weird."

My quiet murmur woke me and I sat up with a start. My skin was no longer burning and the horrible stench was absent. I had no explanation for the dream. *Is that what fate has planned for us next? Why bother sending a message if it's going to be so cryptic,* I complained internally. The dream made no sense, so I shrugged off my misgivings and dressed.

"Are you awake, Natalie?" Geordie asked through the wall.

"Yep." My reply wasn't exactly enthusiastic, but he took it as an invitation to join me. The word was barely out of my mouth before the teen was at my door. I opened it at his knock. Looking down at my bare legs beneath my t-shirt, he forgot what he was going to say.

Igor clumped down the hall, stuck his head in through the door, rolled his eyes at Geordie's stupor and smacked him in the back of the head. "The yellow gas has cleared and we will be leaving in an hour," the Russian informed me, then retreated back down the hall to his room.

"Was that what you were supposed to tell me?" I asked Geordie.

Rubbing his head ruefully, he nodded. "You slept for sixteen hours straight. I thought you were never going to wake up."

Gathering my clothes, I paused in shock. "I was out for that long?" He nodded solemnly. I hadn't realized just how exhausted I'd been.

"President Rivers has arranged a parade for us. They're holding it in Manhattan, because it was the site of the first alien attack," Geordie said. "She has planned a ceremony that she wants us to attend first. I think she's going to give us all medals."

I listened to Geordie's chatter as I dressed in the bathroom. He sounded excited at the prospect of being rewarded for saving the planet yet again. Somehow, I doubted it would be medals they would pin on us. More likely, it would be a target on our backs to make it easier for their soldiers to try to eradicate us.

Gregor sent me a guarded look when we met him in the hallway. Kokoro hadn't had a vision since she'd regained her eyesight, but she was also subdued. Luc and Igor appeared to be resigned. Ishida was younger than Geordie in mortal years, but he'd gained wisdom in his ten millennia of rule. He knew that it was doubtful we'd be rewarded for our efforts.

I'd known all along that siding with the soldiers would end badly. Apparently, most of my friends had all secretly been harbouring the same fears. "We don't have to go to this farcical parade. I can teleport us all out of here one by one," I offered quietly.

My teleporting talent was still too new to have worked out my limits yet. I wasn't sure how many of my friends I could take with me when I transported to a different location. If we had the time, I would have to experiment to find out just what I could and couldn't do.

Gregor had already thought his way through our dilemma and shook his head. "We seven are theoretically immortal now. I believe it would be best if we face whatever it is that the humans have planned. If we do not, there is no telling what fate will throw at us next."

"I thought you'd say something like that," I said glumly. "I guess it's a good thing that I took some precautions."

His gaze sharpened. "What precautions?"

Studying my fingernails with false nonchalance, I shrugged. "You'll see. Just don't be surprised if the humans' treachery backfires on them this time." My smile was grim as I preceded them down the stairs. Geordie was following me so closely he was almost stepping on my heels. He was bursting with questions, but manfully kept them inside. He knew me well enough to know I wasn't going to spill the beans, no matter how much he pestered me.

It was late afternoon and the sun was still a painful ball of light in the sky, not that we could see it directly since it was hidden behind the hotel. Sanderson had anticipated our needs and an enclosed truck waited out the front for us.

"This brings back unpleasant memories," Ishida murmured as we climbed inside. I vividly remembered being escorted by hostile soldiers to the airfield where we had been evicted from our home world.

This time, we were alone in the back of the truck, but we only drove a short distance before stopping. When the door opened, Higgins and a dozen other soldiers climbed in. "Ma'am," he said with a nod at me. "Vampires," he said with another nod at the others.

Geordie bit his lip to contain a giggle and I had to stare hard at the floor so I didn't join him. The other soldiers were familiar and also nodded politely when I met their eyes. They were all armed, but none acted the least bit threatening. They were merely hitching a ride with us to the air force base.

We picked up a few more soldiers along the way. By the time we reached the base, the truck was full and several more vehicles had formed a convoy behind ours. Not all of the soldiers would be heading for Manhattan and the ceremony that was going to be put on for our benefit.

We disembarked from the truck and split into two groups of those who would be heading to the parade and those who would be returning to whichever base they belonged to. Out of the original eight hundred troopers we'd teamed up with back in Manhattan, only two hundred remained. They formed a tightknit group around their commanding officer as we waited for a jet to be readied.

My friends and I waited inside the back of the truck until the last rays of the sun finally faded. Once our jet was ready to be boarded, we filed inside and chose seats in the middle of the craft. Seconds after we had settled into our seats, one of the general's men approached and addressed Gregor. "Our policy forbids foreigners from bringing firearms into our President's presence. I'm going to have to ask you to relinquish your weapons."

I elbowed Geordie when he opened his mouth to whine. He closed it, but his bottom lip pooched out in a pout. He reluctantly handed over his death ray when the soldier stopped next to him and held out his hand. Everyone else gave up their weapons without complaint.

Before the soldier could ask for them, I handed him my swords and sheaths as well as my alien gun. "I'll keep them safe for you, ma'am," he promised. Shouldering the backpack he'd stashed our weapons in, he wandered towards the front of the plane again.

As defenceless as the humans could possibly make us, we descended into New York. We landed at the same airport that we'd left from several nights ago. It was far too soon for the bridges to have been repaired and a ferry waited to carry us back to Manhattan.

Some effort had been made to restore order now that the gas had cleared away. The dead would have to be gathered and disposed of. There were far too many for the usual funeral ceremonies to be performed. I wondered if they'd bury their casualties in mass graves. I shuddered at the thought of being amongst the piles of corpses that would be buried beneath the ground.

Millions of humans had been eradicated all around the country with each Viltaran attack. I doubted they'd ever be able to rebuild all of the ruins that had been left behind after each assault. Manhattan had gotten off lightly compared to the cities that had been used as decoys to hide the true attack against Las Vegas. Reports had come in that my senses had been correct. There had been no survivors amongst the wreckage of the decoy cities.

Igor raised a point that hadn't even occurred to me. "Do you think the soldiers will discover our ship lying on the bottom of the river?" He kept his voice low enough not to be overheard.

Gregor shrugged and grimaced at the same time. "I hope not. I wish there was a way for us to destroy it. Even if the humans did manage to salvage the ship, I highly doubt they'll be able to recreate the Viltarans' fuel source. Earth does not contain the necessary components."

That was a relief. Picturing humankind questing through the depths of outer space gave me another momentary shudder. They'd already led one alien species to their home world. For all we knew, there could be something far worse than the grey skinned extra-terrestrials out there.

Trucks were on standby to drive us to the ceremony. I overheard a soldier mention that it would be taking place in Central Park. Again, Higgins and thirty other soldiers crammed into the back of the truck with us.

Sergeant Wesley was one of them. The smile he gave me seemed to be sincere. None of the troops gave us sidelong, measuring looks. If treachery was about to be unleashed on us, they didn't seem to be a part of it. Either that, or they were all actors worthy of awards for outstanding performances.

Our journey was fairly short, since most of the streets were clear of moving traffic. No one had returned to their jobs as yet. It would take time for the inhabitants of Manhattan to slip back into their normal routines again. They'd need to grieve for their dead first.

I wondered how the little boy I'd saved from being eaten by Kveet imps had fared and if his parents were still alive. *He isn't my problem,* I told myself. I'd already saved the humans three times. As far as I was concerned, my responsibilities towards our former species were now over.

It'll never be over, my subconscious warned me. *Remember the weird dreams about the boats and the caves and the thing that attacked Sydney? They have to mean something. You know there's still more for you to do.*

Our truck came to a stop as my alter ego went silent. It was time to face our destinies once more.

Chapter Twenty-Nine

A crowd had gathered on a large grassy field in the centre of Central Park. Chairs had been lined up in neat rows. The five hundred guests and dignitaries could sit in relative comfort during the ceremony. Most of the people gathered were male and sat with military straightness. Some had flown in from overseas to represent their countries.

A small podium sat on a stage in front of the crowd, waiting for a speaker to approach. General Sanderson and his surviving soldiers stood to the left of the platform in ranks that were as neat as the chairs. Our small group of vampires was directed to a row of seven chairs that were to the right of the podium. Sanderson stood directly across from me. I felt his blue eyes boring into my face, but I didn't deign to acknowledge him.

Sending out my senses, I couldn't detect anyone hiding in the trees waiting to ambush us. There were no humans beneath our feet ready to burst out from holes in the ground to gun us down. My suspicion of coming treachery didn't lessen as we settled in to wait for the show to start.

I cocked my head to the side when I heard a chopper approaching. It took the humans a lot longer to hear it. When they did, they craned their heads to watch as it landed several hundred yards away. Only when the blades had stopped rotating did the doors open. Two men wearing sombre black suits jumped out first, then helped President Rivers to the ground. From their neat haircuts and general alertness, they were probably Secret Service agents. More of the dark suited men stood around the perimeter of the field. They kept their eyes out for enemies as several aides jumped out of the chopper.

Straightening her conservative navy blue jacket, the president strode towards the podium wearing a determined expression. Her assistants scurried after her, hurrying to catch up despite her much shorter stature. In person, she was even more buxom than on TV. Intelligent blue eyes studied us curiously as she climbed the three steps to the podium.

Standing at the lectern, Rivers flicked a rapid glance at Sanderson. He nodded slightly in response. That sly exchange was the sign of impending treachery that I'd been waiting for and I sent out my senses once more.

The parade that had been promised to us was a lie. No cheering, grateful citizens would be lining up to throw rose petals at us as we drifted by in convertible cars after the speeches were finished. Apart from everyone who'd gathered in the field, the area was empty of human life.

My instincts had warned me that the humans would turn on us yet again and I was glad I'd listened to them. I sought for and found the little surprise that my subconscious had suggested I leave behind. It was time to put my contingency plan into action.

President Rivers tapped the microphone to make sure it was on. It gave a high pitched whine that made me wince and Geordie mutter an expletive. "On behalf of the United States of America," she began, "I would like to thank you for aiding General Sanderson and his people in saving us from the threat of alien invasion."

Her expression was sincere, but her eyes darted away from us, to Sanderson, then back again. "There is no way we can ever repay you for the services you have rendered, not just for us, but for the entire world. As a token of our gratitude," she paused to give the general a much more significant glance, "I would like to present you with these medals."

She motioned to her aides and one of them scurried forward holding a small black case. He climbed up to the stage and flipped open the lid to reveal a row of shiny silver medallions.

"Told you," Geordie whispered smugly.

I nodded, but the sick feeling in my stomach made it impossible to respond. Any second now, their treachery would be revealed.

"Please approach the podium, so that I can bestow these medals on you," the woman in charge of the US government said and beckoned us to come forward.

"Let's get this travesty over with," I told the others quietly. We stood and headed towards the platform in single file.

Gripping the wooden lectern tightly, Rivers gave the order that I'd been both expecting and dreading. "Now, Sanderson!"

Pointing at us, the general barked an order at his men. "Cut them down!"

An expectant hush fell over the spectators as they waited for us to be showered with explosive bullets. None of the soldiers obeyed the order that their commander had given them. Sanderson turned to look at his men in confusion. They stood quietly, eyes on me, waiting for their true commander to tell them what to do. "I'm ordering you to shoot the vampires!" he shouted.

"Don't bother trying to give them orders," I told him. "They're under my control now." This was the second precaution I'd taken and I was relieved that I had. I'd secretly placed a light level of hypnotism over the soldiers right from the first night we'd joined forces. Doing so prevented them from turning on us now. I'd strengthened my hold over them during our lengthy journey from Vegas back to Manhattan. They were now my henchmen and would remain so until I decided to let them go.

Using the lectern to hold up her shaking legs, President Rivers stared at me in dismay. "There's been a mistake," she croaked. "General Sanderson acted without my authorisation. I did not intend for him to attempt to assassinate you." Sanderson flicked a glare at her and I felt a stab of satisfaction. He'd just received a taste of what it felt like to be betrayed by someone he'd trusted.

"Sure you did," I contradicted her. "This was your plan all along. Did you really think we'd be stupid enough to trust you walking blood bags again?" My tone was rife with contempt. "We saved your species from becoming slaves twice and you repaid us by killing most of us and experimenting on the rest. Then you did us the favour of sending us into space."

Her eyes darted from side to side, seeking a way out of my trap. There would be no escape from my wrath for any of these people. It was time to turn the tables on the betrayers. I took one step towards the president and stopped when Sanderson snatched Sergeant Wesley's gun out of his hands.

I regretted not turning him into one of my minions as he fired three rapid shots at me. I dodged them easily and they exploded behind me as I sprinted towards him. Snatching the gun out of his hand, I bent it in half and tossed it away. It landed with a soft thump somewhere in the darkness.

"Nice try, General," I sneered. "You should know by now that it'll take a lot more than a few explosive rounds to take me down."

Sanderson's gaze moved past me and his reply died before it was born. Dread widened his eyes.

"Natalie," Geordie said and it came out as a moan. Another premonition of doom washed over me. I had the disturbing sensation that I was about to witness something that would strip me of my sanity forever. My legs were frozen, mercifully preventing me from turning around and facing whatever was behind me. "*Chérie*," the teen tried again.

Kokoro gave a single sob and I knew what I would see even before I finally turned around. Gregor, Igor and Ishida stood close together with Kokoro and Geordie several yards away. There was a gap between them where no space should have been. My friends stared in horror at the small chunks of flesh and fabric that were scattered through the grass. Deep in denial, I searched for Luc and couldn't see him anywhere.

Unable to refute what my senses were telling me, I was standing beside the scattered remains of my one true love before I'd even registered the intention to teleport over to him. Dropping to my knees, I reached out with a trembling hand to pick up one of Luc's. Smeared with black blood, it was uninjured and perfect.

I waited for his pieces to start moving as he tried to heal himself, but they remained still. He hadn't broken down into ooze, which meant he was still alive. Yet I could barely sense him.

It had taken me a long time to learn how to piece myself back together. I'd only done so because I was the weird and wacky Mortis. Luc hadn't even tested his ability to reattach a severed limb, let alone learned how to heal an injury this catastrophic.

He might not be able to fix himself, my inner voice told me. *He could spend the rest of eternity like this.* My head went back and my mouth opened. Howling in rage and sorrow, I called my minions forth from the darkness. My eyes didn't just turn scarlet from my overwhelming anger, they pulsated in their sockets. Half solid and half whirling particles, I rose and floated towards Sanderson. My bedazzled servants closed in around him to stop him from fleeing.

Halting before my betrayer, I floated several inches above the ground. "Do you remember what I said I would do to you if you tried to harm me or my friends?" My voice had deepened and my fangs had descended. The general stared at me speechlessly. "I told you I would reach down your throat with my hand and rip your intestines out through your mouth," I reminded him.

Stricken with terror, my betrayer tried to scream. It was choked off when the particles of my right hand poured into his mouth. Tumbling down his oesophagus and into his stomach, they re-formed and tore through his stomach lining. He screamed in abject agony as I fished around inside him and gripped a handful of his intestines.

The spectators attempted to flee as piercing shrieks issued from the general. A glance was all it took for my human henchmen to fire warning shots. Some of the crowd kept running. They fell to the ground when the next round of bullets shattered their legs.

There would be no swift, painless deaths this night. These humans were going to pay for everything that had been done to my kind. Their deaths had already been fated, but they were going to suffer so much more now that Luc had been reduced to a ruin.

Gurgling in agony, Sanderson clawed at his stomach as my hand began to climb upwards, dragging his intestines with it. He began to choke when Righty reached his throat. His neck bulged and blood burst from his mouth. Higgins caught his commanding officer before he could fall. Sergeant Wesley helped to hold the general in place as he coughed out gouts of red fluid. I didn't try to avoid the splatters that covered me in sticky red. My face was soon bathed in the blood of the man who had all but murdered my beloved.

Sanderson was still alive and was hanging by a thread as my fingers appeared between his lips. Righty wormed its way free, still dragging the intestines until they hung down his chest like the medals that had been promised to us. His eyes met mine and his bloody mouth croaked out his last words. "I'll see you in hell."

"No you won't," I said as the life left his eyes and the breath left his body. "Because I can't die," I reminded the corpse of the man who I'd been longing to kill. Now that the task was done, I felt no satisfaction. My grief didn't lessen with the general's demise and I turned my attention to someone who was equally deserving of pain.

President Rivers backed away from my scarlet eyed fury and tripped down the steps. Landing on her back, she tried to scramble away, but I was on her before she could stand. My knees landed on either side of her chubby legs. "Please, don't kill me," she begged. "I'll give you anything you want!"

"Really?" I asked her around my fangs that were far longer and sharper than usual. "Then give me Luc back."

She began to scream even before my teeth tore into her neck. I could have ripped out her jugular and left her to bleed to death, but she deserved to suffer and so suffer she would. Hauling her to her feet, I turned myself into a whirling mass of molecules and inserted them into the president's flesh. Her heart stuttered and seized up for a moment as I clogged her veins, then it thundered back into action again.

This time when I transformed back to my normal size, I did it with excruciating slowness. The cries of horror and revulsion from the watching dignitaries sounded muffled since I was inside Rivers. Her flesh bulged as I slowly increased my size. Her overtaxed organs failed long before I burst through her flesh. Her body fell apart in chunks that weren't much larger than what was left of Luc. Naked and covered in blood, I wore her skin like a badly fitting suit.

Huddled in a frightened, sobbing group, the guests begged for mercy. Leaving the corpse of their leader, I peeled off her sheets of skin. I dropped them to the blood sodden ground and turned to face them. No one else had tried to run since the others had been gunned down. "There will be no mercy for my enemies," I told them. Gore dripped from my hair and blurred my vision as I sent a mental command to my tiny minions.

Small and silent, the Kveet imps that I'd hypnotized in the sewers beneath Manhattan surged into the bright lights that had been set up to illuminate the ceremony. Something deep inside me had warned me to save these two hundred clones. Instead of exploding them along with the rest, I'd commanded them to hide deeper in the subway. For once, my inner voice had come through for me and I was glad that I'd listened to it.

Pointing at the guests, I spoke in Viltaran. "Food."

Red eyes growing wide in delight at the banquet that was before them, the tiny terrors required no further urging. Racing across the grass, they fell on the humans who'd been disabled first. Their shrieks were cut off swiftly and only tattered clothing and chewed skeletons remained as razor sharp teeth consumed their flesh.

My human henchmen had to shoot most of the remaining guests in the legs to stop them fleeing from the slaughter. Their bamboozled faces remained serene as they did so. I was sure deep down in their subconscious they were horrified by what they were doing, but none of them could resist my dark magic.

Once more, fate had tried to bend us to its will. I hadn't been willing to stand idly by and had taken measures to avoid it. Due to my arrogance, Luc had been struck by the bullets that had been intended for me. If I had allowed Sanderson's projectiles to hit their true target, my love would still be whole and unharmed. Thanks to me, the person I loved most in the world had been reduced to the consistency of chowder.

Chapter Thirty

Kneeling beside Luc's scattered pieces, I picked up his cold, still hand and held his palm to my cheek. I was too stunned to cry. Human screams and piping cries of greed from Kveet imps mingled together. I ignored them all.

Peripherally, I was aware of Kokoro sprinting over to the chopper before it could take off. The engine had powered up as soon as my hand had started to traverse through Sanderson's body, dragging his intestines along behind it.

A small part of me registered that I wasn't alone in my grief. Geordie sobbed in Igor's arms. The Russian's face was stony as he patted the teen on the back. Ishida's head was bowed in sorrow. Gregor had known Luc for several hundred years and they had been very close. He mastered his grief enough to be concerned for the rest of us.

Hunkering beside me, he put a hand on my shoulder. "Natalie, we need to leave." I couldn't be bothered to dredge up the will to acknowledge him. I wasn't capable of speech or even of much thought. "Igor, can you find something to carry Luc's…body in?" he asked.

Gently pushing Geordie away, Igor jogged over to the rows of chairs that were now in disarray. Someone had left their jacket folded over the back of their chair. He grabbed it and jogged back to Gregor.

I watched in a dazed silence as the pair began picking up small chunks of my beloved and placing them in the coat. Geordie and Ishida helped. Working together, they scooped up bits and pieces of rent flesh and added them to the pile.

When they were done, Gregor put his hand on my shoulder again. "Natalie, you need to order the soldiers to destroy the imps."

"Why?" I asked dully, knowing he would keep nagging me until I answered him.

"It would be too dangerous to allow them to roam free. Innocent lives will be lost."

He flinched back when I seared him with my scarlet gaze. "Innocent? None of the meat sacks are innocent! Any one of them would put a bullet in your head just because you exist."

"You don't want any more little children to be eaten alive, do you, *chérie*?" Geordie asked in a small voice. "Surely they do not deserve to suffer?"

The imp feast was still going on. Grey bellies were already beginning to bulge, but they wouldn't stop until all of the humans were dead. The heavy compulsion I'd laid on them wouldn't allow them to. I could have sent them back into the sewers, but my hypnotism wouldn't last forever. Once it wore off, they would emerge and would start hunting down fresh prey again.

Geordie had used the only argument that would have worked on me. I'd already witnessed the death of one child and it had affected me more than I cared to admit. Forcing out a tired sigh, I stood and trudged over to the soldiers.

Higgins and Wesley stepped forward to hear my orders. They, and their fellow soldiers, were deeply enough beneath my spell that they were able to ignore the cries for help from the people they'd disabled. "Once the clones are finished eating the guests, kill them all," I ordered them both.

"Yes, ma'am," Higgins said.

"What then, ma'am?" Wesley asked.

"Then tell your next leader that this is what happens when humans turn on vampires." I indicated the carnage with my free hand. The other one was wrapped around the cold fingers of Luc's dismembered hand.

The soldier who had confiscated our weapons stepped forward and handed me his backpack. As one, the men offered me a salute. I returned the salute with Luc's hand since my other one held the weapons stash. Then Gregor was guiding me towards the helicopter. I took a seat and swapped bundles with Igor, carefully placing Luc's hand inside with the rest of his shattered body. I held the bulging coat on my lap as everyone climbed on board and the chopper took to the skies.

We didn't travel far, just across the river to the airport once more. Kokoro bamboozled our way onto the tarmac and into the cargo hold of a plane that was heading for Europe. The lengthy trip passed in a blur. My friends tried to talk to me, but I was too mired in misery to respond. Luc was my only concern. I needed peace and quiet so I could try to help him heal.

I vaguely remembered swapping planes when we landed and sneaking into the cargo hold of an aircraft heading for France. That trip also passed in a blur and then we were climbing inside a van. When I next glanced up, we were driving through a familiar small town. Several minutes later, Igor parked the vehicle that he'd most likely stolen in a garage that I'd seen several times before.

Geordie and Ishida coaxed me out of the van towards the safe house that was only a few miles away from the abandoned Court mansion. I felt a stir of hope at the familiar surroundings. Maybe Luc would somehow sense that he was now in a safe place and would rally enough to begin piecing himself back together.

In the bedroom that I had previously shared with my one true love, I spread the coat out on the bed and knelt before it. I took Luc's hand in mine again and tried to will him to regenerate.

Several nights and days passed without any signs of change. I heard the others whispering about us downstairs in the living room. I knew they were concerned for my mental health. It was obvious to them that Luc was too far gone to be able to piece himself back together. They didn't share my faith that he would return to me. The fact that he hadn't broken down into slush kept my hopes alive.

Igor was the first to give up and leave, but he didn't go alone. Entering the room, his heavy hand rested on my shoulder briefly. I hadn't heard him approach and started at the contact.

"I will be gone for a few nights. I'm going to Kazakhstan to see if my car is still where I left it," he said in Russian. I sincerely doubted it would still be there after all this time. He was just using it as an excuse to leave.

"Geordie and Ishida have decided to accompany me on the journey."

I nodded to indicate I'd heard him, but remained silent and focussed on Luc.

"Goodbye, *chérie*," Geordie whispered from the doorway.

"We will see you soon," Ishida said and ushered his friend away as he began to sob brokenly. Igor squeezed my shoulder in silent commiseration at my misery, then left.

It was Gregor and Kokoro's turn to desert me the next night. They stood arm in arm in the doorway as Gregor explained their reasons for running away. "Just go," I said, cutting him off in mid-sentence.

"We will be back, Mortis," Kokoro said softly. I flinched at the name that had been given to me over two thousand years before I'd been born. My entire life had been planned down to the last detail and I'd had no say in how it would turn out. The one time I'd tried to thwart fate, it had backfired on me in a way that I'd never anticipated.

More time passed and I spent it kneeling on the floor in penance for my arrogance at believing that I could prevent Sanderson's final great betrayal. Eventually, I slept.

Turning in a full circle, a sea of tall grass surrounded me. It was long enough to brush my fingertips and tickled the crosses on my palms. I came to a stop and noticed the ground sloped upwards to form a small hill. A figure waited at the summit. I knew instantly that it was Luc without needing to see his face. The shape of his body was forever etched into my memory.

"Luc!" He didn't turn around at my happy shout. He stared out over the horizon at a low, full moon and didn't even seem to know that I was there.

I ran towards him, but it was like running through thigh deep mud. A breeze picked up and horror raced down my spine when Luc began to dissipate. "No! Luc, stay with me!" He ignored my screams and continued to stare at the moon.

Clawing at the air, as if it would help me reach him in time, I ran a few more steps. I gave a low moan of fear when ragged holes appeared in my beloved's body. The wind increased and more and more of him disappeared. Remembering that I could now teleport, I appeared right behind him and he finally turned around. He reached out for me and I did the same. Our fingertips met, a sad smile touched his mouth, then a blast of wind scattered his particles far and wide.

Screaming Luc's name, I stumbled forward and teetered on the edge of a cliff. Waves crashed on the rocks far below, sending sprays of foam and water in every direction. Then a hand pushed me over the edge and I was falling.

Snapping awake, I rubbed my face with both hands then froze. Luc's hand had been in mine when I'd fallen asleep. I stared uncomprehendingly through my fingers at the empty coat. The chunks of flesh were gone and hadn't been replaced with watery goo.

Wild hope surged through me. I stood and sent out my senses, searching the house, then the surrounding area. I swept my senses towards the abandoned Court mansion a few miles up the road in increasing desperation when I came up blank. In a final effort, I scanned the entire country and several more countries that surrounded France. I found no vampires close by.

Bereft, I stared down at the bed and could see no trace of my one true love. Luc was gone and not even his particles remained. My fingers tore furrows in my cheeks that healed instantly as I howled out my anguish. I screamed in torment until my voice gave out and I collapsed to my knees again.

Luc was gone and nothing would ever bring him back. Fate had won and I would live forever with the knowledge that I had killed the only man who had ever loved me and whom I would ever love.

Chapter Thirty-One

I wasn't certain just how long I'd been mourning when I sensed vampires approaching. It could have been days, or maybe even weeks later. There were three people and that meant it was probably Igor, Geordie and Ishida. It was highly unlikely that some of the other vampires scattered throughout Europe had stumbled across the safe house by accident.

As soon as the trio stepped into the bedroom, they would see that Luc was gone. I couldn't stand the thought of having to share my grief with them. They would blame me for Luc's death or, far worse, they might expect me to somehow move on and attempt to resume my life.

The thought of having to face their accusing stares forced me into action. The door opened below and footsteps thundered on the stairs. "Nat, we're back!" Geordie called excitedly, but I was already gone before he reached the doorway.

Standing in the shadows beside the garage, I took a last look at the house that had offered me safety and shelter. This was where I had made the friends who I cared about so deeply, but who I would now have to leave behind.

"Where is she?" Ishida asked from the room I'd just vacated on the second floor.

Igor broke the news to the teens. "Lucentio is gone." The grief in his voice brought a fresh lump to my throat.

"What do you mean, 'he's gone'?" Geordie asked with foreboding.

"He's dead," Ishida clarified. "He was unable to heal himself. Even with our new abilities, he could no longer sustain his flesh."

"Where is Natalie?" Geordie asked, voice quavering with fresh sorrow.

"She has left us," Igor said. His apprentice burst into sobs and was comforted by the other two.

I turned and walked away before I could be tempted to run inside and beg for their forgiveness. I'd been cursed to bring death to our kind. They would all be far safer if I just left and never returned.

I walked until dawn neared, but I had no particular destination in mind. The safe house was the closest thing I'd had to a home since I had left my mortal life behind. Moments before the sun rose, I became a swirling mass of molecules. Leaving my blood stained clothing behind, I rose into the air and allowed the wind to carry me away.

As a consciousness without form, I drifted aimlessly for what might have been a week or more. I didn't realize I'd had a destination all along until I re-formed my body and found myself standing in a familiar cemetery. It had been spring in the northern hemisphere and it was autumn back home in Australia. Any normal vampire would have been cold, but the chilly air had no effect on me at all. I was numb both inside and out.

Naked and alone, I walked through the darkness, picking my way around the graves. I unerringly found the mausoleum where my life had been so cruelly stolen from me. The door creaked when I pushed it open. It was dustier and dirtier inside than I remembered. A faint trace of the sludge that had once been my maker remained in the middle of the cement floor.

A filthy, threadbare blanket lay in one corner. I remembered stealing it from an old dog that had to be long dead by now. Picking it up, I shook some of the dirt out of it, then wrapped it around my bare body. Four stone sarcophagi contained mummified corpses that were well over a hundred years old. The dead would be my only companions from now on.

Dull and tarnished, I spied the cross that I had speared through Silvius' heart. It still lay in the middle of the puddle that he'd left behind after burning to death from holy flames. I picked it up and sat it back on the sarcophagus that I'd accidentally broken it from.

Its twin, which I'd also accidentally taken from one of the other stone coffins, had given me my holy marks. I wasn't sure what had happened to it after I'd battled the imposter who'd pretended to be me. One of the Court guards would most likely have disposed of it carefully.

My new home was dank, cheerless and seemed very fitting for someone who had almost caused the entire extinction of her own species. After Luc's death, I had no right to attempt to seek any form of happiness. I deserved to be alone and to suffer for what I'd done.

I had only one goal left now. I knew my task might very well be impossible, or would at least take me a very long time to accomplish, but time was the only thing that I had left. Lying down on the cold, hard floor, I closed my eyes and proceeded to will myself to die.

Printed in Great Britain
by Amazon

23353121R00175